T0283504

OUT

A NOVEL

OF THE

SILENCE

MARIE THEODORE

GREENLEAF
BOOK GROUP PRESS

This is a work of fiction. Although most of the characters, organizations, and events portrayed in the novel are based on actual historical counterparts, the dialogue and thoughts of these characters are products of the author's imagination.

Published by Greenleaf Book Group Press
Austin, Texas
www.gbgpress.com

Distributed by Greenleaf Book Group

For ordering information or special discounts for bulk purchases, please contact Greenleaf Book Group at PO Box 91869, Austin, TX 78709, 512.891.6100.

Design and composition by Greenleaf Book Group and Kim Lance
Cover design by Greenleaf Book Group and Kim Lance
Cover image © Seyedomid Mostafavi/Getty Images

Publisher's Cataloging-in-Publication data is available.

Print ISBN: 979-8-88645-230-3

eBook ISBN: 979-8-88645-231-0

To offset the number of trees consumed in the printing of our books, Greenleaf donates a portion of the proceeds from each printing to the Arbor Day Foundation. Greenleaf Book Group has replaced over 50,000 trees since 2007.

Printed in the United States of America on acid-free paper

24 25 26 27 28 29 30 31   10 9 8 7 6 5 4 3 2 1

First Edition

This book is dedicated to my amazing children, Lindsey, Randy, and Christopher, my reason for being. Without them, there is no me!

To my wonderful mother, the one who gave me life and sacrificed everything. Mom, I always wanted you to be proud of me . . .

A special appreciation goes to my greatest fans and inspiration— Oprah Winfrey, Tyler Perry, Steve Harvey, and Pastor Joel Osteen. Steve has inspired me to jump. The words "your greatest gift is when you do your absolute best with the least amount of effort" were like a song constantly playing in my mind. I just knew I had to follow my dream and write my book.

Last, and most importantly, my Heavenly Father who inspired me the most and gave me strength through every page!

CHAPTER 1

Alexa, 2024

A LEXA SAT BEHIND HER DESK, head bent over a stack of paper, when there was a soft knock on the door.

"Mrs. Montgomery?"

Alexa looked up to see her secretary's head poking out from the other side of the doorway.

"What's up, Sally?" Alexa asked, putting her pen down.

"Mr. Barrow wants to talk to you."

Alexa sighed and looked down at the pages strewn across her normally clean desk. "Does it have to be now?" she asked.

"He said the sooner, the better."

"All right." Alexa stood, stretching as she did. "Thanks, Sally."

Alexa strolled past Sally and down the hall to the district attorney's office.

As she walked, she could feel the gazes of several men flicking over her. It was something she was used to. Even at forty, Alexa Montgomery was stunning: brown hair, chocolate-colored eyes, and a petite frame that accentuated her voluptuous curves. Her flawless dark skin and toned, long legs completed the package. She ignored the looks and kept walking.

When she arrived at Barrow's office, she could tell something was wrong. He was paler than normal and looked nervous. He was biting his nails, too, which was always a bad sign. When Alexa walked in, he jumped slightly.

Barrow was an older man, short, with thinning gray hair, but trim. He was, as always, in an impeccable suit and tie, but the tie was rumpled this morning, and when he saw Alexa, he looked worried.

"What's wrong, Andrew?" she asked.

"Ah, it's . . . well . . . you see . . . why don't you take a seat?"

Alexa's eyes narrowed. Her arms folded as she scrutinized the DA, the same way she would examine a witness on the stand. It didn't take a genius to realize that there was something he needed to tell her that he really didn't want to.

"I'm fine where I am," she said, leaning against the wall. "So why don't you just tell me why you wanted me to come in?"

"I—you see . . ." He licked his lips and scratched his head. "Would you mind closing the door?"

She did.

"Now quit stalling," Alexa said, brushing her hair out of her face. "What's wrong?"

Barrow let out a deep breath before saying, "Casimir Johnson was just arrested."

Alexa froze, her mouth slightly open. The words barely seemed to register, and it took her a long time to regain control of her limbs. When she did, her perfectly manicured nails dug into her arm.

"For what?" she asked. Her voice was low and deadly. Her mind was flying back to a trial fourteen years ago, when a smug, short man had leered at her from across the courtroom.

"Assault and battery," he said. "They're talking about kidnapping and attempted murder, but he hasn't been charged with those yet."

"What did he do?" she asked. Her voice, normally smooth and sensual, was harsh and demanding. "What did that asshole do this time?"

"I don't know all the details," Barrow said. "From what I've heard and seen in the police report, he attacked a young woman after meeting her at a club."

Of course he did. Alexa's fingers dug farther into her flesh. "I want the case," she said.

Barrow sighed, and his shoulders slumped. "I thought you would," he said. "But you know I can't give it to you."

"What?!" Alexa all but shrieked. No wonder Barrow had wanted the door closed. "Andrew, you know I—"

"I know exactly why you want this case, Alexa," Barrow said, and he seemed genuinely upset. His voice sounded tired and tinted with guilt. "Trust me, I know. But you know that his attorney will claim a conflict of interest immediately."

"I don't care," Alexa said. "Depending on the judge, I can get him to agree."

"I'm not taking that risk, Alexa," Barrow said. "I want this man behind bars as much as you do. But there's a risk that might not happen if his lawyer manages to call a mistrial."

"Who's his lawyer?" Alexa demanded, but she already knew.

"Henry Thompson," he said. At the look on her face, he added, "I'm guessing you remember him."

"We've gone up against each other on more than one occasion," she said. She didn't need to add that Thompson was Casimir's lawyer the first time around. He knew already. "Andrew, you have to give me this—"

"I don't, actually," Andrew said. "I know you want it, but this is ultimately my decision."

"Who's getting the case?" she asked.

"I'm giving it to Jacob," he said.

"Jacob O'Brien?" Alexa stormed toward Andrew. "You can't be serious? He's a raging misogynist. You can't actually think that he'll handle this case properly? Casimir's going to walk."

"You don't know that," Barrow said. "I think he'll do a good job."

"He's corrupt," she said.

"Alexa," Barrow said, his blue eyes finally meeting her brown ones. "You don't have any proof of that. You're overreacting."

Alexa stared him down, her eyes shooting daggers. But he didn't waver.

"Why did you tell me, then?" she asked.

"I thought you had a right to know," Barrow said. "I know your history with him. I wanted you to hear it from me rather than someone else."

She raised a perfect eyebrow. "Like Jacob?"

"Yes, like Jacob."

"So you agree he's not a great choice."

"I didn't say that," Barrow said. "I was just trying to be respectful."

Alexa took a deep breath, squeezing her eyes shut even as she was screaming internally. This wasn't fair. She deserved to prosecute Casimir more than anyone else. But she also knew that she wasn't going to win the argument.

"And there's no way I can convince you to change your mind?" she asked.

Barrow shook his head.

"Great," she snapped. She spun on her heels and yanked the door open. "I should get back to work then."

This time, when she walked down the hall, there was none of her typical cool composure. She stormed down to her office, bristling with anger. And as she made her way back to her office, her mind started drifting back to fifteen years ago, when all this began.

CHAPTER 2

Carmella, 2009

CARMELLA JOHNSON'S BRUISES still hurt. Purple splotches, slowly turning to an off-greenish color, covered her upper body, vibrant and visible despite her dark skin. Her full lips were split in two places, cuts ran across her forehead and her arms, and if she moved the wrong way, everything would start crying out in pain. She drummed her right fingers against the black plaster cast on her left arm as she waited, trying not to move too much.

She was in a medium-sized room with too-bright lighting, but comfortable chairs. What parts of the wall weren't covered in books were a pleasant shade of red. A clock on the wall made an infuriating ticking sound that grated her ears.

She didn't want to be here. She'd rather be anywhere else in the world at this point. But here she was, as requested.

Maybe she could leave, sneak out before anyone came in. She could run away and change her name so Casimir would never find her. She could have a fresh start. All she had to do was run now.

She stayed where she was.

A beautiful Black woman strolled purposefully in a moment later. It was impossible to tell her age, but she had to be fairly young. Her dark eyes found Carmella, and the smile that the woman had been about to give flickered, replaced with horror and something like anger as she took in Carmella's battered appearance.

"That asshole did this to you?" the woman asked.

Carmella had been expecting stuffy formality and some white guy in an overly expensive suit, not swear words or the woman in front of her. Her shoulders relaxed, and she gave the faintest of smiles—the most she had given in days. It hurt a little.

"Yeah," she said. "Ain't the prettiest, is it?"

"You're still beautiful," the woman said. "No bruises or anything that guy did to you will change that. I'm Alexa." Alexa held out her hand, and Carmella shook it.

"Carmella."

"I know. I'm the prosecutor assigned to your husband's case. Thanks for coming in. I just wanted to go over some groundwork and give you an idea of how the next few months will go down."

Alexa walked around the desk to sit down, looking at Carmella intently, every inch of her focused on the woman in front of her.

"All right then, go ahead."

"It'll take a bit to go to trial," Alexa said. "In the meantime, we'll have the discovery period, and I'll start prepping a case. We'll need to do a formal interview at some point. Did anyone take photos of the bruises and arm?"

"The police did when I was in the hospital."

"Good. Anyway, I know you've already spoken to the police, but I'd like to talk to you more to get a better idea of how to shore up the case against him. When you testify—"

"Wait, what?" Carmella stiffened, every inch of her suddenly on alert.

"Testify," Alexa said, glancing back down at the pages in front of her. "We'll need you to give a statement on the witness stand during the trial. You'll probably get an official subpoena."

"Hell no, I ain't doing that." Carmella sprung to her feet, half-ready to make a bolt for the door.

Alexa blinked, a slight frown creasing her face. "What?"

"I ain't testifying."

"Why?"

"I don't want to," Carmella said. "So I ain't."

"You're the one who went to the authorities and reported him, didn't you?" Alexa asked. "What changed your mind?"

"Nothing's changed my mind. I still wanna see him behind bars," Carmella said. "I'll do an interview or whatever will help put him away. But I didn't realize I was gonna have to testify."

"And you don't want to?"

"That's what I've been saying," Carmella said. She stood from her chair and paced the room. "You don't know Casimir like I do. He'll get off, and he'll come find me."

"With your testimony, he's almost certainly going to wind up behind bars," Alexa said. "It's the strongest piece of evidence we have."

"Then he'd get someone on the outside to get me." Carmella gestured, then winced at the pain shooting up her body. "He has those kinds of connections. He ain't a good guy."

"I know he isn't," Alexa said. Her eyes were hard obsidian, her face gravely serious. "Which is why I want to do my job and throw his ass in jail. If I didn't before meeting you, I definitely do now. He did a number on you."

"Then do it. The police took pictures. Show them in court. Ain't that enough?"

"It might be," Alexa said tentatively. "Or it might not be. I know his lawyer: Henry Thompson. He's good and ruthless, known for getting scumbags like Casimir off by spinning a web of lies that makes his client look like a paragon of virtue. My guess is that he'd say that anyone could have beat you up like this. Or maybe that you fell down the stairs. He'll cast reasonable doubt, and that's all he needs."

"Then I can do an interview or something," Carmella said. "I just don't want to be in the same room as him."

"I completely understand, Carmella," Alexa said. "I wouldn't either. But again, it won't have the same impact. Juries respond better to real-time reactions and people in person. It's easier for the defense to spin a bad light onto a video interview than it is on someone physically on the stand."

Carmella closed her eyes, trying to block out all the unpleasant thoughts trying to creep in, but it didn't do any good. Instead, she just saw flashes of what happened a few nights ago—her head slamming into the wall so hard that it made a dent, the baseball bat lying on the ground, his feet stomping across the filthy floor to the door as he stormed out, leaving her there on the ground, her entire body screaming in agony. The arm beneath the cast began to itch unpleasantly.

She felt sick. She knew that Alexa was right, that testifying in court would help the case. She knew that it was the smart thing to do. But the thought of being in the same room as Casimir made her stomach twist into a pretzel.

Alexa was waiting patiently while Carmella stood there silently and tried to figure out what to say and what she wanted to do. She had known Casimir for years, had been charmed by him when they'd first met. There was a point when she had loved him, even. But that had vanished over the past few years. And now here she was, her body still aching, knowing that the man needed to be put behind bars but terrified of what might happen if she helped.

"If I say no," Carmella said, "you gonna make me anyway?"

"Of course not," Alexa said, shaking her head. "Forcing you to testify isn't going to have the same effect, and I don't want to make you do anything. I want it to be your decision."

Carmella appreciated that, but that didn't make her feel any more comfortable. The prosecutor was still waiting, her brown eyes boring into Carmella.

It was Carmella's choice, and she was the only one who could make it.

"No," she said, shaking her head. And she gathered her things and hurried out of the office.

CHAPTER 3

Alexa

"IF ANYONE CALLS, TELL them I'm not here," Alexa said to Sally as she stormed past. Before Sally could even confirm, Alexa had stomped into her office. The door rattled as she slammed it shut.

Sitting in her chair, she closed her eyes and rubbed her face, trying to keep herself from screaming.

It wasn't fair. She deserved to prosecute that asshole. Barrow knew that. Otherwise, he wouldn't have called her into his office.

"Conflict of interest, my ass," she muttered when she had managed to get a bit of control back. She still wanted to throw something into the wall—preferably Andrew Barrow or Jacob O'Brien—but she was at least calm enough now to know that it was a bad idea.

She sat in silence for several minutes, staring down at her desk, as she thought about what Barrow had told her. She was furious. He knew she was good. She was one of the best at her job and one of the people first in line for the DA position whenever Barrow decided to retire. She would have whooped Casimir's ass in the courtroom and finally seen him go to jail.

She could have convinced the judge, too, most likely. She was on good terms with all of them, and if she had asked them to approve her being on the case, then they would have done it. But Barrow didn't want to take that chance.

The worst part was that there was some truth to Barrow's concerns. Even if she got the judge to approve, despite any perceived conflict of interest, Casimir's lawyer might still have used it to his advantage. But Barrow had given the case to O'Brien, who was perhaps the worst option he could have picked. O'Brien was arrogant, smug, lazy, and almost certainly corrupt. He hated Alexa, and Alexa hated him. She couldn't believe Barrow had chosen O'Brien, and the fact that he had made her furious.

She gritted her teeth and clenched her fists. She needed to calm down so she could at least focus on her other cases. But it was nearly impossible for her to focus with all the rage and anxiety currently flowing through her. She closed her eyes, taking deep breaths and trying to think of anything other than the problem she had just been presented with.

Just as her pulse was beginning to slow, the phone on her desk rang. The large digital screen told her it was Sally trying to reach her. Sighing—half-considering ignoring it entirely—she reached out and grabbed it.

"What is it?" Alexa asked, trying not to sound too mad at the older woman. Sally was sweet and good at her job. She didn't deserve to be snapped at, no matter what sort of mood Alexa was in.

"I'm sorry to bother you. I know you said no calls, but your husband is on the line."

Alexa slumped back in her chair, unable to stop the small smile spreading over her face. Somehow he always seemed to call when she needed him to most. If anyone could make her feel better right now, it was Joe.

"Patch him through," she said.

There was a click, and then a pleasant, smooth voice said, "Hey, babe, you all right? You aren't answering your cell."

Alexa pulled out her cell phone and saw three texts and a missed call.

"Sorry," she said. "I must've had it on mute."

"Something the matter?"

Her jaw clenched again, and she said, "Casimir was arrested."

There was a long pause on the other side of the phone before Joe said, "Really?"

"Yup."

"Good, they got that asshole for something then," Joe said.

They should have gotten him for something fourteen years ago, Alexa thought, her fingers gripping the receiver a little too tightly.

But Joe could clearly tell that wasn't all of the story.

"So what's the problem then?" he asked.

"Andrew's giving the case to Jacob O'Brien."

"Fuck," Joe said. Then, "Fuck. I'm sorry, babe."

"Thanks."

"I'm guessing you wanted it pretty badly."

"Course I did," Alexa said. "Especially when the other option is that asshat O'Brien."

Joe laughed. "And let me guess," he said, and his voice was teasing, mildly flirtatious. "You're already thinking of ways to get in on that trial, aren't you?"

Alexa grinned. "I don't know what you're talking about."

"That's my girl," Joe said fondly. "I was actually just trying to reach out and make sure we were still on for this evening. It's been too long since we had a date night."

"After what happened today? Absolutely. I'm going to need a glass of wine. Or three. Or a whole bottle."

"Whatever you want," Joe said. "I'm looking forward to it."

"Me too. I've got this new dress you haven't seen yet."

"What do you mean I haven't seen it yet?" Joe said, laughing. "We live together."

"I bought it on my lunch break," she said. "Trust me, it's worth every penny."

"When it comes to you, everything is worth every penny," Joe said, and her smile grew wider. There was something about Joe that always made her happier and seemed to make everything a bit better, no matter how bad the day was. He always knew just what to say and when to say it.

"You're gonna be all right, babe," Joe said. "You're strong and brilliant. And even if you don't get this case, you're going to be okay, and you'll get through it. And that asshole is gonna go down for what he did."

Alexa made a face. She was still frustrated at the situation and probably would be for a while. Joe might be able to make her feel better in a way that no one else could, but even he wouldn't be able to soothe this wound. She was going to have to do that herself.

"I know this might not be the best time," he said, bringing Alexa back to the present, "but I'm really excited to see this new dress. And I'm more looking forward to seeing it on the floor of our bedroom."

Alexa arched an eyebrow, one edge of her mouth quirking upward in a knowing smirk as a delightful squirming sensation began between her legs.

"Is that so?" she asked, her voice a soft purr that oozed sex.

"You know it is."

"Well, in that case, I'll see you in a few hours. Seven-thirty, right?"

"Yep. See you then. Love you, babe."

"I love you, too." Alexa hung up, her head clearer than it had been since the news broke. She looked at her computer. She still had a lot of work to do, and 7:30 was hours away. She had to focus and not fixate on what she had to look forward to this evening.

—

ALEXA WAS BORN IN PORT-AU-PRINCE, Haiti, to Emmanuel and Roseline Etienne, and there were both good and bad moments throughout her childhood.

When she was younger, she didn't notice the bad. She and her brother and sister lived in a spacious, beautiful home in Petion-Ville, a stunning neighborhood in Port-au-Prince filled with colorful houses that rose up the hillside. Each of them had their own bedroom, and the yard was big enough to run around and play in. The walk-in closets had felt massive when she was little, and the kitchen and pantry even more so. The luxurious French-style furniture, all carefully picked out by Roseline, showed exquisite taste and the lifestyle she was trying to create for herself and her family.

Roseline was a stay-at-home mom and did everything she could for her babies, including shielding them from some of the more unpleasant realities of their lives. Roseline was only nineteen when she was forced to marry Emmanuel, twelve years her senior, who already had three other kids out of wedlock, whom he pretended didn't exist.

Later, Alexa could never be sure how Emmanuel wormed his way into Roseline's life. But he had somehow managed to charm both Alexa's mother and grandmother, and when Roseline got pregnant, Marie, her mother, had strong-armed her young daughter into marriage. Her father, Daniel, on the other hand, had been against the union from the beginning. But ultimately, Marie had won out.

For the first few years, things had been good between Roseline and Emmanuel. Alexa and her siblings, David and Stephanie, had gone to a good Catholic school and had a normal childhood. They had played with other kids and had fun, doing everything from playing tag to running around the playground and cooling off in the pool. It had been a normal, fun life.

It didn't last.

Alexa was eight the first time she came home from school and saw a bruise covering her mother's eye.

"What happened, Mommy?" Alexa asked.

"Oh, sweetie." Her mother gave a warm smile, even as her hands were shaking, and her eyes were filled with tears threatening to spill over. "It's nothing. I just fell."

"Are you okay?" Alexa asked, her brown eyes wide and filled with worry.

"Yeah, yeah, I'm fine. Did you have a good day at school?"

"Madeline showed me a trick where you can cross your eyes. Do you want to see?"

And life moved on.

It wouldn't be the last time Alexa would come home to see new injuries on her mother. At first, she didn't understand what was happening; her mother was still trying to shield her children, even while she was privately suffering. But it kept getting worse, and soon the bruises and split lips were an everyday occurrence.

Alexa would be kept up most nights by her parents arguing about everything from finances to cleaning the dishes. The longer it went on, the more disillusioned and aware she became of the troubles that were going on at home. And by the time she was ten, when she fully began to understand the arguments and the connotations behind her parent's ever-increasing fights, she slowly began to realize one thing: Her father had only married her mother for money.

It wasn't until Rosaline and the children moved to the US that Alexa learned the whole story: It all came back to her grandfather, a man whom she had never met.

Daniel, Alexa's grandfather, was a wealthy businessman, well-known and well-loved in Haiti. He was shrewd and cunning but fair and kind to his workers. Most everyone called him "Gro Boss," and he became famous for being able to get anyone anything they needed. And no matter how difficult the object might have been to acquire, he always made it seem easy.

He grew his empire from nothing and loved Rosaline dearly. Gro Boss was the type of man who believed in hard work and dedication—which was one of his biggest problems with Emmanuel. Emmanuel was well off, but he still tried to form a relationship with his father-in-law for no other reason than the older man's money. But Gro Boss had seen right through it and had refused to give him anything. The last time, Emmanuel had stormed out of Gro Boss's house, calling him cheap and greedy, and the final bridge between Rosaline and her father was burned to ashes.

After that final encounter, Emmanuel lost any interest in his family. He stayed out late and grew harsher toward his wife. It got worse and worse, until Alexa was about eleven.

She still remembered the last time she had ever seen her father. She had been eating an afternoon snack after school, just about to start her homework. Her mother had been cleaning the kitchen, wiping down the counter before she began making dinner: griot, Alexa's favorite pork dish. Her father had strolled in. It was the earliest he had come home in a month.

Without preamble and without greeting his daughter, he turned to Rosaline.

"I want you out," he said, getting straight to the point. "Unless you go to your father right now and get him to give you money, I'm not taking care of this family anymore. You can go to the States for all I care, but you're not staying in this house anymore."

Rosaline's jaw had twitched, and she had given a glare that years later her daughter would use in the courtroom to stare down the defense. And at that moment, Alexa realized what a prideful, strong woman her mother was, despite everything she had been through.

"Alexa," her mother said, her eyes never leaving Emmanuel's face. "Go tell your siblings to pack. It looks as though we'll be staying in a hotel this evening."

Two weeks later, they were in the States, moving into a much smaller house. It was cramped for four people, but as she grew up, Alexa grew to appreciate and love it even more than their grand house in one of the nicest areas of Port-au-Prince for what it symbolized and for what her mother had done, both to protect her children and to rise from the ashes like a phoenix after years of abuse and neglect.

CHAPTER 4

Sally

SALLY KEPT HER HEAD DOWN the rest of the day, not wanting to bother Alexa any more than she had to. She wasn't sure what had happened, but it clearly hadn't been good. She had been working for Alexa for the past seven years or so, and she had rarely seen the woman that furious. She might have witnessed it once or twice, but not more than that.

So she kept to herself and made sure Alexa wasn't bothered. She redirected all of Alexa's calls, as requested, reworked Alexa's schedule for the rest of the month, and printed out some of her boss's more important paperwork for Alexa to sign when she had a moment.

Even at sixty-two, Sally Montachek was a beautiful woman, above-average height, with surprisingly few wrinkles, save for lines around the eyes and mouth. She was slender, having kept the same hourglass figure throughout her life. Her hair was miraculously still blond, though thinner than when she was younger, and now perpetually in a bun.

It was a little past five, and people were already trickling out of the building, but Sally stayed behind. She'd always been the type of person who couldn't stand leaving anything half-finished at work. Besides, she was nearly done. She squinted at the computer, pulling her glasses up from around her neck where they hung whenever she wasn't using them. After she had responded to the email, setting up a meeting for next week between Alexa and the defense attorney handling one of her cases, she stood, stretched, and walked over to Alexa's still-closed office door. It looked like her boss was staying late.

She knocked gently on the door. "Alexa?" she said. "I'm leaving."

"Have a good night, Sally." Alexa's voice was muted by the door but still audible.

As Sally was walking toward the exit, she stopped as she saw the man in the middle of the hall. He was tall and well built, with olive skin and short, black hair. He had his head down, cheerily whistling a tune Sally didn't recognize.

Luca glanced up at the sound of her heels on the tile floor and gave a dazzling grin as he straightened, stretching slightly from being hunched over.

"Hey there, Sally," he said, still giving her that heart-melting smile as he leaned against his mop. "How are you doing today?"

"I'm fine, thanks," Sally said, trying not to think about how much she liked her name coming from the young man's lips, or the way her heart was beating just a little faster. "And yourself?"

Luca had been working at the district attorney's office for about two years now, and he had never failed to give Sally a warm smile and a "hello" as she walked past. She had never spoken to him outside of work, but it was easy to imagine him strolling down the street with a different woman every evening. He was charming, young, and good looking, and Sally tried to ignore those facts every time she walked by him.

"Much better now that I'm talking to a beautiful woman," Luca said. His dark-blue eyes, the same color as the sky after a storm, moved up and down her body, and she felt hot all over just from his gaze.

"Flatterer," she said teasingly. "I have to be twice your age."

"Mmm, not quite," Luca said, his eyes glittering. "Besides, that don't matter much to me; I prefer older women."

She couldn't hide the delighted blush creeping up her face. He saw it, and his grin grew wider still. He stepped around his mop so that there was nothing between them. He was close—a little too close. She could smell the alluring spice of his cologne and see every one of his dark, thick eyelashes.

"You got a stray hair," he said, and reached out and brushed it behind her ear. Sparks flew from where his fingers brushed lightly against her temple, and his hand lingered a second too long.

"Thanks," she said.

"What are you doing right now, Sally?" he asked. His hand went gently but confidently to her shoulder, and her breath almost hitched.

"Going home," she said.

He raised an eyebrow and cocked his head. "You think you could be a few minutes late?"

Reality came crashing back to her, and she stepped back, a little ashamed. His hand fell away from her without protest. "No," she said. "I have to get home to my husband."

Her husband. She had a husband. She needed to remember she had a husband. Even if she couldn't remember the last time they'd had sex, she was still married to Vladimir, still loved him, and needed to remain loyal.

Luca shrugged casually, clearly unbothered by the rejection, and moved back. "I just figured I would offer," he said. "I hope you don't mind. It's just hard to help myself around sexy, older women."

And there it was again, that old heat rushing through her, something she hadn't felt in what close to ten years.

She imagined it then: dragging him into the nearest broom closet, stripping him to see the firm, taut muscles beneath. She'd pull down his pants to see his cock before taking it in her hand and—

She kicked the thought away as far as she could, into the dark recesses of her mind, begging it never to resurface.

"You're fine," she said. "But I should probably go."

"Of course," Luca nodded, unabashed and seemingly unfazed by the conversation they'd just had. "You take care of yourself, Sally."

I might need to when I get home, Sally thought as she hurried down the hall. She could feel his gaze on her ass as she walked away. *Just to get this out of my system.*

All she could think as she stepped out into the warm August air that moved through the skyscrapers of New York City was: *Thank God for my vibrator.*

She took a deep breath, clearing her mind, then strolled down the street to the nearby parking garage. It had been a long day, and she needed to get home.

For more reasons than one.

CHAPTER 5

Alexa

ALEXA MET JOE AT THE Rooftop Plaza, one of the nicest restaurants in Manhattan. She stepped out of the elevator to a stunning view of the surrounding landscape and the glittering lights of the buildings below. The moon was bright overhead, and the rooftop restaurant was lit with hanging lanterns and elegant lights around the perimeter that gave the entire area a stylish, glowing appearance.

Joe was already waiting at the host stand when Alexa arrived. His jaw dropped when he saw her.

"Damn, babe," Joe said, walking over to her and kissing her passionately. "You weren't kidding about the dress."

Alexa smiled. It was a stunning, crimson dress that clung to her body in all the right places and went to midthigh, showing off long, sexy legs. The cut of the V-neck dipped low between her breasts, making it nearly impossible not to look. The fact that it was backless let everyone know she wasn't wearing a bra.

"You clean up nice yourself," she said, gesturing at the perfectly tailored dark-blue jacket and matching pants. "The suit's a nice change from the scrubs. Though you still manage to look great in those, too."

Joe Perilli was tall—a little over six feet—with dark hair that was already salted with gray. His mustache and goatee accentuated his strong jaw and high cheekbones. His green eyes glinted in the lantern light as he took in his wife's appearance.

"Trust me, I look like an ogre next to you," he said, kissing her again. "How the hell did I get so lucky?"

The hostess took them back to a table nestled in one corner of the rooftop: one of the more private tables, which was just fine for Alexa.

"Did your day get any better?" Joe asked as they settled into their seats.

"A bit," Alexa said. "It was still exhausting, and I'm still mad, but I at least got work done. But I'd rather not talk about it."

"Fine by me." Joe's hand reached out below the table to her thigh. "I'd rather talk about how hot you look in that dress. I can't get enough of it." He leaned forward and kissed her, squeezing her thigh at the same time in a way that made her moan with longing.

"Don't do that to me," she said.

"Why not?" he asked, rubbing her leg.

"Because you're going to make me want to skip dinner entirely."

"Well, if you need a bit of release—" Joe cut himself off as a waiter walked up to them. He was young, somewhere in his twenties. He didn't look as though he'd been sleeping well: His tan skin seemed pale and unhealthy, there were bags under his dark eyes, and his lush, dark hair was disheveled.

Despite this, he still wore a warm smile on his face as he came up to them. "Good evening. My name's Tony, and I'm going to be your waiter this evening. Can I get you started on something to drink?"

"Scotch on the rocks," Joe said.

"Pinot grigio," Alexa said.

"All right," Tony said, scribbling in his notebook. "I'll have those out for you in just a minute."

"Are you okay?" Alexa asked before Tony could leave.

Tony turned back around, still forcing that smile. "I'm all right," he said. "Just been a long week. My sis—" he coughed and looked away. "Just some personal things. But I appreciate the consideration."

And he walked briskly away. Alexa watched after him, her brow slightly furrowed. But then Joe kissed her neck, and her mind was diverted to a more interesting place.

—

THEY SKIPPED DESSERT AND HURRIED home to their large house on Long Island as fast as they could. Joe's hand didn't leave Alexa's thigh the entire time they were in their car, and the gentle caress of his fingers on the inside of her thigh was enough to send her into a frenzy of longing.

The instant they were through the front door, Joe was pulling the dress off her, his knuckles brushing against bare skin. Alexa shivered with delight as electricity shot through her to rest below her stomach. Leaving her dress crumpled on the living room floor, they raced upstairs to their bedroom.

He stripped, revealing lean muscle as he did. He looked even better with his clothes off. Alexa looked down to see his cock springing up, already erect. It was the perfect size, Alexa had always felt. Not too small and not too big. Just right.

He kissed her fervently as she fell into his arms and lowered her slowly to the bed. His hands were magic, running deliciously across her body. His lips moved from hers to her neck, her collarbone, and then her breasts— first the right, then the left.

"God, you're so sexy," he said between kisses. "Your body is absolutely incredible."

He kept lowering his head until it was level with her pussy, which was already soaking wet. He ran his fingers between her legs, feeling her swollen lips and smirking his approval.

"I've been waiting all day to taste you," he said. "I couldn't get you out of my mind."

Then he lowered his head, his tongue skillfully brushing against her clit, flicking gently. Her delighted gasp turned into a moan of longing as his tongue ran between her lips before thrusting it inside her.

How was he so good with his tongue? She groaned and clutched the bedsheets as he continued eating her pussy, each sweep of his tongue sending new spasms coursing through her, building the ever-growing need racing through her. She wanted more than his tongue, but it felt so good that she let him continue, her back arching as he continued pleasuring her expertly.

When he came up for air, his eyes were filled with lust, and he licked his lips.

"You taste so good, babe," he said before moving up and kissing her. She could smell herself on his lips and his breath, and it made her even hungrier for him than she had been moments earlier.

"Stop teasing me and fuck me," she said, though her words were immediately followed by a gasp as his fingers pressed against her mound.

"You sure about that, babe?" he asked teasingly. "You look like you're having a good time."

She glared at him, not saying a word. Joe laughed.

"All right," he said. "As you command."

His dick pressed lightly against her vagina, still teasing her as he ran it along the outside, circling her womanhood tantalizingly. Finally, just when she was about to snap at him again to stop taunting her, he thrust himself into her, cutting off her irritation. She cried out in pleasure as he filled her, every pump sending new longing and delight through her.

He gripped her hips as he continued to glide in and out of her, his own soft grunts demonstrating his pleasure. Her heartbeat was speeding up, and her entire body burned. Her mind began to go blank, save for the overwhelming need for him and his cock. Her head flew back in ecstasy, and her breathing grew rapid and shallow. Every one of his movements— every caress of his hands and every breath that blew across her hair—she felt tenfold as she grew increasingly aware of him and how his cock felt inside her. She began bucking her hips, thrusting in time with him as her body desperately needed him and begged for the release that only he could provide.

He leaned over her, his mouth lowering to her neck where he nipped gently, the way he knew she liked, sending a breathless gasp escaping from her mouth. Her toes curled, and her back began to arch even higher. His kiss moved up her neck even as he continued thrusting inside her.

The heat in her stomach was continuing to build, burning hotter and brighter with each sensation, each pump of his cock. It was nearly unbearable, and she thought she might break at any second.

He gave a hard thrust just as he nibbled her ear, and she shattered. She cried out in delight as she rode the wave, savoring every moment of pleasure. Moments later, she felt Joe finish inside her with his own groan of pleasure, his dick throbbing inside her as he came. He gave her a soft kiss and slid out of her.

"You're amazing, babe," he said, brushing a strand of her now-messy, dark hair behind her ear.

"Funny," she said, still breathing heavily. "I was just about to say the same thing."

CHAPTER 6

Carmella, 2004

CARMELLA WRIGGLED THROUGH THE crowd and made her way over to the bar.

The club was packed, but the overly loud club music blasting throughout the dimly lit space made it nearly impossible to hear any of the conversations around her. Bodies pressed against one another, the heat beginning to grow a bit stifling. Her mouth was dry, but her head was swimming pleasantly from the alcohol.

She wedged herself up against the bar and waved at the bartender. The bright-red crop top; short, black skirt; and high heels were enough to draw the eye of just about every man (and several of the women) in the immediate area, so it didn't take long for the man to notice her and come over.

"Two vodka cranberries, please," she said, glancing over her shoulder. Her friend Georgia was barely visible through a gap in the people. Her hips were swaying to the music, her eyes closed as she grinded against a stranger. Carmella smiled. She was glad Georgia was having fun. It had been a long week for both of them at work, and Georgia had just gone through a pretty nasty breakup, and they'd agreed spur of the moment to go out and have some fun.

The bartender came back a moment later, holding two identical glasses. "Tab?" he yelled, and she nodded.

She'd just wrapped her hands around the glasses, the outsides of which were already dripping with condensation, cooling her fingers and palms pleasantly, when she felt someone a little too close behind her. Slowly, she turned. This time, the crowd had pressed together into a mass, and there was no sign of her pretty, redheaded friend dancing on the club floor. That view was blocked by a broad-shouldered, shorter man. In her heels, she was nearly a head taller than him.

"Hey," he said.

Carmella arched an eyebrow. "Hey, yourself."

She studied the man briefly. He wasn't unattractive necessarily, but he wasn't conventionally attractive, either. His black hair was slightly greasy, and his brown eyes were unremarkable, but there was still something alluring about the man, something inexplicable that made her feel drawn to him in a way she wasn't used to.

It was his smile, she decided. It was incredible and made his otherwise round face seem chiseled. No, it wasn't just that. There was something else there, too; something that wasn't as easy to define. It was the charisma, the self-confidence. He wasn't intimidated by Carmella, and it was clear that he had every confidence that she would say yes to whatever he asked. He wasn't timid or nervous like others might have been. She decided she liked that.

"I'd offer to buy you a drink," the man said, grinning lazily, "but it looks like you beat me to it. Can I at least get the next one?"

"If you can find me," Carmella said.

"Oh, don't worry," he said, his eyes glancing up and down her body as he took in the long legs, the taut stomach, and her firm breasts—perky, despite their size. "There's not a chance in hell that I'm going to miss you in a crowd."

"That so?"

He took a step closer, and the scent of cologne and Listerine wafted toward her. "I make a point of keeping track of attractive women," he said. He held out his hand, and the two of them were close enough that his fingers nearly touched her breast. "Casimir."

She shook it. "Carmella."

"Do you want to dance?" he asked.

The beat of the music had changed to something more alluring and sexual, the kind of song that was more suited to a single partner than jumping up and down in a crowd.

She cocked her head, looking him up and down again. "Think you can keep up with me?"

He laughed. "Trust me, baby," he said, and his hand went to her waist without her permission, his fingers brushing against her ass just a little. "I'm more worried about you keeping up with me."

Then, without waiting for a response, he pulled her onto the dance floor by her hip, both vodka cranberries still in her hands.

She managed to get the drink to her friend before it spilled all over her dress, and Carmella held onto hers as best she could on the dance floor. She would have put it down somewhere, but Casimir held on to her the entire rest of the evening, his hand rarely away from one part of her body or another, subtly but effectively keeping her in place. But it was so expertly done that she didn't even notice he was doing it.

She should have guessed then—by the possessiveness, the presumptuousness, the way he glued himself to her the rest of the night, barely letting her speak to anyone but him, including Georgia—that there was something off about him, that he was bad news and she should stay away from him. But none of it registered as they grinded and moved against one another on the dance floor, surrounded by dozens of other people.

When she finally said for the third time that she needed to sit down and have some water, he capitulated, leading her to an empty table on the edge of the dance floor before disappearing toward the bar. When he came back, there was a plastic cup of water in one hand and a new vodka cranberry in the other.

"I thought you might want a refill," he said, placing both glasses in front of her before sliding into the seat directly to her right. His thigh pressed against hers.

"You're pretty sure of yourself, ain't you?" she said, raising an eyebrow as she drank some of the water before switching to the other drink. It was strong.

He gave a wide smile, and his arm slipped around her back, his hand coming to rest on her shoulder.

"I've learned that women like a bit of confidence in a man." His thumb brushed gently against her neck, sending shivers through her body. She forced herself not to squirm as a fire began to kindle between her legs.

"Confidence, maybe; not cockiness."

"You mean you don't want some cock?" His free hand went to the inside of her thigh, moving halfway up her skirt and stopping just short of her pussy. From anyone else, it would have been creepy and way too forward, and she would have shoved the guy away immediately, cursing him out and telling him to get the fuck away from her. But from Casimir, it felt perfectly natural, absolutely fine, despite knowing him for only an hour. He squeezed, almost proprietarily, and her back arched reflexively. She let out a soft gasp.

"Yeah, that's what I thought."

She didn't answer, but it seemed she didn't need to. He leaned forward, and his warm breath caressed her neck.

"You're coming home with me," he said, his voice a command. "You know that, right?"

He was doing all the right things to turn her on. She wasn't wearing panties, and she could feel the inside of her legs getting wet. She nodded unthinkingly.

"Good." He squeezed her thigh again, this time harder. There was an unspoken but vividly clear message in the gesture, one that was impossible for her to mistake for anything else, even though she missed the danger behind it.

You're mine.

Later, Carmella would wonder how she'd overlooked it. She knew the signs, knew enough of the red flags that it should have been obvious. She shouldn't have fallen for him or his tricks. But in the moment, she'd been captivated by his spell.

And she'd be his captive for the next five years.

—

WHEN CARMELLA WAS eighteen, she moved out of her mother's house.

It wasn't because of a falling-out or anything like that. She still loved her mother and the rest of her siblings, but their place was too small for their family, now they were all older. Someone needed to move out. And since she was the oldest, she was the one who had to make that sacrifice.

She didn't mind. Ever since she was fifteen, she'd wanted more space, somewhere to call her own. And this way, she'd be able to send her mother more money. There weren't many job opportunities for her in the small, upstate New York town where they lived.

So when she graduated from high school, she moved to New York City, enrolled in community college, and began looking for a job. It wasn't long before she found a decent secretary position for some real estate firm that paid enough that she was able to send home a decent amount to her family, even if she had to eat canned food and ramen for dinner most nights.

It wasn't easy. But her life hadn't been easy for some time, not since long before her abusive father had left. He hadn't been physically abusive (at least not to the kids), but his words were enough to leave deep scars that still hurt years later. She'd heard them all: *lazy, good for nothing, nothing but a financial drain.* And she'd internalized them more than she would ever realize, for years to come. It was easy to think you were worthless when you heard it your entire childhood.

There was one time when she'd come home from school, her mother had had a new bruise, and her father was lounging on the couch as if nothing had happened. When her mother asked her how school had been that day, before Carmella could even answer, her father had interjected.

"Don't know why we even bother," he said, his eyes not moving from the television. "You're not smart enough to do anything with it. I don't get why some kids have to go to school. It's not like they're going to make anything of themselves. If you ask me, she's going to be either whoring herself out by the time she's sixteen or waiting tables her entire life."

"That's not fair," her mother said. "You can't talk to her like—"

"I'll talk to her however the hell I want," he interrupted, standing from the couch and stalking over to his wife, even while his daughter watched. He jabbed a finger into her chest. "This is my house. You can't tell me what I can and can't do."

"She's your daughter," her mother said. "How could you say she's going to be a whore? She doesn't even understand what that means. She's ten."

"Well, she better learn soon," he said. "She's gonna be doing it soon enough."

Her mother was getting angry now. "You need to sto—"

He hit her. It was the first time Carmella had seen it, but it wouldn't be the last. Every time after that, until her mother finally left, it grew less and less shocking and seemed more and more normal. And her father always made a point to remind Carmella, especially when he caught her staring at him after he slapped her mother or gave her a new bruise, that she was good for nothing and wasn't worth his time and that she would probably wind up a slut on the streets somewhere.

But she tried hard to make something of herself, tried to put her father's insults behind her and push them to the back of her mind. More than anything, what fueled her through that time in her life was a desperation to prove that her dad was wrong. She knew by then that she would never see him again, and she had no desire to do so in the first place. But that drive was what kept her going, even when she had to go without heat one winter, when her kid brother got injured in a bike accident and her mother didn't have the health insurance to pay for it. Carmella had given her mother everything but what she needed for groceries and tuition until the medical bills were taken care of.

And the hard work paid off. She finished community college with her associate's degree in business two years after she moved out. She got a better job as an office manager in the same company, and she began to save money, planning to start a business of her own, though she wasn't sure what it would be.

Things were beginning to look up. She gained more confidence and made friends, and it was easier and easier to put her father's words behind her.

It all seemed to be going well.

At least until Casimir forced his way into her life that night at the bar.

CHAPTER 7

Alexa

"ALEXA," A SMUG VOICE CALLED from behind her. "Wanted a word."

Sighing, Alexa closed her eyes momentarily. She had just finished a long meeting with a defense attorney who had failed to hand over all his evidence during discovery, and she was trying to convince him to give her the rest before she involved the judge. He'd been reluctant, and they had gone in circles for an hour, but she had finally convinced him. She desperately needed coffee, and the last thing she wanted to do was deal with Jacob O'Brien.

"What is it, Jacob?" She didn't turn to look at him or stop moving toward the break room, where freshly brewed coffee awaited her.

She knew her not stopping wouldn't deter the man, even if she wanted it to.

O'Brien sauntered up to her and started matching her stride. He was tall, with a perpetual five o'clock shadow that enhanced his features. He dyed his hair a soft brown, but the creeping gray was visible at the roots.

"I heard you threw a fit when Andrew gave me the Johnson case instead of you," O'Brien said, his hands in the pants pockets of his expensive suit. "Everyone outside of his office could hear you yelling."

"That so?" she said dryly. She sped up, and O'Brien kept up with her. It had been two days since Barrow had called her into his office to break the news to her. She was still fuming about it, even as she accepted the situation. But O'Brien mocking her for it was rubbing salt into the wound, and it was all she could do to keep her temper.

"Oh yeah," he said, smirking. "I don't think I've ever heard of someone wanting a case that bad. And everyone's talking about it."

"I don't particularly care," she said.

They reached the break room. There was enough coffee in the carafe for two cups. She opened the cupboard to grab a mug, but O'Brien reached over her head and plucked a large mug from the top shelf, then strolled over to the coffeepot.

"You know Andrew's pushing me to add attempted murder to the charges?" O'Brien poured the entirety of the remaining coffee into the oversized mug. "It's so stupid."

Alexa watched with growing anger as he casually added an exorbitant amount of milk and sugar to the mug. Gritting her teeth, she began rifling through one of the lower cabinets for more coffee to make a new pot.

"We're out of coffee," O'Brien said, slurping from his mug. "This was the last of it until Joanna restocks it."

Great. Her fists clenched, and she forced herself not to sigh. She crouched again, this time rummaging around for a decent caffeinated tea. She found the most tolerable one—which wasn't saying much—and started the percolator.

"The whole thing is bullshit," O'Brien said. His eyes never left Alexa's face as he kept track of her reaction. "I don't get why the police arrested him in the first place. And attempted murder? Come on, we all know that girl is lying. I mean, have you heard her story?"

You know I haven't, Alexa thought, even as she imagined punching O'Brien in his smug face. She needed to leave before she did something she regretted. The percolator needed to hurry up.

Instead of enacting her fantasies of pummeling him into the ground, all she said was, "Nope. Haven't heard anything."

"The whole thing is stupid," he repeated. "The girl—I think her name is Maria something-or-other—is saying Casimir brought her to his place without her asking. Then, when she said she didn't want to fuck him, he raped her and beat her to a pulp. Then he got her into his car, drove a bit, threw her out into an alley, and drove off. It's one of the most far-fetched stories I've ever heard. And a guy once told me a dragon burned down his house and was framing him for arson and insurance fraud."

"And what about the story isn't true?" Alexa asked. "You know he's been up on charges before."

"Oh, I know," he chuckled. "And if I didn't, I would have after your outburst the other day."

"What about the story isn't true?" she repeated, trying not to clench her hands into fists.

"Well, I'm sure she went to his place," he said. "But if she did, I'll bet it was consensual, and she fucked Casimir willingly. Then, when she felt guilty about it later, she lied to preserve her image. It happens all the time."

Guys like you *think it happens all the time*, Alexa thought but didn't say. Instead, she asked, "And the bruises?" in as calm and rational a voice as she could muster.

He shrugged, taking another loud slurp of coffee that should have been Alexa's. "My guess? She liked it rough. Probably why she needed to explain them away in the first place with that stupid story. Otherwise people would've known she's a whore."

She almost pounced at him then, prepared to tear him limb from limb. She would have been arrested for assault, but it would have been worth it to beat some sense in him. What stopped her was his expression. He was grinning ferally, smirking at how he was annoying her and riling her up. The reaction he was getting out of her was better than sex to him right now. That was the entire reason he was doing this. Well, if he wanted to piss her off, two could play at that game.

"You got some white under your nose, Jacob," she said. "Might want to clean up better when you do coke in your office."

His eyes flashed with alarm, and he quickly wiped his hand beneath his nose. He looked at his hand, then scowled when he saw nothing. Alexa smiled sweetly.

"Well, it's good to know that my suspicions about you were right."

He glowered at her, every inch of his body now tense, practically shaking with anger.

"You can't prove it," he said.

"Not right now," Alexa agreed. "But we'll see."

The percolator clicked off. Finally. Alexa poured hot water into the mug and bobbed the sachet tag up and down as she sauntered toward the exit.

O'Brien's hand reached out and grabbed her arm as she passed, spinning her violently enough that hot, tea-stained water splashed against her fingers and onto the floor.

"What the hell?" she asked, glaring up at O'Brien even as the hot water scalded her fingers. There was no smugness or mockery in his face now; it was pure rage.

"Make no mistake," he hissed, his fingers still gripping her bicep. He leaned forward so his face was in hers and spoke so quietly that no one else could hear them. "That bitch is lying, and I'm going to make sure everyone knows it by the end of this."

For a long moment she stared, her mouth open in shock as his words sunk in.

"You're going to throw the case, aren't you?" she said. "If it gets to trial, you're going to intentionally do a shitty job so Casimir wins the case."

"I don't know what you're talking about," he said, but his eyes said something entirely different. He released her arm and stood straight. "Well, I need to get back to work. Take care."

He strolled out, whistling, leaving Alexa standing in the break room staring after him in shock.

After the shock wore off, the anger resurged, and her blood began to boil. O'Brien was going to lose the case on purpose. She couldn't let that happen. Even if Casimir was innocent and the girl was lying (about as likely as her winning the lottery three times in a row, but innocent until proven guilty), that wasn't a reason to not do his job properly.

She clutched the mug tighter in her hand. She needed to get Jacob O'Brien off the case. She needed to be the one to prosecute.

The only question was how?

CHAPTER 8

Maria and Tony, One Month Earlier

TONY PACED BACK AND FORTH in the kitchen anxiously, checking his phone every two minutes as he waited for his sister to call or text him.

She was late. She should have been home an hour and a half ago, but he hadn't heard anything from her. Her phone went immediately to voicemail, and that frightened him.

He knew she'd gone to the club with her friends. She'd texted him a photo of four girls' heads smushed together as they all smiled for the camera. But that was the last he'd heard from her. This wasn't like her, and he knew something had happened.

He had just made up his mind to go out and look for her when he heard the sound of a key sliding into the front door of their apartment. His shoulders sagged in relief. Maria was the only other person with keys.

There were soft shuffling noises, as if his sister was trying to make as little noise as possible. She emerged from the hall into the kitchen and startled when she saw him, but her surprise was nothing compared to the shock and horror that slammed into Tony like a sledgehammer when he saw her.

Maria looked terrible. Her face was swollen, red in spots that promised to be large purple bruises by morning. There was crusted blood beneath her nose, and her lip was split.

"*¡Mierda!*" Tony said. His phone clattered to the ground as he bolted toward her. "Are you okay? What the fuck happened?"

She flinched as his hands went gently to her shoulders and looked away.

"I'm fine," she said. Her voice was dry and husky, with no sign of her normal, musical lilt.

"Bullshit," Tony said. "Anyone with eyes can see that's not true. Here, sit down on the couch. I'll get you some water."

He guided her to the sofa and sat her down before dashing toward the kitchen and grabbing her a glass of water. As he did, he grabbed the Advil as well.

"Take these, too," he said when he returned to the sofa. Maria had laid down, her head resting on the armrest and her knees drawn in close to her chest. She sat up long enough to follow her brother's request before curling up again.

Tony crouched beside her so they were at eye level. His hand went to her hair, stroking it comfortingly. It wasn't until then that he realized her hair was covered in grit and dirt.

"What happened?" he asked.

"Nothing," she said, then burst into tears. Her whole body convulsed as she sobbed, tear tracks spilling down her swollen and grime-covered face. Tony let her cry, continuing to stroke her hair as she did, waiting patiently and feeling his own pain with every sob.

Finally, after several long minutes, her cries softened to sniffles and eventually died away.

He waited another five minutes before asking again, "What happened?"

She shook her head violently, burying her face in the armrest.

"It's okay," Tony said soothingly. "You can tell me. It's safe."

When she still didn't say anything, Tony stood and walked back into the kitchen. He wet a washcloth and came back to the sofa.

"Here," he said. "Sit up for a moment."

She obeyed mechanically, trembling slightly. Her brown eyes were as wide as a doe's, and they kept darting around the apartment as if she expected someone to emerge from the shadows.

Tony wiped her face, trying his best to be gentle while also getting her clean. Removing the dirt and dried blood from her face made her instantly look better, but not by much.

"Please tell me what happened," he said softly.

His sister hesitated again, but then her shoulders slumped, and she relented.

"I was at the club," she said. "And this guy came up to me while I was dancing."

Tony winced. He knew how much his sister loved to dance, how she moved so gracefully and beautifully. She looked even more stunning when she was dancing than normal. She had been dancing ever since she was four, and even seventeen years later, she was still incredible at it. It wasn't surprising that so many men watched her whenever she stepped onto the dance floor.

Even when she wasn't dancing, she was a gorgeous woman. Tanned skin and wavy, auburn hair accentuated her almond-shaped eyes and angular face. Her curves were well-defined, even as she kept the lean muscles of a dancer. But right now, she seemed small, the vivacity she normally possessed diminished by whatever had happened.

"He seemed nice at first," Maria said, not looking at her brother. She spoke to the floor. "Kept dancing with me and offering to buy me drinks. He was on the older side but seemed harmless enough. And the more I drank, the nicer he seemed. He kept making me dance with him, and whenever I tried to go talk to my friends, he'd find some way of convincing me not to.

"After a while, I started feeling really drunk. I told him I wanted to go home, and he offered to take me there. So I said yes.

"I was so drunk that I didn't realize until he got me to his apartment building that he had taken me back to his place instead of here. When I tried to get away and told him that I had meant my home, he ignored me and dragged me into his apartment. I was too drunk to fight, and when I tried to scream, he covered my mouth.

"He locked the door when we got in. And then he—"

She hiccuped and began crying again. Tony sat on the couch next to her, wrapping his arms around her and holding her, trying to give her some brotherly comfort.

"It's okay," he said, patting her gently. "It's okay."

"Then, when he was done," she finally managed to get out, even as she glossed over the traumatic events that had happened in the man's apartment, "he threw me back in his car and then tossed me into an alley. I had to walk home cause I didn't have enough money for a cab. He stole my wallet."

"Why didn't you call me?" he asked. "I would have come and gotten you. Or called you a cab." He would have done that in a heartbeat, and he knew she knew that. He and Maria were incredibly close, and there was nothing he wouldn't do for her.

She gave a tired smile that made her split lip more prominent, and she wiped her eyes again. "My phone broke while he was hitting me. It fell out of my pocket as I was trying to get away from him, and he stomped on it."

"Asshole," Tony said.

"I tried to fight him, Tony," she said, tears clearly on the verge of spilling over again. "I promise. But he was too strong, and I was drunk. And whenever I tried to do anything he didn't like, he just started hitting me. I'm sorry."

"You don't have anything to be sorry about," he said, still holding her. "This isn't your fault."

"It feels like it is," she said, pulling away from him and wiping her nose. "If I'd been more careful—"

"No, don't say that," he said. "That's not true. Those kinds of guys, if they want something, they're going to get it one way or another. And you're here now. You're safe. That's all that matters."

He meant it from the bottom of his heart. Ever since their parents died, all Tony and Maria had were each other. Tony loved his sister dearly and didn't know what he'd do without her.

I could have found out tonight, Tony thought, panic and relief jolting through him at the same time.

"Who did this to you?" he asked, his anger rising. "What asshole did this? I'm going to make him pay."

But Maria was shaking her head violently, her eyes wide with fear and horror. "Please don't," she said. "You don't know what he's like. He'll kill you."

"Who?" he repeated. "Who was it?"

"Casimir Johnson," she said.

Tony blanched. Everyone in this area knew Casimir's reputation. He wasn't a crime lord or anything like that; he was too lazy. But he had the connections he needed to throw his weight around, and people who crossed him tended to have a hard time of it after. And he was usually able to cover his tracks, purely because people were terrified of who his friends were.

"You gotta go to the police, Maria," he said.

"I can't," she said, her eyes wide with horror. "He'll come after me."

"I'll protect you," he said.

"I can't," she said.

"I know you're scared, and that's okay. But he's just gonna keep doing this if someone doesn't say something." Maria didn't answer and instead turned away from him. The angle made the cut and bruise on her cheek even more noticeable. "And we've gotta get you to the hospital," he added.

Maria opened her mouth to argue, but Tony shook his head. "You're too beat up, and I'm worried you might have a concussion or something worse. You're my little sis, and I'm gonna make sure you're looked after. We'll talk about the police later. But right now, we're getting you to a doctor. Come on."

Without waiting for her to respond, he stood up. He gently lifted her off the couch, and the two of them moved slowly—Maria limping rather than walking normally—toward the front door.

"We'll fix this," Tony promised. "You're going to be all right."

But how, he wasn't sure just yet.

—

TONY AND MARIA GREW UP in Bogotá, Colombia. Even though he was barely a teenager when they moved to the United States, he remembered the incredible food and marvelous entertainment that seemed to be on every street. He remembered the eclectic races and cultures that made up the melting pot of Colombia. It had been a vibrant, multicultural city that had helped shape his childhood in a way he could now barely describe.

His parents, Harry and Metilda Gonzalez, seemed to have a perfect life with a fairy-tale love story.

Metilda had been petite, not even five feet tall, with long, black hair—which Tony had inherited—that cascaded down to her waist. She and Harry had married when she was only sixteen, and she had completed high school after they were wed. But despite her young age, they had been deeply in love, and nothing seemed to come between them. Their arguments were resolved smoothly and always ended with a tender kiss. Even though Metilda had never learned to drive or how to manage finances, she taught herself and kept the house spotless and the bills paid.

And she could cook better than anyone Tony had ever met. Their house had always been filled with the mouthwatering scents of whatever she was making: empanadas, pescado frito, arepas, pan de bono, or even chocolate santafereño. He had gotten spoiled with delicious food as a child, and as he grew up, he would come to miss it. When he was older, he would be grateful that he had clung to his mother's side as a kid whenever she had been cooking. She had taught him as much as she could in the too-short time they had together. But at least now, whenever he cooked and his apartment filled with those same tantalizing smells, he could be transported back to Colombia and his mother's kitchen—somewhere he'd never be able to go again.

Harry was six foot and stocky, with Maria's lighter, auburn hair and a beard. He had been attractive, with his strong muscles and piercing stare, and Tony remembered more than one woman stopping him in the street or eyeing him from across the shop. But his father didn't seem to notice. He was too preoccupied with his job, dedicated to a fault. He was the type of man who had a schedule and stuck to it like glue, never wavering no matter what the situation was. In his entire life, he had only missed two days of work: The first was the day Tony was born, and the second was when Maria came into the world four years later.

Every day, even on the weekends, Harry woke up at three a.m. On workdays, he was out the door by four and wouldn't return until six that evening. On his days off, he would either do as many household chores as he could or relax in front of the television with a six-pack.

He and Metilda didn't make much, and with Tony and Maria, their funds were stretched even tighter. But they still had a good life and were entirely devoted to one another.

When Tony was twelve, his family made the decision to move to the United States, hoping for better opportunities, both for the family as a whole and for Harry's job. They moved to a small apartment in New York City, one that had only two bedrooms, so Tony and his sister had to share a room. At first, Tony had hated it. He was old enough to want his privacy. But after complaining about it for the third time in a month, he saw the pain and guilt in his mother's eyes when she told him they couldn't afford anything else, and he didn't bring it up again.

They thought things would be easier in the United States, but they were wrong. The American Dream, it seemed, did not apply to everyone. Harry couldn't find a job. At first, he put the same effort into job hunting as he had his old job. He would get up every morning, go to the library, and get on one of the public computers to go job hunting. He would surf all the websites, sending out a minimum of five applications a day, sometimes as many as fifteen or twenty. He would even go so far as to search the paper for job opportunities. And every day, when he logged on to the computer, surrounded by silent library patrons at their own cubicles, the clacking of their keyboards the only real indication that others were there, he would check his email, only to find it as quiet as the rest of the library, with no emails anywhere to be found.

The longer it went on, the more discouraged he got, and the more time at home he spent sitting in front of the television and drinking beer they couldn't afford. Tony watched, helpless, as his father continued to sink further and further into a constant, drunken depression.

Finally, one of Harry's friends whom he met during one of his trips to the library found him a job. It wasn't a fantastic job, but it would at least pay the bills and take some of the weight off Metilda's shoulders. But it was clear he was still miserable, and every moment he wasn't at work, he was sitting in front of the TV.

Tony, for his part, waited anxiously to turn fourteen, when he would be able to get a job so he could help his family. When he was finally old enough, he found work as a busboy and put in as many hours as was allowed. And every paycheck, before he gave it to his mother, he set aside enough money for Maria to take dance lessons like she had back in Colombia. It had been two years since she took classes. Tony loved his sister, and the one thing he wanted more than anything was to give her back something she loved.

But that didn't change the problems his family was experiencing. Harry got worse and worse as the years went on. Tony was thirteen when his father hit Metilda for the first time. He remembered it clear as day, the horror and anger that washed over him in a great wave as his mother stumbled back, her hand going to her cheek where he had slapped her. Harry had turned and seen Tony standing there, his mouth open in despair.

"Mind your own business, boy," Harry said. "It'll be better for everyone."

It got worse. The more his father drank, the more he hit Metilda. And it wasn't long after that that he began striking Tony and Maria as well. Tony tried to protect his sister whenever he could, but there were times when he couldn't, and it broke his heart every time.

He could have endured it if it were just him, if Harry had left Tony's mother and Maria alone. But he didn't. He wanted to do something, to stop his father, but he didn't know how. And he was afraid.

Later, he would blame himself, tell himself that if he had acted sooner, he could have stopped what happened next. But by the time he finally got up the courage to tell someone about what their father was doing, it was too late.

He was fifteen when he came home from school to an eerily silent house, and the smell of shit and piss hit him like a truck when he stepped inside. He gagged, and as he did, he had to wonder why he was smelling something so rancid instead of the familiar, mouthwatering scents of Metilda's cooking.

"*Ma?*" he called, and when there was no response, his stomach clenched. It was too quiet. The television wasn't on. It was always on when he came home because his father was always sitting in his chair watching whatever was on until it was time for him to go to work. But there was nothing, only that putrid smell that seemed to permeate the apartment, seeping into the walls.

He walked hesitantly down the hall, glancing around to peer into the small rooms, only to find nothing out of the ordinary. It wasn't until he got to the kitchen that he found the source of the stench.

Both his parents lay dead on the floor, blood pooling around them. His mother had been shot three times: once in the stomach and twice in the head. Her skull was cracked open. It turned out brains were gray, not pink.

Onions and peppers lay scattered across the floor as if she'd been carrying them when she'd died. Some of them had drying globs of blood on them that matched the ones on the top row of cabinets and part of the counter. Raw chicken breast sat patiently on a cutting board.

His father, on the other hand, had a single wound. The gun was still in his mouth, and his brains were splattered on one of the windows.

He killed her, Tony thought, his legs going numb and unsteady. *He actually killed her.*

Then he ran into the bathroom and threw up in the sink.

The story was fairly clear, both to him and the police. The worst part was trying to explain what had happened to Maria, who was only eleven. He didn't let her see the bodies, but she was smart enough to know that something bad had happened. They had turned into orphans in a single afternoon, all thanks to their father.

After that they went into the foster system, though, mercifully, they managed to stay together and in New York. When Tony turned eighteen, he requested guardianship over Maria and worked to provide for her. It was hard, but they managed.

And then Casimir had to come and ruin it.

CHAPTER 9

Carmella, 2004

CASIMIR PROPOSED TO CARMELLA in between cigarettes in his apartment.

"Been thinking," he said, smashing the still-burning butt into the overflowing ashtray. "Don't think we should keep going like this."

Carmella's brow furrowed as she lounged on the couch next to him, her feet propped in his lap. She shifted up and looked at him, her head cocked.

"What's that supposed to mean?" she asked. "You breaking up with me?"

Her heart lurched at the thought. It had been a month since they first met at the club, but it had felt like a lifetime. From the moment she woke up in his bed the morning after their first meeting until now, it had felt as though he were a permanent fixture in her life. He called her every day, would show up at her house unannounced, and had seemingly wedged his way into her friend circle and every other facet of her life. She didn't mind. Casimir was charming, once you got past the rough patches. Her friends loved him, and there was something about the overprotectiveness that she found endearing. The fact that he might be breaking up with her didn't fit the pattern, but she still felt an ominous prickling creeping up the back of her spine.

"Nah." He bent forward to look at the coffee table in front of him, considered the bag of pot and rolling papers, then shrugged and went for another cigarette. "Nothing like that. You're too sexy for me to do something that stupid."

"Then what? Move in together?"

He flicked the lighter and inhaled as he brought the flickering flame to the end of the cigarette.

"Closer," he said. His gaze swept up and down her body, eyes proprietarily lingering on her breasts. "Nah, I wanna keep you close so I can keep an eye on you. I don't want no man getting his hands on you besides me."

"Then what?"

He raised an eyebrow. "You really this stupid?"

She folded her arms. "If it's what I think it is, then stop dragging it out."

One side of his mouth grinned while the other held on to the cigarette still dangling between his lips. "Then go on and stand up."

She obeyed and watched, heart pounding, as he went down on one knee, wedging himself between the coffee table laden with drugs and the filthy sofa he refused to get rid of. He fished around in his pocket and dug out a small, black box.

He took out the cigarette, blew out a large puff of smoke, and said, "I want you to marry me."

It wasn't a question so much as a demand, the way he said most everything. But in the moment, Carmella didn't notice or care. They had only known one another for a month, but she was certain he was the one. He seemed perfect for her, and she wouldn't realize until years later the facade he'd put on in order to trap her.

"Yes, of course," she said.

Grinning, he stood and embraced her. His kiss tasted like stale tobacco smoke as he slipped the ring on her finger.

She blinked, surprised, as she studied the ring properly for the first time. The band was yellow gold, and there was a large, oval diamond surrounded by smaller ones. It was undeniably beautiful, but she couldn't hide her shock.

"It's huge," she said. "You sure you can afford it?"

Later, much later, when the setting was loose and she went to fix it, the clerk would tell her it was fake. The diamond nearly as big as her thumb was just cubic zirconium, a cheap knockoff. Casimir had been lying to her the entire time. But by then, she was wearing long sleeves nearly all the time and sunglasses even inside, claiming she was cold and had migraines when really she was trying to hide the bruises. So the fact that he had skimped on the ring and then lied to her about it no longer surprised her. She still got the ring fixed and never confronted him about it. It wasn't worth the beating she'd get for it.

But at that moment, she believed it was real, and the sparkle it gave in the dim light of the apartment mesmerized her, even as the elation of Casimir proposing washed over her like a tsunami.

"You're worth it," he said as she admired the oval diamond. "You're getting only the best from now on." His hand went between her legs and cupped her womanhood, the other hand holding her shoulder. "And I ain't just talking about fancy jewelry."

And he spun her around and pushed her into the bedroom.

—

CARMELLA WOULD HAVE BEEN happy with a simple wedding. Hell, she would have been happy going to the courthouse with a couple of witnesses and doing it there. She didn't need anything fancy. All she wanted was Casimir.

But he had insisted, saying he wanted her to feel like a queen. But even then, Carmella wondered if it was actually because *he* wanted something fancy and was using her as an excuse. She wasn't blind, and she knew the type of people he was hanging out with. They were the unsavory type, but powerful, and showing them he could afford something extravagant would be a great way of getting into their good graces. She didn't like the fact that he was getting involved with them, but the one time she had expressed her concerns, he had waved them away.

"Don't believe everything you hear," he said. "They're good people. Getting friendly with them is going to bring us straight to the top."

When she'd tried to protest, he'd just walked away, saying, "I ain't hearing nothing more about it."

So she went along with it and the lavish wedding. But she didn't mind. Casimir handled almost everything, from the venue to the menu, asking for her input but handling everything else, saying that he wanted it to be perfect for her and he didn't want her to worry. So the only thing she really had to worry about was her dress and those for her bridesmaids: her sister and Georgia.

As the planning continued, one thing became very clear: Casimir really was going all out. Fancy champagne, an open bar, expensive food, a venue with a stunning view of a river and mountains for the actual wedding, and a massive house for the reception.

"Are you sure we can afford all this?" she asked.

"Course we can," Casimir said, lighting a cigarette as they went over the final seating arrangement. "I wouldn't be paying for it if we couldn't."

"How?" Neither of their jobs was terrible, but it seemed impossible they could pay for something like this on their salaries.

"Won a shit ton of money at poker a couple of months ago," he said. "We've got money for this and then some. Relax. I told you I got this covered."

She wanted to protest, to say that money could go toward a house, or savings if they ever wanted a kid. They shouldn't blow it all on a fancy wedding. But when she opened her mouth, he shot her a warning look, and she clammed up, trying to ignore the prickling sensation crawling up her spine.

He's just stressed, she thought. *Once things die down a bit, he'll be back to his normal self.*

The wedding itself was gorgeous and everything that Casimir had promised. Everything went perfectly, and Carmella couldn't remember the last time she had danced that much and smiled so widely.

But when they got into the limo afterward, as she kicked off her shoes,

Casimir said, "I think we did a good job. Reggie and the rest of that group had a good time. Did you see the looks on their faces when they brought out the cake?"

Carmella gave him a funny look as the words set in. "I guess," she said. "But I was more focused on us getting married."

"Of course." He leaned over and kissed her. "Me too. I just thought it was funny. Now come on, we need to get ready for the honeymoon tomorrow."

CHAPTER 10

Alexa

ALEXA DRUMMED HER FINGERS on her desk, staring at the computer screen in front of her but not registering what was on it. A new email popped up with the familiar, slightly obnoxious chiming sound. She ignored it.

If anyone had walked in at that moment, they would have seen her brown eyes glazed over and her face contorted in an irritated scowl. Her chin was resting on her palm, and her mind was far away from the emails that had piled up in her inbox over the day.

It was O'Brien again. Because of course it was. It was always him. Ever since he had gotten that damn case, he'd been insufferable. Every time they crossed paths, he would give her that self-satisfied smirk and ask a snide question about her cases. From anyone else, it might have come across as courteous and interested. But from him, it was a clear jab, rubbing it in that he had gotten the case instead of her. Whenever they came across one another in the break room, or she came across him talking to another attorney, his hazel eyes would flick over in her direction, his mouth would tilt up into the faintest of smirks, and he'd change topics, going on about the Johnson case and how tedious it was and what a waste of time it was going to be. If any of the other lawyers he talked to noticed the abrupt change in topic or his blasé attitude about it, they didn't let on or say anything.

The entire thing was just to get a rise out of Alexa. She was certain that he would love for her to try and punch him. But she had kept her cool, determined not to stoop to his level or let him get to her. Unfortunately, that wasn't really working for her. The anger was rising and threatened to boil over at any minute.

And what she had seen just an hour ago had put her over the edge.

She had been walking down the hall toward the break room, desperate for another cup of coffee, which always took her directly past O'Brien's office. When she strolled past, her mind on a completely different case, he and another man had been in deep discussion in front of his open door. As she neared, the two men laughed amicably. The other man's back was toward her, and it wasn't until they turned to go into O'Brien's office that the man turned, and she instantly recognized the man's side profile.

Henry Thompson hadn't changed much over the last twenty years. His hair was gray and thinning now, and he was a bit paunchier than he used to be, but besides that, he looked almost the same as he always had.

O'Brien clapped the other attorney on the back as they moved into his office. Neither of them noticed her watching.

It wasn't unusual for attorneys to talk to one another when they were on opposite sides of the same case. But seeing them together made the hair on the back of her neck stand on end. The way they had acted with one another hadn't felt as though they were meeting in a professional capacity or as if they would soon be going head-to-head in a trial. They had acted like old friends. Again, it wasn't unusual for friendships between defense attorneys and those in the DA's office to emerge. But those two . . . she didn't like the thought of them together.

Something dug painfully into the flesh of her palm. When she looked down and unclenched the fist she hadn't realized she was making, there were deep nail marks embedded in the skin.

She needed to get O'Brien off this case. There was no way that Maria would get a fair hearing if O'Brien continued as prosecutor. She felt bad for the woman. How much courage must it have taken for her to come forward? And now she was having to deal with a misogynistic asshole who had openly admitted to Alexa that he planned to throw the case.

Not for the first time, she wished she had been able to record that conversation. She could tell Barrow what O'Brien had said until her face turned blue, but it wasn't going to do her any good without proof. Innocent until proven guilty—that was the type of person Barrow was, even outside of the courtroom. While normally Alexa appreciated it, right now it was a massive inconvenience.

She needed evidence of something, some sort of criminal activity O'Brien was up to. But the man was smart and knew how to cover his tracks. She wasn't going to be able to just go up to him and record him. And besides, she didn't know what she was looking for. He did coke, that much was obvious, but she couldn't go sneaking into his office to look for his stash even if she wanted to. He kept the office door locked whenever he wasn't there.

And if she found the evidence, what then? Blackmail? Take it straight to Barrow?

She groaned and rubbed her forehead. Her head was beginning to throb painfully, and she couldn't think straight. She had to find a way to knock O'Brien off the trial and insert herself instead. But besides that, she had no idea what to do or how to do it.

Another ping from her email reminded her that she had other cases that needed her attention, even if she didn't want to give it at that moment. She owed it to those other clients. And until she could come up with a plan, stewing over the Johnson case was as pointless as playing poker with a card shark.

So she pushed O'Brien to the back of her head and opened the email.

—

"YOU SEEM TENSE, BABE," Joe said when he plopped onto the couch next to her that evening. "What's on your mind?"

"Nothing," Alexa lied, taking a sip of wine. "Just a long day at work."

She knew she could have told Joe what was going on. He was smart enough that he almost certainly could guess the general theme, if not the specifics. It wasn't as though she had kept her frustration over the Johnson case a secret. But she was tired, and her brain was going into overdrive as she tried to figure out what to do about the problem. And she didn't want Joe to think she was overly obsessed. Besides, his own job was incredibly stressful; being a neurosurgeon didn't give him much time to decompress. He didn't need more problems. So she kept her issues to herself.

Joe gave her an amused but exasperated look. "I know when you're lying," he said. "But if you don't want to talk about it, I'm not going to force you. But maybe I can make your evening a bit better."

He shifted on the sofa and turned her back to him. His hands went to her shoulders and began lightly massaging them, sending tingles shooting down her spine. She closed her eyes and smiled. This was one of the many reasons she loved her husband. No matter how his own day had gone, he always put in the effort to take care of her and make sure she felt loved.

He ran his hands down her back, one finger gently caressing her spine. Her back arched instinctively, and she nearly purred as her eyes closed. He lifted her shirt over her head, revealing a lacy, red bra. His hands went to her lower back, massaging gently as his magic fingers slowly moved upward.

"Mmm," Alexa said as he unclasped the bra with a skillful, practiced motion. She turned her head to look back at him. "Careful," she said, "or I might not be able to control myself."

"That doesn't sound like a bad thing." His breath brushed against her collarbone, and her body gave a delightful shiver. He kissed her neck from behind, his hands still massaging every inch of her back. "In fact, maybe that was my plan the whole time." He leaned over and kissed her once. His lips were soft and warm, and her body instinctively craved more. The next kiss was deeper and more passionate. His hand wrapped around her waist to her stomach, pressing her against him.

Cold air and arousal stiffened her nipples, and his fingers roamed up toward them. He pinched one, and she jerked slightly. He let out a soft chuckle, even as his lips remained pressed against hers.

He broke the kiss for just long enough to get off the couch and spread her across it, taking off his pants before he crawled back on top of her. She licked her lips as her gaze locked on his fully erect manhood, and a fire burned between her legs. She stopped him before he could move to take off the rest of her clothes.

"Uh-uh," she said, propping herself up. He cocked an eyebrow as she reached out and took his cock in her hand. She squeezed lightly and began stroking, first slowly, then picking up speed. His eyes closed, then flew open as her mouth wrapped around the shaft, and her tongue ran across the head. "I'm in charge tonight."

Joe looked at her, then grinned widely. "If that's what you want, babe, then I'm not gonna complain."

And he didn't.

CHAPTER 11

Sally

SALLY YAWNED. HER EYES HURT from staring at the computer for hours, even with her glasses on. She blinked rapidly, even as she tried to focus back on the email in front of her—something about rescheduling one of Carmella's appointments that was supposed to happen the following day. But the rest of her boss's week was incredibly busy, and there was virtually no time for the switch.

She spun her chair around, preparing to go talk to Alexa about whether she was okay with coming in early or staying late sometime in the next few days. But her office door was closed. Her head swiveled around as she frowned. The office was ghostly silent, and none of the familiar faces were anywhere to be seen.

Glancing at the clock on her computer, she blinked in surprise. It was nearly six. Time rarely got away from her like this. Used to be, when she was younger, she was out as soon as the clock struck five, ready and eager to get back to her husband. But now, it was almost as though she looked for excuses to stay late, as if part of her dreaded going back home. It was ridiculous. She was over sixty; she shouldn't want to stay at work this late.

But here she was, sitting in the office completely alone.

But then a familiar whistle crept through the halls toward her, and she realized with a painful jolt in her stomach that she wasn't alone at all.

She stayed frozen, eyes glued on the hall where the whistling was growing louder. The sound of old, squeaky wheels trailed along with the nameless tune, as well as the gentle sloshing of water in a bucket.

Luca emerged through the hall, looking as dashing as ever. His hair was messy this evening, as though he hadn't bothered brushing it before coming into work. He managed to make the janitor's costume seem attractive and effortless, and he had his usual easygoing air about him that was irresistibly attractive.

Her heart was racing, sounding like a drumline, and part of her wanted to hide, to hurry out of the building before he could see her. She still remembered the last time she had seen him, remembered the way her pulse had quickened and how her mind had blanked when he had touched her. She was almost afraid to see him. She had carefully tried to avoid him ever since that last encounter. Now, with him approaching, with him now in sight, she didn't know how she would react or what she would do. Or if she would be able to control herself again. Last time had been hard enough.

She was frozen like a deer in headlights, and she remained rooted to the spot. She would have said it was out of anxiety, but that was a lie. The truth was, she wanted to see him again. And so she stayed where she was.

It took him a minute to see her. He was staring at the floor, whistling as he readied the mop. But after a moment, he paused and glanced up. His eyes found Sally and crinkled as he gave another of those charming smiles. He set the mop against the wall and sauntered over to her, hands in pockets.

"Hey there, Sally," he said. "I haven't seen you in a few days. Been keeping yourself busy?"

"Always," Sally said, giving a soft chuckle. Her fingers went unconsciously to her hair as if she were trying to smooth it, blushing like a teenager.

"You should tell Mrs. Montgomery that she should give you more time off," Luca said. "Sounds like she's a bit of a tough boss."

"Alexa's wonderful," Sally said. "I'm the one who keeps pushing myself too hard."

"You gotta take some time for yourself." Luca sat down on the side of her desk. "You gotta learn to relax and have a bit of fun."

"I know how to have fun," Sally said.

He looked at her, his dark-blue eyes boring into her in a way that made her stomach twist into a knot. "You sure about that?" he asked.

She didn't answer and instead turned her attention back to her computer. Her face was on fire, and she knew that she couldn't look at Luca, not with the intense way he was looking at her. She coughed and stood, turning off her computer as she did so.

"I'm positive," she said. She started to move past him, determined not to look at him. "It's been nice talking with you, Luca, but I have to get go—"

His hand reached out and gently brushed against her wrist, not stopping her, but a clear request for her to stay.

"I'm sorry," he said. "I'm coming across as an asshole, aren't I?"

"No, not exactly," she said, but still unable to look at him. "But this isn't okay."

He was too close, and even as she tried to avoid looking at him, she couldn't help herself.

"I'm sorry," he said. "I'm not trying to be pushy, and I know you're married. I want to respect your wishes. So if you want me to just leave you alone from now on, I'd be more than hap—"

She kissed him.

She wasn't sure when she had decided to do it, but all of a sudden, her hands had grabbed his shirt and pulled him closer. She slammed her lips against his, still holding onto his uniform for dear life, as if she would fall into oblivion if she let go.

Luca's hands wrapped around her, one hand reaching into her hair, inadvertently pulling it out of its bun, but she barely noticed. His other hand went to her back and pulled her in closer, pressing her against him.

Her brain had gone blank, all of her attention on his lips as they continued to kiss. She was drowning in him, even as his grip on her tightened.

But then she felt him stiffen, his cock pressing against her body as it grew and hardened. The feeling brought her back to her senses, and her eyes flew open. She pushed him away, taking several steps backward as the horror of what she had just done hit her like a truck. Her hand went to her still-tingling lips as she willed her heart rate to slow. Her breasts heaved.

Luca stood silently, unmoving as he watched her. His cock was still bulging against his jeans, but he made no move to restart the embrace.

"I'm sorry," she said as her brain reeled, trying to fully process what had happened. But there was just a numb white noise filling her head. "I've got to go."

"Sally," Luca called, but she was already running away, leaving the office and hurrying out of the building as fast as her shaking legs could carry her.

—

IT TOOK SALLY A LOT LONGER to get home than normal. She went the more circuitous subway route as she tried to clear her head and get the taste of Luca off her lips. But it was nearly impossible. All she could think about was the way she had grabbed fistfuls of his shirt when she had pulled him toward her and the delicious smell of his cologne enveloping her.

How could she have been so stupid? She was married, and Luca was thirty years younger than her. It wasn't possible, and it wasn't fair to Vladimir. She had been married to Vlad for over forty years now, and he deserved better.

Her heart was still thudding as she reached the front door of her home and fumbled for her key. She and Vlad lived in a quaint home that was nestled at the end of a cul-de-sac. They had lived there since they had moved nearly twenty years ago. When she opened the door, the first thing she noticed was that the stairs leading to the basement were open, then the sound of clanging metal and steady grunts filtering upward from it. A delicious scent that might have been Indian food came from the kitchen deeper inside the home. Taking a deep breath and forcing herself to relax, she plastered a smile on her face and walked down to the basement.

Vlad had redesigned their basement over ten years ago, converting it to a gym. In a way, Sally sometimes saw that as the turning point when everything had started going to shit.

She and Vlad had married as soon as she had gotten out of high school. He was two years her senior, and they had been high school sweethearts. So when he proposed to her beneath a full moon in the park where they had gone on so many dates, the answer was simple.

Back then, everything had seemed perfect. She still remembered how stunning Vlad had looked in his tux: over six feet and, even then, more or less entirely made of muscle. His blond hair had been thick and luscious instead of thinning to the point of nonexistence, and his blue eyes had been locked on her the entire time she had strolled down the aisle on her father's arm.

Those first few months had been filled with sex and new discoveries. About half a year after the wedding, maybe five minutes after Vlad had rolled off her, panting heavily from the third round of sex in two days, he turned toward her and propped himself up on his elbow.

"I've been thinking about joining the military," he had said. "But I don't want to make any big decisions like that without talking to you about it first."

"Why?" she had asked.

He had shrugged. "Make a difference, I guess. That and it's a good way to provide for you."

"Your parents aren't going to be happy about it. They worry too much."

"They'll be fine once they get used to it. But I'm more concerned about what you think."

She had smiled, leaned over, and kissed him. "If that's what you want, then I say go for it."

And for a long time after, everything had gone great. They raised three beautiful children, the oldest of which had given them their first grandbaby three years ago, and the youngest of which was finishing up a graduate program in business. They had traveled across the country for Vlad's job, and Sally had managed to pick up secretarial work wherever she went. They had ultimately settled in New York, and Vlad had finally retired from the military a few years ago after forty years of service. They seemed to have the perfect life—at least on the outside. No one except Sally had begun to see the rot festering beneath the surface.

The clanking sounds of metal against metal grew louder as she walked down the steps. Their home gym was nice; Vlad had designed it himself. It was filled with weight machines, dumbbells, pull-up bars, and all the other things you would find typically at a gym. Mirrors were put up all over the wall, and the entire floor was covered with padding. Vlad was sitting at a weight machine, his hands over his head as he pulled the bar down below his chin. He was shirtless, his body slick with sweat. Even though he was nearly sixty-five now, his body was in better shape than most twenty-year-olds. His hair was thin and gray, but his muscles and abs were solid steel.

He glanced up when he saw Sally clear the last few steps and paused his workout, the final scrape of metal dying away. He grabbed a nearby towel and mopped his face.

"Hey, Sal," he said. "Good day at work?"

"It was all right." She tried to keep her face impassive, and a sudden panic washed over her. Would he be able to sense what had happened? Could he smell Luca's cologne on her?

But he just nodded, not even getting off his seat. He tossed the towel to the padded floor and reached back up to grab the bar.

"Supper's going to be ready in about thirty minutes," he said. "Just needs to simmer a little longer."

"Sounds great," she said. "I'm starving. I'm going to take a shower if you want to join me?"

It was an invitation, a rather blatant one. But Vlad simply shook his head.

"I wanna finish this workout first," he said. "I'll have a quick one before dinner."

Something sad clenched Sally's stomach, and her face flushed as she looked away.

"Okay," she said. "Thanks for cooking."

And she went upstairs.

When they had been younger, Sally and Vlad had sex nearly every day. Even into their forties, the intercourse had been at least twice a week. But in the last fifteen years, Vlad had begun to change. Instead of sex, he had become more interested in exercise. It was all he seemed to do now that he was retired. She knew he spent at least two hours in the gym a day and would often go on runs on top of that. Part of her wondered if he had some sort of body dysmorphia or exercise disorder—both of which were apparently real things, and he definitely showed some of the signs. But she had never broached the subject with him.

Regardless, he had been showing Sally less and less attention. At this point, she couldn't even remember the last time they had had sex. Last month? The month before? It might have been their anniversary. It was getting to the point where it was hard to believe he loved her anymore.

As she got in the shower, and the warm water washed over her naked body, she closed her eyes and tried to remember the way it used to be. But instead of her husband in his youth, her mind went to Luca and how she had begun to burn as though on fire when their lips had met. His bulge against her hips had told her he had responded in a way her husband hadn't for years. And that feeling of being wanted again, of feeling desirable, was something she hadn't felt in a long time.

Why had she stopped herself? They had been alone in the office. No one would have known. She could have let him take her there on her desk, his strong hands gripping her hips and pulling at her hair as his hands explored her body.

Her fingers slid down her stomach and between her legs, and she began stroking herself. She let out a soft moan as her fantasy continued. She could practically feel Luca's hands on her, his lips brushing against her nipples.

She kept rubbing, her fingers moving faster and her hips shifting with the movement. She could feel that delicious pressure building as she continued imagining her fingers gripping Luca's dark hair as he slid her skirt and underwear down, and his mouth went to her clit. She pictured his hands gripping her wrists firmly, forcing them against the desk and holding her in place as he worked his magic.

She exploded, and her eyes flew wide open. She gasped, her body convulsing and her toes curling. She moaned as she rested her head against the tiled shower wall and tried to push away the gnawing guilt at the fact that she had just masturbated to cheating on her husband with a virtual stranger. And what was worse was that she had been more turned on by that fantasy than she had been by her husband in years. And it hadn't been enough. She could already feel that yearning and need for release building again.

She ran her fingers through her wet hair, trying to push the image of Luca out of her mind. But nothing she did seemed to have any effect.

Groaning in frustration, she closed her eyes again and turned the water to cold.

—

DINNER WAS PLEASANT, as it always was. They talked about their days and gossiped about the next-door neighbor's teenage daughter, who definitely had thrown a party the weekend before while her parents were away. But it was bland and generic and, despite the rotating topics, felt the same as it did every day. It was impossible not to notice, even as Sally pushed the unpleasant thoughts away.

"Man, I'm full," Vladimir said, putting his knife and fork down and pushing away slightly from the table. He patted his flat, toned stomach. "I'm going to need to work out extra tomorrow to work all this off."

"You know, there are more fun ways to do that," Sally said, giving a small, knowing smirk. She stood and walked behind her husband, rubbing his shoulders before bending down and kissing his cheek.

After the shower, she had still been riled up, unsatisfied by just her fingers. She wanted a good, proper fucking, and she wanted it from her husband. She wanted to try again; she needed to try again, if for no other reason than to get Luca out of her mind.

But Vlad shifted in his seat and gave her a chaste peck on the cheek.

"Not right now, honey," he said. "I'm a bit tired. But I appreciate the offer. Right now, all I'm up for is watching the Yankees crush the Red Sox in thirty minutes."

Her hands slid away from him as some final thing inside her broke.

"That's fine," she said, and her voice was distant to her own ears, as though she were far down a tunnel and the words were detached from herself. "I've got some reading I can catch up on."

"Well, if you want to do it in the living room while the TV's on, I'd love to have you." He stood and stretched, giving her a brief kiss on the lips before heading toward the living room. Sally watched, rooted to the spot, as the last of her resolve died away.

CHAPTER 12

Carmella, 2005

CARMELLA CAME HOME after work to the apartment in shambles. She stood in the doorway, her mouth partially opened as she took in the sight in front of her. The apartment was a decent-sized one-bedroom with a living room and eat-in kitchen. All of her pots and pans—normally neatly arranged so they all fit in the cabinets—were scattered on the floor and linoleum counter as if someone had ransacked the cabinets while robbing the place.

Her stomach plummeted, and she hurriedly glanced at the door. The locks were intact and so were the doorframes. It didn't look as though anyone had busted in. So what had happened?

And then she noticed the dozen cardboard boxes scattered across the room.

There was a noise from the bedroom, and Casimir walked out, lugging a full box.

"Good," he said when he saw her. He hauled the box toward her and dumped it at her feet. "Go put this in the car."

"The fuck's going on?" Carmella asked, folding her arms and not moving an inch.

Casimir's eyes narrowed. "Thought it was obvious enough that even a dumb bitch like you could figure it out. We're moving."

She took a step back in shock, and her hands fell back to her sides. Casimir had never spoken to her like that before. There had been the occasional dirty talk when they were in bed, but that was different.

"I can see that," she said when she managed to get over her initial shock. "But why?"

She walked over to the kitchen and peered into one of the boxes. Her favorite mug had shattered on the floor, and three of the plates she had inherited from her mother were broken because he hadn't bothered to pack them correctly. There was no padding, and he had tossed things in without care.

"Cause I lost my job, and we can't afford this place no more."

"What? When?" She rounded on Casimir, the broken plates momentarily forgotten.

"Two months ago," he said, putting his CDs in a box with far more care than he had used on the kitchen supplies.

"You lost your job two months ago? When the hell were you going to tell me?"

She couldn't believe it. None of this made any sense. She tried to wrap her mind around what she was seeing and everything that had just happened.

"I'm telling you now, ain't I?" he asked, glaring over at her from where he knelt on the ground. "Now shut the fuck up and help me pack. We gotta get out of here before the landlord starts sniffing around for the rent."

"You didn't pay our rent, either?" she asked. This wasn't happening. This couldn't be happening. In the span of thirty seconds, her entire life had been upended.

"No shit. We couldn't afford it."

"What? How?" There had been nearly ten grand in their bank account a month ago. There was no way that they had lost that much money so quickly.

"Spent it on poker," he said.

That was when she snapped. The rage boiled over, and she stomped toward him. "You spent all our money gambling? Without even asking me?

You ain't got no common sense. You ruined our lives and didn't even tell me. You're a fucking ass—"

The slap was so hard and fast that she fell to the ground. Dazed, she propped herself up on her elbow, her other hand going to her stinging cheek. Tears of pain blurred her vision and blood filled her mouth.

A shadow fell over her, and she looked up. Casimir was looming over her, suddenly six feet tall from where she lay on the ground. Staring up at him, she felt very, very small. A lump formed in her throat, and she swallowed.

She wanted to say something, to stand up and storm out the door, to tell him, "Later, asshole." She had told herself her entire life that she would never let herself get kicked around and beaten up like her mother had, that she would be smart enough and strong enough to leave as soon as a guy so much as laid a hand on her. But she stayed on the ground, suddenly very afraid and timid in a way she had never been before.

"I told you to shut the fuck up," he said and kicked her in the ribs. "Now listen to me when I talk to you, bitch. Get up and pack."

He kicked her again, and she cried out, curling up on her side as she tried to make herself as small as possible.

This wasn't happening. There was no way Casimir was towering over her, calling her a bitch and kicking her. It was Casimir—he'd never done anything like this before in his life.

And yet, there he was, and here she was.

"I said get up."

A fist tangled itself in her hair and yanked her to her feet so hard that it felt as though he would pull her hair out by the roots. The hand jerked her head so that she was face-to-face with Casimir. He was surprisingly strong for such a small man, and she couldn't get free no matter how hard she tried to pull his hands away. His face was twisted in anger, contorting his features into those of a wolf.

"Next time I tell you to pack," he said, "pack."

His breath, reeking of decay and cigarettes, washed over her, and flecks of spittle splashed her face.

"Let go of me," she said, trying to pry his fingers out of her hair. But he slapped her again, and the only thing that kept her from falling over was his hand grasping her locks.

"That's it," he said. "I've had enough of your lip. It's time I put you in your place."

Then, ignoring her screams of pain, he dragged her into the bedroom. She tried to get away, to drag her heels and make it as difficult for him as possible, but the only thing that resulted was a blazing pain in her scalp. She dug her nails into his arm, but she might as well have been digging into stone for all the effect it had.

Despite all her fighting, he managed to haul her into the bedroom. He threw her onto the bed, and before she could get back to her feet, he had slammed the door shut so hard that the walls rattled, and one of the photos fell to the ground with a crack. He didn't seem to care. He locked the door and stalked toward her.

"Stay down," he barked as she tried to scramble off the bed and to her feet. He grabbed her by the hips and yanked her toward him so her flailing legs were off the bed. With what felt like hardly any effort, he flipped her around onto her stomach. One hand grasped the back of her head and slammed it into the mattress. She squirmed, hands scrabbling futilely as the comforter began to smother her. She couldn't breathe, and all she could smell was the musty fabric.

With skillful ease, as though he had done exactly this a thousand times before, he pushed up her skirt and jerked down her panties. His hand loosened against her head just enough to allow her to gasp frantically for air, then to cry out in shock as he jammed a finger into her vagina.

"You ain't wet yet, bitch?" he asked. "Don't worry, I'm gonna fix that."

"Casimir, please stop." The words were choked sobs, even as she tried uselessly to move away. "I don't want—"

He forced her head back against the bed, muffling the words.

"I told you I was gonna teach you your place," he said, holding her down. "And that's exactly what I'm gonna do."

He leaned forward, and his entire body pressed against her, holding her in place. She could feel his hard cock through his jeans, pressing between her ass cheeks. A rustle of clothes later, his dick pressed against her again, only this time there wasn't anything between it and her bare skin, and it moved slowly down toward her womanhood.

She squirmed and screamed, limbs flailing even as the sheets made it difficult to breathe. Adrenaline raced through her as she panicked. She slammed her legs together, squeezing them against one another so he couldn't move any farther. But he just grunted and kicked her legs apart, sending dull pain racing up from her ankles as his feet kept her legs spread wide for him. She kept trying to fight, but no matter what she did, she was stuck, and no amount of struggling could make a difference.

Even though she knew it was pointless, she kept on going, trying to reach her arms back to claw at him. But he grabbed her wrists and jerked them painfully behind her back, pinning them there with one hand.

"Hold still, cunt," he snarled. "Or I'll make this even worse."

Then, with another grunt of effort, he forced himself inside her. At first, it was barely the tip, but he kept pushing and thrusting, until he was fully inside and the chafing was unbearable. Tears dampened the comforter she was pressed into.

"Fuck, that pussy feels good even when it's dry," he said.

He continued pumping, jabbing into her and making her buck with the pain that shot through her every time he rammed too far. The chaffing got worse, burning as he kept going. A distant part of her wondered if she would start bleeding because of it.

But the dryness didn't last long, and eventually her body responded instinctively, ignoring Carmella's own fear and protests.

Casimir noticed the change and laughed. "That's right. Take it. You like having me inside you, don't you, slut?"

Her entire body went slack as the fight slowly died out. She stayed still, letting Casimir have his way with her. All she could do was close her eyes and hope that he would finish soon, all while listening to the near-constant stream of slurs and insults, eventually blending together so she could barely tell one from the other.

The thrusts grew more rapid, and his breathing turned to grunts. She waited, legs still dangling off the edge of the bed. Finally, there was one last pump and a satisfied, disgusting groan as he finished inside her.

He slid out. Carmella stayed where she was, trying to ignore the burning sensation between her thighs and gulping down her sobs. A moment later, a towel fell across her back.

"Clean yourself up," Casimir said, already zipping up his pants. "Then get me a beer and start packing like I told you. We gotta be out day after tomorrow."

CHAPTER 13

Alexa

IT WAS A LONG, GRUELING DAY, AND when Alexa got home, she flopped immediately on the couch, closing her eyes and relishing sinking into the soft cushions.

A glass of Chablis materialized in front of her, a hand attached to it.

"Hey, babe," Joe said, kissing her on the forehead as she took the glass and took a long sip. "How was court?"

She yawned before taking another sip, sitting straighter. "Closing arguments today," she said. "Jury is still out, so hopefully they'll figure out a consensus sometime tomorrow."

Joe nodded, sitting down next to her, placing his own glass of red on the end table. She never discussed all the details of a case with Joe, but she told him enough that he got vague context without her telling him anything confidential. So all he knew was that she was dealing with a murder case and that she thought the defendant was a scumbag. That, and that she wasn't a huge fan of the defense attorney.

"Think Lawson got the best of you?" he asked jokingly.

Alexa snorted into her wine. "That man's an idiot," she said. "You should have heard some of the questions he tried to ask my lead witness. They were all badgering or leading. You'd think he'd just gotten out of law school. At one point he said, 'You said you were afraid of my client. Do you regularly have instances of paranoia?'"

Joe let out a low whistle then snickered. "I'm betting the judge loved that. So I'm guessing that means you have this one in the bag?"

"I hope so," she said. "For the victim's sake. But we'll see what happens. You never know with juries."

"Well, if it's Lawson going up against you, I can't imagine he's gonna win."

Alexa sighed. "He's just doing his job," she said. "The point of defense attorneys isn't to get guilty men out of a conviction. They're there to make sure everyone gets a fair trial. I can respect that, even if some of them aren't the brightest. That doesn't mean there aren't some defense attorneys who give everyone else a bad name. But I can say that about some of the prosecutors I work with, too. You get bad eggs in every profession."

"I don't have to guess who you're talking about there," he said. "O'Brien still being a pain in the ass?"

"Of course he is." She rolled her eyes but didn't go into details. She hadn't told Joe anything about her plan to get O'Brien off the case, but he was smart enough to guess she had something planned, even if he didn't know what it was yet. Granted, she didn't either. It had been a week since she'd seen O'Brien and Thompson together, and she still hadn't been able to come up with a concrete plan to get O'Brien off the case. And time was running out. If she didn't figure out something soon, it would be too late. It had been over two weeks since Casimir was arrested and arraigned, and the prosecution had six months from that initial court appearance to come to trial. O'Brien would take every minute of that time drawing things out, and she had to wonder just how much effort he would put into collecting evidence. The thought made her stomach churn with disgust, and she took a large sip of wine. "But I don't want to talk about it right now."

"I can understand that." He cuddled next to her, slipping his hand around her shoulder. Without prompting, he switched topics seamlessly. "I spoke with Chloe today."

"How's she doing?" she asked.

"She's good," he said. He always had a soft smile on his face whenever he talked about his daughter. "Worried about her final project that she has to start this term, but she's doing okay overall."

"That girl worries about everything and then blows everyone else out of the water," Alexa said. "She's gonna do fine."

Joe bobbed his head back and forth in a you're-not-wrong gesture. "She'll figure that out eventually," he said. "She's always been a bit of an overachiever and a perfectionist."

"I figured that out the first time I met her," Alexa said. "It's one of the reasons I liked her."

Alexa's stepdaughter was as bright as her father and in her last year of undergrad at Yale, Joe's alma mater, getting her degree in computer science. His other kid, James, had just started his sophomore year at Duke, though he seemed to want to study just about everything rather than limit himself.

"Anyway, she said to tell you hi."

Alexa nuzzled into Joe as he turned on the television. "That's nice of her. What about you? How was your day?"

"Pretty standard," he said. "Needed to prep a guy for surgery and give him the normal spiel about what to expect and what he would need to do. I guess I'll find out tomorrow if he listened. Surgery's at ten tomorrow, and assuming nothing goes wrong, I'll probably only be a little late for dinner."

"I don't know how you do it," Alexa said musingly. "I'd be terrified poking around in people's brains."

"It's definitely not the easiest thing I've ever done," he said.

"That's a massive understatement if I ever heard one."

"But it's worth it," he said. "I can't save everyone, but I'll always try my hardest."

Alexa smiled and leaned up to kiss him. "I know," she said. "That's one of the many reasons I fell in love with you."

"Funny," Joe said. "I could say the exact same thing about you."

The rest of the evening they sat curled on the couch. Alexa made popcorn, and they watched old movies that neither of them had seen but always meant to.

This was one of the many things she loved about Joe. The sex was phenomenal, but they also had no trouble just spending time together and doing normal things, and those things didn't always go together. She had been with people who could fuck her brains out, but who she couldn't connect with on a deeper level. But with Joe, it all came effortlessly. He was her soulmate on every level, and she couldn't be luckier that they had found one another.

CHAPTER 14

Joe

JOE PERILLI WAS FIVE YEARS OLDER than Alexa. He grew up in middle-class Massachusetts with his parents and younger brother. It had been a good life but, he realized as he grew up, perhaps a bit sheltered. His parents, now in their seventies and still happily married, made sure he never wanted for anything, and his life was devoid of many of the hardships financial difficulties brought.

Even from a young age, he had loved medicine and the human body. The first time his anatomy class examined the brain, he and his classmates had studied it by looking at parts of a frog's brain, poking certain locations to stimulate different parts of its body. The intricacy of the brain and its complex connections to the rest of the body had fascinated him, and he took that interest with him through life. He'd known even then what he wanted to do with his life, and he set to it with abandon, getting the best grades possible, graduating valedictorian, and going to Harvard, before starting med school at Yale.

Not long after starting med school, he met a young woman lounging on the lawn outside of Sterling Memorial Library, a great Gothic building that cast long shadows across the green grass when the sun hit it the right way. The woman was alone, reading a book with a black-and-red cover.

Joe was about to keep going when he stopped and pivoted, something compelling him to approach her.

"Excuse me," he said.

The woman closed her eyes in exasperation before looking up, still holding her book.

"Sorry," he said. "I normally don't do this, but I was hoping you could help me out."

"Let me guess," she said. "You lost your number and want mine?"

"No, nothing like that." He swung his backpack around and fished in the pocket, pulling out a book identical to the one she was reading. "I'm about a third of the way in and am totally lost. I was hoping you could explain to me why Andrea is supposed to go to the lake when she knows there's a serial killer there. I can't find any reason why she would do that other than a plot contrivance, and it's driving me insane."

The woman's eyes lit up, and she shifted from lying on her stomach to sitting upright, her beautiful eyes suddenly alert and sparkling with enthusiasm. "I know," she said excitedly. "That bugged the shit out of me for two hundred pages. But you do find out why eventually. I think the author could have made it a bit more explicit, though. I won't give anything away, but it does feel like it comes a bit from left field, considering everything."

"Is it still worth finishing?" he asked.

"Absolutely," she said. "Besides that problem, it's fantastic. I'm about fifty pages from the end now."

"That's a relief." Joe stuffed the book back in his bag. "In that case, I'll let you finish in peace."

"Hold up," the woman said as he was turning around. "Got some pen and paper?"

"I think so."

He handed both over. The woman scribbled hurriedly and handed both back. "Great, here's my number. Call me when you finish. I'm dying to talk to someone about it."

"In that case, I'll try to finish it soon." He stuck out his hand. "I'm Joe, by the way."

She took it, smiling warmly as her blue eyes looked him up and down. "Jenn," she said.

A year and a half later, after she finished her master's program in economics, she became Jenn Perilli. Her blond hair and brilliant smile could charm anyone who came near her. They had two beautiful children together as Joe finished his program and residency. They moved to New York when he got a job with NYU.

The ovarian cancer that took Jenn came suddenly and struck quickly. They had been married for twelve years.

CHAPTER 15

Carmella, 2006

CARMELLA WAITED UNTIL she heard the slam of the front door before leaving the shower. The filthy tiles felt grimy against the soles of her freshly cleaned feet as she dried herself off with a towel, every motion making her wince in pain because of the fresh bruises on her shoulders, upper arms, and rib cage.

Glancing in the cracked mirror, she saw that the bruise on her cheek from last week was finally beginning to heal, the sickly yellow beginning to blend with her dark complexion so it didn't stand out as much—though the shiner on the other eye and the split lip he had given her this morning were going to last for a long time, so the other one's vanishing felt like a moot point.

Sighing, she wrapped the towel tighter around herself and stepped out of the steamy bathroom and into the rest of the apartment, though calling it an *apartment* felt generous. It was a cramped place, with an ancient stove and fridge tucked in the corner of the small living room, along with two sections of cabinet space, making up the "kitchen." Off to one side was their even smaller bedroom. It was at least half the size of their old apartment, if not closer to a third.

The ancient, threadbare carpet that covered the small living room was always filthy, no matter how hard Carmella tried to clean it. Old takeout cartons and magazines scattered the ground—all thanks to Casimir. And drugs of all sorts were stashed around the house. If the police came and raided them right now, they'd be in a shitload of trouble.

It had been over a year since they had been forced to move apartments. Though he still constantly complained about them not having enough money, he never bothered trying to get a job. Instead, all he did was sit on the couch and drink. He had gotten fat and lazy and expected her to do everything he ordered. And if she didn't, she was punished.

So Carmella was forced to get a second job just to pay the bills. She was constantly tired, and the regular beatings didn't help. Today was her one day off a week, and every ounce of her body screamed at her to sleep and relax. But there were chores to do, and if she slept instead, Casimir would call her worthless and hit her again when he got home—if she was lucky. He could always do worse. He had already done worse.

Ever since that day when he first raped her, everything had changed. Casimir no longer showed her the same amount of affection or devotion. Their second wedding anniversary had been last month, and he hadn't remembered. At this point, he didn't seem to see her as anything other than his personal maid/punching bag/fuck toy.

She bent down to pick up a pair of Casimir's dirty underwear and hissed in pain as her ribs shifted and pressed against one of the bruises. She clutched her side and wished, not for the first time, that they had health insurance. But they didn't, and even if they did, there was no way Casimir would let her go anywhere near a doctor.

She hated it here. She hated every moment of her life now. She hated Casimir for hitting her, and she hated herself for staying with him after everything he had put her through.

She thought about leaving every single day. But she stayed. Because she was afraid.

She had tried to leave once a month after their move, and after the second attempt, he had really beaten her up. She was packing her suitcase hurriedly, throwing everything in haphazardly, worried that at any moment Casimir would come home from the bar or underground casino or wherever he was that night. But she had time. He wouldn't get home for another hour, so as long as she got everything packed and was gone by then, she'd be fine.

Then the front door to their apartment had unlocked, and Carmella had frozen.

The bedroom door was wide open, and Casimir had been able to see her hunched over something laying on the bed.

"The fuck you doing?" he asked. Before she could get away, his hand darted out and grabbed her bicep, squeezing painfully. His dark eyes stared down at the open suitcase, half-filled with jumbled and wrinkled clothes, and his eyes narrowed.

"You running off on me, cunt?" he said.

"No—" She tried to wrench her arm from his grip, but his fingers only tightened, burying themselves in her flesh. He cut her off with a slap.

"Don't fucking lie to me," he said. He hit her again, this time harder and in the stomach. She doubled over, eyes bulging as she tried to get her breath back.

"Stay there, bitch," he said. A moment later he returned, this time holding a thick leather belt. It was looped around his fist as he clutched it like a whip. "Shirt off. Bra, too."

When she didn't comply, he struck her again, repeating the command. This time she obeyed, her hands shaking.

He walked around her twice, and she stood upright and still, her bare chest cold in the winter chill. She wanted to leave—all of her instincts screamed at her to do so—but she was terrified of what would happen if she moved so much as an inch.

Finally he stopped circling her and came to a stop in front of her. The belt dangled from his hand, swaying from side to side.

"I'm gonna teach you a lesson," he said, his voice low and dangerous. "And you're going to listen, or I'll teach it to you again."

And the belt darted out, striking across her left breast. Without giving her any time to recover from that first searing pain, he kept going. "You.

Ain't. Going. Nowhere," he said, a stinging slap of the belt emphasizing every word.

Every lash left a burning band along her body wherever it struck. She told herself to move, but her feet wouldn't listen to her. It was as though they had taken root in the carpet. She squeezed her eyes shut, flinching at each stinging mark of the belt. She wouldn't let herself scream or cry out. The strangled chokes of pain were all the satisfaction she would give him.

He stopped at ten lashes, but it felt as though every part of her was on fire when he finished. He flung the belt on the bed, then reached up and grabbed her by the neck, squeezing tightly and nearly cutting off her airway. He yanked her down so she was bending slightly and they were at eye level. His breath had the rancid smell of pot and cheap whiskey, and it washed over her face in nauseating waves.

"Next time I see you doing something that stupid, I ain't gonna stop at the belt," he hissed. "You're mine, and you ain't leaving unless I say so. You got that, bitch?"

She nodded, and when he released her, she meekly unpacked, putting the now-empty suitcase back under the bed.

That incident had burned itself into her brain, and after that point, all she tried to do was as much as she could to avoid him beating her again. After that day, he had seemed to gather more and more of her life in his hands, controlling more of her with each day. He wanted her to get another job? She better go out and start looking. She wanted to go out for drinks with Georgia? Fuck no, not unless she cleans that damned kitchen. She got a hole in her shirt and needed a replacement? Think we got that kind of money, bitch? It had gotten to the point where it felt like she had to run every minor decision by him. And if she argued with him, she would get the belt, or the fist, or whatever struck his fancy at that moment. He was slowly choking every part of her life.

She hadn't tried to leave, even if she fantasized about it regularly. Because if she did, he would find her somehow; she was positive of it. He had finally gotten all those connections that he had fought so hard to get. And even if she did leave, what would she do? She didn't have any money; the bank account was in Casimir's name. She'd be homeless for who knew how long. And she was tired and worn down. At this point, the most she could do was pray that Casimir would get hit by a subway on his way home.

She hated how she sounded, hated herself for being stupid enough to get in this position in the first place, and hated the fact that she had lost all her will to fight and get out of the problem.

Her mind was still going along this hate-filled train of thought when the phone rang.

"Hello?" she asked.

"Carmella? This is Marissa," a woman's voice said.

It took Carmella a minute to place the name. She was the girlfriend or wife of one of Casimir's friends.

"Hey, Marissa, what can I do for you?"

"Nothing." There was a pause on the phone as Marissa hesitated. "Um, I don't know if this is a good time or if I should really even tell you. Trey told me not to, but I felt bad not saying something."

Carmella sighed and closed her eyes, leaning her back against the wall. "What is it?" she asked.

"Um, so, the other night, me and some of my friends were out at a club. Night Pulse?"

"Yeah, I know it." Not that she had been there in a while. Casimir would have had a fit if she so much as stepped foot inside.

"Yeah, well, Casimir was there. He was dancing with some girl. They started making out and then they walked out together."

"What night was this?" she asked. It was the only thing she could think to say.

"Thursday, I think."

Thursday. Casimir hadn't come home that night. Carmella's entire body sagged with disbelief as the words sunk in. After everything he had done to her—all the beatings and slurs, the way he had manipulated her and taken over her life—he had to add cheating. She shouldn't have been surprised, but she was. He was beating her and making her clean up after him and fucking her whenever he wanted, regardless of whether she was in the mood. Why wouldn't he be cheating on her as well? It was just another way of showing her how worthless she was.

"Thanks, Marissa," Carmella said. "I've gotta go now."

She hung up without waiting for the other woman to respond. Tired and exhausted, she walked over to the couch and slumped down on it.

She felt so stupid, so worthless. Of course he would do something like this. In that moment she hated him more than she ever thought possible. She had to do something; she needed to take back control over her life. Because if she wasn't able to grasp onto something, she knew she would slip away forever.

She curled up on the couch, lying down and facing the back cushions, wrapping her arms around herself protectively. She needed to get out from under Casimir's thumb. The only question was how.

CHAPTER 16

Sally

THIS TIME SALLY WAITED, staying long after the rest of the staff had left the building, pretending to be backed up on paperwork. But that was a flat-out lie.

Her eyes kept darting toward the clock on her computer screen, and her heart beat double-time and so violently that she could feel it in her throat. Her leg jittered up and down as she stared at nothing, her ears pricked for a familiar sound.

It wasn't until nearly six that she heard it: a tuneless whistle and squeaking wheels. Luca emerged, looking down at the floor, almost a perfect recreation of the last time they had seen one another a few nights earlier. He looked up, and this time, when he saw her, he looked almost alarmed and perhaps a little uneasy.

"Hi," Sally said, and she hated how squeaky her voice sounded. She suddenly was very conscious of the makeup she had put on, of the fact that her hair was out of its bun, cascading down her shoulders. Her glasses were sitting next to her keyboard rather than dangling from her neck. Her dress was low cut, her skirt shorter than normal, and her bra was a lacy, black push-up she'd bought two days ago.

"Hi," Luca said. He looked her up and down, and the surprise was evident on his face. "You're looking good."

Her face flushed. "Thanks," she said.

"Date night with the husband?" he asked, taking his mop out of the bucket and sweeping it across the tile floor.

"Not exactly," she said.

The mop stopped as the implication behind the words hit Luca. He looked up, stunned. Even with his mouth open and gaping, he was incredibly attractive.

"No?" he said.

She shook her head and stood up, walking toward him. He straightened, leaning the mop against the wall as he took a closer look at her. His eyes lingered on her breasts.

"What about your husband?" he asked.

There was a slight hesitation, and for a moment, she almost backed out of her decision. She had agonized over it, wondering whether what she was doing was a horrible idea. And undoubtedly, it was. But she couldn't keep living like a spinster and was tired of feeling unwanted, like she was second to her husband's gym. She needed more, needed something that her husband couldn't—or wouldn't—give her anymore.

But it was nearly impossible to put this into words that wouldn't sound trite or dismissive. She couldn't articulate any of the things she wanted to.

So instead, she kissed him, and that was all that needed to be said.

Luca responded instantly, holding her close, pressing her body into his. His mouth moved from her lips to her neck, moving down toward her collarbone. He raised his head back up so his lips were nearly kissing her ear.

"Are you sure?" he whispered. Warm breath brushed against her ear and caressed her neck, sending shivers jolting through her body to rest below her stomach. If she had any doubts, that sensation, that feeling of finally being wanted after ten years, was enough to convince her.

"Yes," she muttered, her eyes closing.

Without another word, he pushed her against the wall. She gave a loud gasp as his hands gripped her wrists, holding her in place. He noticed, and she could feel his lips curl into a grin against her neck.

"Like that?" he asked. And when she nodded, he pulled her arms above her head, grasping them there in one hand. A warm, calloused hand slipped up her shirt toward her breasts. "Good to know. Next time I'll bring handcuffs."

A thrill ran through her, making her stomach lurch. *Next time.*

With a practiced, effortless motion, he whipped her shirt off and unclasped her bra. He sucked in a breath as he took in her bare torso, the bra dangling from his fingers, falling to the ground.

"Damn, girl," he said. "You are stunning."

"I'm old," she said, but couldn't hold back the schoolgirl giggle.

"I told you before," he said. "I like older women. And that doesn't mean you can't be beautiful."

His hand went to her breast and cupped it, squeezing tightly. Her entire body erupted in shivers, goosebumps running up and down her body. It had been so long since she had been touched.

Almost instinctively, her hand shot out and grasped Luca's cock through his uniform. He jerked slightly.

"Feel how hard I am?" he asked. "That's all for you."

She squeezed harder.

"If I didn't know any better," Luca said, "I'd say you wanted my cock."

She nodded, her eyes staring deep into Luca's piercing blue ones. He stared at her with a longing she hadn't thought possible. His body pressing against hers radiated heat, his firm muscles pushing against her, and she was acutely aware of every inch of his body. His full lips were parted, curling into a smile.

"Then beg for it," he said, even as he moved to lower her skirt. "I wanna hear how badly you want it."

Her gut lurched, and her toes curled instinctively. The idea of having to beg for him sent a thrill through her that she couldn't properly artic-ulate. And she wanted it—she wanted him. It was all she could think about. Her heart raced, and the craving doubled. This was what she had wanted, even if she had been denying it to herself. And as much as she hated to admit it, she didn't feel the guilt that she probably should have. It felt *right*.

"Please," she said, her voice sounding almost hoarse as his fingers deftly lowered her panties. One finger ran between her lips, circling her vagina as another played with her clit.

"Please, what?" he asked, raising his eyebrows and smirking. That self-confident, almost cocky smirk made him even more attractive than he had been moments earlier. He was enjoying taunting her, making her plead.

"Please let me suck your cock," she said and was surprised by just how much urgent need saturated her voice.

His smirk grew wider, and he reached up, tangling one hand in her hair and gripping tight. And with gentle force, he pushed her down to her knees.

With trembling fingers, as if she were a virgin who barely knew what she was doing, she unbuckled his pants. Even through his boxers, she could see the massive bulge, and when she pulled his underwear down, it sprung out, fully erect and almost throbbing. She licked her lips unconsciously as she saw it. His cock was even more incredible than it had been in her dreams: large and thick, but not too much of either for it to be uncomfortable. It was just right.

His hand still in her hair, she took him in her mouth. He groaned as her tongue stroked his shaft, and she savored the taste of him as her hand grasped his cock and began moving in time with her mouth. It had been years since she had given anyone a blow job, but the motion came back to her with surprising ease. She let out a soft, contented moan.

"Fuck, Sally," he said. "You're amazing."

She grinned around his cock but didn't let up until he pulled her upward by the hair and clashed his lips against hers. With strong hands, he hoisted her up and held her against the wall. Her bare legs locked around his waist. Slowly, breathing heavily as her heart pounded with excitement, she slid down onto him. She gasped as his manhood filled her, making her whole in a way that she hadn't been in a long time. Then the gasps turned into ragged breaths as he began pumping, pushing her up against the wall even as her legs remained wrapped around him. Every thrust sent him deeper into her, sending her closer and closer to the edge. Spasms of ecstasy jolted through her like lightning.

"Oh, god," she cried out. "Fuck me harder."

He obliged, his pumps growing faster, harder, more intense, punching into her rapidly. The pressure inside her built and built as he continued. She could see his face beginning to glint with sweat as his eyes bore into her. His hands gripped her hips tighter as the rhythm sped up and intensified.

"That's right, baby," he said, his voice husky.

Her nails dug into his back as she neared the precipice, her entire body moving along with his as that need and pressure built and grew. It was phenomenal. It was sex in a way that Sally had never experienced before. And now that she had a taste of it, she never wanted to go back.

The thrusts had turned to a rapid, steady rhythm, and her own breath began to hitch as the fire began to climb insurmountably. It kept growing, and she wasn't sure how long she could stand it. Her toes curled, and her back began to arch, pressing her bare breasts against his chest. The burning kept growing to a crescendo until she exploded. She cried out in ecstasy, her body moving up and down his shaft as she rode the wave of pleasure. She dragged her nails across his back, and he bucked.

He paused, panting hard as his cock throbbed inside her. He looked at her as she continued to straddle him, taking her in. She had never seen that sort of longing from Vlad, and it nearly made her ready to continue.

"I need a break," he said, giving a sheepish grin. "You're taking a lot out of me."

He slid her down the side of the wall and slipped out of her, leaving her feeling slightly empty and more than a little disappointed. Then he cocked his head, raising his eyebrows and giving her another of those dizzyingly attractive smirks that made her want to jump him all over again.

"You think you could help me out a bit with that amazing mouth of yours?" His thumb went to her lip and stroked it softly.

Sally smiled, mimicking the head tilt as she pretended to consider. "I think I can handle that," she murmured.

Without another word, she went down to her knees again, admiring his manhood and feeling that sensation below her stomach jolt back to life. She ran her tongue along the shaft, licking the taste of herself off him, before wrapping her lips around his cock once more.

It didn't take long. His hands knotted in her hair and gripped tighter, pulling slightly at her scalp in a not-unpleasant way. Then he groaned as his cum filled her mouth. It tasted delicious, not like Vlad's, which, when she had given him head years ago, had been a roulette wheel as to what it would taste like.

When she was done, she stood again, looking up at Luca. His eyes searched her face hesitantly.

"Are you all right?" he asked, and there was something endearing about it. He was genuinely concerned. His hand reached up and smoothed out some errant strands of hair that had appeared on her forehead.

She smiled.

"I'm absolutely fantastic," she said.

CHAPTER 17

Alexa, 2017

"WE'RE GOING TO BE LATE, GIRL," Alexa said, fidgeting in the back seat. "This is why you don't primp for thirty minutes before going to the airport. Who you cleaning up for, anyway? We're going to be on a plane for over sixteen hours."

"You never know who's going to be there," Michelle said, grinning as she redid her lip liner for the third time. "For all you know, there could be some rich, old guy sitting in first class with an extra seat looking for an attractive woman to shower with gifts." She winked to say she was kidding, and Alexa snorted as she rolled her eyes fondly.

"If that happens, I expect a million bucks for my birthday and Christmas each year," she said. She shifted again, looking around her at the packed street. "Why is it always this crowded?" she asked. "And why are people so stupid they can't drive properly?"

"We can't all be as perfect as you," Levi called jokingly from the driver's seat. "Granted, if you were that perfect, you'd be the one driving."

It was midday, and Michelle and Alexa were on their way to the airport. Or they would be, if the traffic wasn't so bad. It was frustrating enough that they were going to be couped up in a tin can for hours on end. The fact that they had to do it in the car beforehand as well just felt like unfair punishment.

It'll be worth it, Alexa told herself, trying to calm the growing irritation. And it would be. She had been looking forward to this conference for over a year. Once she had found it, she and Michelle had booked it instantly. "Transforming Your Inner Self." It had seemed too perfect, and it was something she had been working on for years. Even if it was in Nanjing, China, there was no way the distance was going to stop her.

They moved a few feet before halting again. Alexa grimaced as her stomach lurched uncomfortably. Her friend Levi had offered to drive them, and the two women had accepted eagerly, but they hadn't realized just how bad traffic would be.

Next time, we're taking the subway.

She peered out the side. They were getting close to the departures area, but it still felt miles away, and it might as well be, considering how long it was taking.

"You're too impatient," Michelle said teasingly, turning around in her seat to look back at her. "We're going to be fine."

"I know," she said, a bit grumpily. "But I want to get there as soon as possible."

"You know you're just going to be waiting in the terminal instead of a car, right?" Levi asked, glancing back at her through the rearview mirror.

She stuck out her tongue.

—

JOE LEANED FORWARD AGAINST THE wooden bar, propping his elbows up as he waited for the bartender to finish making his drink. Behind him, the din of the airport filled the air, permeating the restaurant he was sitting in as people passed. He watched them; he'd always been a fan of people-watching. There was a harassed-looking woman with two small children in tow (he certainly remembered those days, both with fondness and exasperation), a man in an overpriced business suit talking loudly on a cell phone, and a small group of young girls in their twenties giggling over something, along with a myriad of other people.

"Here you go, sir," the bartender said, placing a glass of red wine in front of him.

"Thanks."

"So," his friend Mark said. "Looking forward to the conference?"

Joe nodded. "Not so much the flight, but I'm interested to see what it's all about. Plus, I've never been to China. Seemed a shame to pass up the opportunity."

"Carla taking care of the kids?"

Again, Joe nodded. It wasn't unusual for his late wife's mother to help out with the kids. In fact, she always seemed eager to do so. He suspected it was because it made her feel closer to Jenn, now three years gone.

"Chloe's getting to that point where she thinks she can take care of things at home herself," Joe said, smirking and taking a sip of his drink. "I told her there's no way in hell until she's eighteen. She loved that."

Mark chuckled. "Sounds about right."

The two men sat in companionable silence as they drank. There wasn't really any need for conversation. The two men knew each other so well that sometimes simple conversation felt beyond them. They had known each other since before med school, had been the best man at each others' weddings, and had taken regular trips together for years now.

Which was why the two of them were sitting in an airport bar at JFK, waiting until it was time to board their flight.

Eventually, Joe glanced at his watch.

"They'll probably start boarding in ten minutes," he said, waving over at the bartender to grab his tab. "Might as well start wandering in that direction."

When they arrived at the gate, he was surprised at just how crowded the area was. Despite the fact that boarding hadn't even started yet, a massive throng had lined up, waiting for their turn to board. He glanced at the desk and saw two flight attendants talking to one another, but they didn't seem quite ready yet.

His eyes scanned the rows of seats where several people were still lounging. Then his eyes locked onto one figure in particular.

It was a woman with beautiful chocolate skin and dark hair. Even sitting down, he could tell how toned her legs were. She was talking to the woman next to her, grinning and laughing. Even through the noise of the crowded airport, he could hear her laugh as she threw her head back in mirth. It was rich and decadent and loud. Maybe a little too loud. But it didn't matter.

"She's cute," Mark said, stepping next to him and following his gaze. "They both are. Think they're on the same flight?"

"Possibly," Joe said, not taking his eyes off the woman. "But who knows? And if they are, I'm not going to bother her while she's stuck in a small space and can't leave. That's just creepy."

Mark tsked. "Missing an opportunity there, bud."

"Rather that than make her uncomfortable," Joe said. He was about to turn around when the flight attendant called the start of the boarding process, and the woman's head turned toward him.

Her eyes met his, and her eyebrows raised slightly. She wasn't embarrassed by the stare; that much was obvious. Her lips remained a straight line as she kept eye contact for a long minute. Then her gaze swept up and down his body for the briefest of moments before she smirked and turned back to her friend.

He kept an eye on her even as they started boarding. He waited in line as people stopped along the airplane to find their seats and throw luggage in the overhead bin. He and Mark slipped into their business-class seats. As he got settled, his eyes kept glancing upward at the line of people, hoping to catch a glimpse of either the woman or her friend.

But when the woman walked by, she didn't glance in his direction.

"Told you, you should have talked to her," Mark said, nudging him playfully. Joe rolled his eyes.

"Let's just get through the flight," Joe said and began playing with the touch screen monitor in front of him, trying to pick out the first movie of a very long flight.

—

"DAMN," MICHELLE WHISPERED AS they waited to board. "You see that guy checking you out?"

"Mm-hmm." Alexa nodded. "Pretty cute. But I'm not looking for anything right now. Been there, done that. It's too much work. Besides, we're in an airport. The guy's probably from Ohio or Canada or something. It wouldn't work out."

"That doesn't mean you can't have a little fun," Michelle said, waggling her eyebrows. "Maybe join the Mile High Club?"

"Maybe on a shorter flight," Alexa said, grinning mischievously. "I don't wanna fuck a guy then have to walk past him every time I need to use the restroom."

But despite the claims that she didn't want anything, she couldn't stop herself from noticing the handsome man as she sauntered past, even as she forced herself to keep moving and to only notice him out of the corner of her eye. There was something about him that pulled her toward him. And some deep, intuitive part of her whispered in her ear that one day that man would become very important to her.

CHAPTER 18

Alexa

A LEXA GAVE A FIERCE, WOLFISH grin as she looked down at her computer. It was the type of smile that put fear into the hearts of the opposition in the courtroom and one she only gave when she knew she had her prey trapped and cornered.

Thank you for your inquiry! We'll reach out to you shortly.

She exited the window and forced herself not to look at her email. It would take them a while to get back to her; she might as well do some other work. Glancing outside, she saw Sally—more relaxed and happy than Alexa had seen her in years, it looked like—sitting at her computer, her legs primly crossed.

"You're staying late today," Alexa said, stretching and moving to the open door. "I hope I'm not that much of a slave driver."

Sally jumped slightly and turned around, her cheeks turning a brilliant pink—or was that new makeup?

"No, of course not." Sally tittered, smiling. She took off her glasses and polished them hurriedly, one of her signs of nervousness. "I just got in late this morning. I've actually been meaning to ask you if it would be okay if I switched my hours a bit. I've been having some things at home that need taking care of in the mornings. Would you be okay with me switching from, say, ten to six?"

Alexa frowned, chewing the inside of her lip as she considered. "It's easier for me if you're here the same hours I am." At the crestfallen, almost panicked look that crossed Sally's face, she added, "Everything all right?"

"It's fine," Sally said, though it was obvious she was lying.

"Come on, out with it."

"I can't really talk about it, Alexa," Sally said.

Alexa let out a long sigh as she ran her fingers through her hair, considering her secretary. She'd been loyal to her for years now. The least she could do was repay the favor.

"All right," she said. "But leave me notes for the morning if there are any major changes, all right?"

Sally's entire body straightened, and her face lit up. "You're amazing, Alexa," she said. "Thank you so much."

Alexa gave a warm smile, one that was far less sinister than the one she had given just a few moments before at the computer screen. "It's the least I can do," she said. "I hope things at home start getting better."

"Oh, I think it will," Sally said. "Thank you again."

Something twinkled behind Sally's beautiful hazel eyes, still vibrant and lively despite her age. Alexa was just about to ask her about it—clearly something was going on, and not just the pushed-back hours. But before she could ask, her cell rang. Glancing down, she saw an unknown number, but she could guess who it was, and an excited jolt lanced through her.

"I have to take this," she said, slipping back into her office and closing the door behind her. "Montgomery speaking," she said.

A husky voice answered, "Mrs. Montgomery, it's Larry Winston. I just received your request. How are you doing?"

"I'm doing well, thank you," she said. "Thanks for calling back so quickly."

"Don't worry about it." There was a puff of air, as if the man on the other side of the line had just exhaled smoke from a cigarette. "Normally I've found that potential clients would rather not talk over the phone. Would you like to meet somewhere?"

Alexa glanced at her watch. "How about I treat you to dinner?" she asked. "I know a good place in Hell's Kitchen. That's near you, right?"

"It certainly is." Another long pause and something that sounded like a puff. "Tell me the address, and I'll be there. Seven?"

"Perfect." She gave him the name of the restaurant and hung up. After that, she sent Joe a quick text that she was going to be late home from work.

There was noise and hushed whispers outside, and then the clack of heels echoed down the hall. Sally, presumably. Alexa didn't think much about it. She stayed in the office for another hour, getting everything ready for later that night. Then, when 6:30 came around, she locked her office and hurried out as fast as she could. Smirking, she strolled outside into the evening air and turned toward Hell's Kitchen, heading for her meeting with Larry Winston, private investigator.

—

LARRY WINSTON WAS ABOUT AS STEREOTYPICAL as it was possible to be for a PI. It was so blatant that he could have strolled out of a 1940s film noir. He was younger than she had expected, rail thin with dark hair hidden beneath a fedora. His face was nondescript, even with the stubble, and his clothes were slightly crumpled. When he shook her hand, she could smell the cigarette smoke.

"I have to ask," she said. "Is this for show, or do you really dress like this all the time?"

Winston cracked a grin as he glanced down at the menu. "Bit of both," he said. "You'd be surprised how many people feel more comfortable when I look like this at the first meeting. They think it means I'm more legit."

The waiter swung by, and Winston glanced over at Alexa. "Is it going to be too cliché if I order bourbon on the rocks?"

"A bit," Alexa said. "But I'll allow it."

They ordered, and Winston turned back to her, his face serious. "So, you want some guy tailed? Cheating husband?"

"Scumbag coworker, actually," she said, fishing around for the file. "I know he's corrupt, but I need evidence."

She slid the file over to him and he flipped it open, scanning the pages with a practiced eye. He glanced back up at her.

"The guy works in the district attorney's office?" he asked. When Alexa nodded, he glanced back down. "And you're looking for evidence that he's corrupt."

"Yup," she said. Winston gave a low whistle. "Is that going to be too difficult?"

"It depends." He closed the file but didn't hand it back to her. She took that as a good sign. "I can only do so much as a PI. I can't stalk the guy, and I have to respect places where he's entitled to privacy. New York's also a one-party consent state, meaning I can't just record him having a conversation with another guy. I would have to be actively involved in it. But I'll see what I can do."

"Assuming I can pay," Alexa said, her smile turning a little wry. He grinned back.

"Assuming you can pay, yes," he said. "It's $100 an hour."

She nodded, considering. It was a little pricier than expected, but she had done the calculations earlier on what she was willing to pay.

"Go up to twenty hours," she said. "Focus on after work. If you can't find anything, let me know, and we'll go from there."

"I think we can arrange that. I do require a five-hour retainer, though."

"That's what your website said." She pulled out her wallet and scribbled a check. "Though this dinner doesn't count as part of the twenty."

"Deal. But still, tell me a bit more about what's going on here."

So Alexa told him.

CHAPTER **19**

Maria, One Month Earlier

C ASIMIR SAW HER FROM ACROSS THE DANCE floor as he sat drinking with his buddies. She was with a group of friends, all of them giggling and having a good time. She was young, but that didn't matter to him. He liked them younger. They tended to be more pliable.

He kept eyeing her, keeping track of the girl for the next hour or so. She was pretty, probably Latin American or something like it, with auburn hair and a sharp face. Her lips were full, and he wanted to know what that mouth could do wrapped around his cock. Well, at least he knew what he was going to be doing tonight.

The entire time he kept his eyes on her, she never realized she was being watched. Again, that was the way he liked it. He didn't want them scared off before he was able to make his move.

He waited, taking his time. He knew how to be patient and when to strike. Clubs were his favorite places to pick up women, and he had become an expert at it.

Finally she separated herself from her friends, moving toward a table and plopping down. She fanned herself, and Casimir watched her breasts heaving up and down beneath her low-cut shirt as she caught her breath.

The way she made her tits move up and down, and the way she was showing them off in that skimpy outfit, told him everything he needed to know. She wanted attention. And he was gonna give it to her.

"I'll see you boys later," he said, standing and nodding to them without an explanation. Then he weaved through the crowd, his eyes locked on the woman, still alone.

Without saying anything, he sat down in the chair next to her. The woman started and looked over at him.

"Hey there," he said.

"I'm so sorry," the woman said. "Is this your table? I didn't realize."

"It is," he lied. "But I ain't gonna run a pretty thing like you off. Keep sitting."

The woman's face turned a brilliant red. The blushing virgin type? Or just a tease who knew how to play a guy? He was inclined to think the former. That was fine with him.

"Thanks."

He raised a finger. "I do have two requests," he said. "One, I wanna know your name."

"Maria," she said. "And the other?"

"Let me buy you a drink."

She glanced down at the almost full drink next to her, then back up at him.

"I didn't say it had to be this minute."

"Well, if you insist," she said, still blushing.

And it was as easy as that. Over the next couple of hours, he kept giving her drinks: shots, Long Island iced teas, the strongest booze he could get his hands on from the bartender. She didn't seem to notice. Her smile grew giddier, and her cheeks flushed red with drink. He moved slowly, inching toward her until his chair was right up against hers. He slipped his arm around her and stroked her neck with his thumb.

"I should get back to my friends," she said and moved to get up. His hand, resting just above her perfect left tit, pushed her back into her seat, subtly but effectively locking her in place.

"Don't do me like that," he said, holding his drink up to her lips. "At least help me finish this last round."

"As long as it is the last round," she said. Her words were slurring now.

"It is. I promise."

It wasn't. There were two more rounds. Thirty minutes after the last one, her eyes were glassy and unfocused, her clothes slightly askew. She had stopped saying she needed to get back to her friends by this point. Her head was resting on his shoulder, and his hand was fully on her breast now. It was firm and perky, just as he'd thought.

"I should probably get home," she muttered, though it was barely audible through the noise.

"Do you want me to take you there?" he asked.

She nodded into his shoulder, and he smirked.

—

CASIMIR WAS IN THE SAME apartment he had been in for almost twenty years. It had not aged well, and neither had the building. Graffiti was splashed all along the front, and a homeless man was pissing in the alley next to it. The windows were grimy—those of them that didn't have large spiderweb cracks running along the surface—and the putrid stench of rotting trash from the dozens of overstuffed trash bags out front was enough to make anyone gag.

As the two of them walked, none of the few people ambling the streets at that hour bothered the couple or found anything suspicious about the two. So they continued uninterrupted, Maria oblivious to the fact that Casimir was steering her in the wrong direction from her apartment. By the time they reached his apartment, she was still pretty drunk. But the cold air had sobered her enough for her to realize that something was wrong.

"This isn't my apartment," she murmured. She moved to turn, to head down the street, but his arm, wrapped around her to help prop her up, pulled her in closer.

"Shh, shh," he said. "Relax. It's all right."

The girl's eyes widened as clarity pierced through the fog of drunkenness, and she squirmed and writhed, trying to get away. But the feeble pawing did nothing to stop him from his goal.

"Calm down," he hissed, pulling her into the building. She tried to scream, but Casimir clamped a large, sweaty hand over her mouth, nearly suffocating her as it pressed against her nostrils. "Shut up, bitch, or I'll give you something to scream about." Truthfully, the girl could scream all she wanted, and no one would bat an eye or call the police. This wasn't that type of building. Everyone minded their own business and ignored the occasional scream or gunshot, so long as it didn't involve them.

So he dragged Maria into the elevator even as she desperately tried to kick out with her legs. Her fingers clawed uselessly at the hand pressed against her mouth as she drunkenly tried to get away. He didn't mind. He liked them feisty. They were more fun to break. Then the heel of her shoe slammed into his shin, and he winced.

"You're gonna pay for that," he snarled in her ear. He grabbed her tit and squeezed painfully. The girl bucked and tried to scream again. "Fight all you like, bitch. You know you want it, and you're gonna get it. So you're gonna take it like the bitch you are, and you're gonna like it."

When he opened the door to his apartment, he shoved her inside. He slammed the door behind him and turned the lock. It made a satisfying click, keeping the wide-eyed girl—who no longer looked a bit drunk— trapped and helpless.

Just the way he liked them.

"Now," he said, strolling toward her and grabbing her wrist before she could make a dash for it. "We gonna do this the easy way or the hard—"

The bitch bit him on the arm.

Crying out in pain and rage, he let go, and she tried to dart past him toward the door. But his hand lashed out, grabbing her by the hair and yanking hard, throwing her to the floor.

Casimir stood over her, one dirty shoe resting on her chest, just between her tits. The girl looked up, her face pale as she took in the livid expression on Casimir's face. His hand went to the vivid, red bite mark on his forearm and rubbed at it.

"Hard way it is, then," he said and grinned.

CHAPTER 20

Alexa, 2017

"DAMN, THIS IS A NICE HOTEL," Michelle said, eyes wide as they stepped into the spacious, luxurious room. The marble-tiled bathroom to their right was huge. They strolled through the kitchen/living room into the bedroom, where a basket of chocolate and champagne lay on the table.

"No kidding." Alexa yawned as she plopped her suitcase on the ground.

"They even give you champagne?!" Michelle asked.

Alexa grinned. "That was me," she said. "Figured we could use some after that flight, so I added it when I booked the room."

"Have I ever told you how much I love you?" Michelle unwrapped a truffle and plopped it into her mouth. She groaned and threw her head back. "God, that tastes so good."

"Don't say I don't do anything for you," Alexa said, flopping down on the bed still fully clothed.

"When have I ever said that?" Michelle asked, already unwrapping another chocolate.

"Last week when I couldn't go out for drinks cause I had to be in court in the morning?"

"Doesn't count." Michelle pulled the bottle out and waved it at Alexa. "So we opening this now or later?"

"Let's do it after dinner," Alexa said. "The hotel restaurant is supposed to be pretty good."

"Great idea." Michelle popped a third chocolate into her mouth. "I'm starving."

—

"PLANE RIDE COULD'VE BEEN WORSE," Mark said, yawning. "Though my entire body is stiff."

"There's a joke in there somewhere," Joe said.

"Yeah, yeah. Go on and follow the nice waitress."

Joe did, and the woman led them deeper into the restaurant.

The hotel bar was massive and opulent. The floor-to-ceiling windows showed a 360-degree view of the city, and the high ceiling was lined with gold and ornately painted. The entire area was illuminated with bright lights, and a large, modern-looking sushi bar stood to one side.

The restaurant's size was impressive, and the entire place was filled with mouthwatering scents that made his stomach growl in anticipation.

But as his gaze roamed across the restaurant, he froze as his eyes locked on one person—one very familiar-looking person.

Then he stumbled as Mark ran into him.

"What's with you?" Mark asked.

"Does that woman look familiar to you?" Joe asked, jerking his head in the direction of the chocolate-skinned woman who was currently laughing with her friend while sipping a glass of wine.

Mark blinked. "Shit," he said. "Is that the woman from the plane?"

"If it isn't, it's her twin," Joe said, still looking at her. Part of him willed her to turn toward him so their eyes could meet the same way they had before boarding. But another part of him hoped she didn't notice him gawking at her.

"You gonna go talk to her?" Mark waggled his eyebrows.

Joe shrugged, turning away and heading toward the hostess who was waiting awkwardly a few yards away.

"You can't keep hiding under a rock," Mark said as they sat.

"What's that supposed to mean?"

"I mean that it's been three years," Mark said. "I'd get it if you said you weren't ready, but I've seen you date before. But you've still seemed . . . I don't know . . . *afraid* of women."

Joe barked out a disbelieving laugh. "You're joking, right?" he asked. "Afraid? Since when? And I've gone on plenty of dates in the last year."

"Afraid to make genuine connections," Mark said. "Those dates always fizzled out. And like I said, if you aren't ready yet then that's fine, and only you can know that. I just want to make sure you aren't shooting yourself in the foot."

Joe went silent for a long moment as he thought back to Jenn. How tired she looked in the hospital bed, and how peaceful she had been in her coffin. He remembered his promise to her: that he would live his life and be happy.

Had he really been avoiding connection all this time? Even by accident? He wasn't sure. But as he glanced over his shoulder at the woman, he knew he couldn't pass up the opportunity.

The woman's friend got up just as a waitress brought Joe his scotch. He glanced down at it, then back at the woman, then took a long swig of his drink.

"I'll be right back," he said.

"I hope not," Mark said, grinning widely and winking. "Good luck."

—

"EXCUSE ME."

Alexa glanced up and blinked in surprise. It took her a moment to recognize the man with the goatee and piercing gaze. He grinned, and it made his already handsome face even more attractive.

Still, she tried to keep her face aloof, as if she weren't admiring how good-looking he was.

"Yes?" she asked.

"I saw you on the plane," he said. "But I wasn't expecting to see you here as well. Are you here for the conference?"

"I am, actually," she said. "I'm guessing you are too?"

"I am. Honestly, looks like I lucked out."

"And why's that?"

"I thought that would be obvious," he said. "Cause I'm going to get to see more of you."

"Hmm." She took a sip of her wine as she looked up and down, again, still trying to play coy. "You're probably right there. Are you from New York?"

"I am. And I'm really hoping you are too."

"Well, seems like you're lucky on two counts."

The man's face brightened. "That is lucky. Do you mind?" He gestured at one of the empty seats, one of the ones unused by Michelle, who had stepped out to the bathroom.

"For a few minutes. We're about done with our meal." As if on cue, a woman appeared and placed a check next to her.

"I'll take what I can get." He sat, moving the seat closer to her. "I'm Joe, by the way."

"Alexa."

"So why do you want to *transform your inner self?*" he asked.

"Mostly I just think it's time to leave some things behind. It's been a few years, but I have a hard time letting go of some things. This seemed like as good an option as any. What about you?"

"Honestly?" He leaned forward conspiratorially. "I just wanted a vacation." She laughed.

"You're honest," she said. "I like that in a man."

"And you have an amazing laugh," he said. "I like that in a woman."

In what had to be some of the worst timing possible, Michelle rematerialized, finished in the bathroom. Alexa glanced down at the check and, reluctantly, signed and added her room number. She would have been happy spending another couple of hours down here with this man, but she didn't want Michelle to feel snubbed. "I've got to go," she said, glancing over at him. "Are you going to the opening seminar tomorrow?"

"Absolutely."

"Find me there," she said, standing.

"I definitely will."

She could feel his eyes on her as she sauntered away, and she may have moved her hips more than was strictly necessary.

CHAPTER 21

Carmella, 2007

THE CLUB MUSIC WAS LOUD AND thumped almost painfully in Carmella's ears, and the lights pulsated erratically, though supposedly in time with the beat. Given she hadn't been in a club for over two years, you'd think it would have been sensory overload. But to her it screamed of freedom.

Casimir was out of town. She had asked him what he was doing, but he had just waved her off and told her to shut it. Her guess was he and some of his friends had gone off to Atlantic City. But it didn't matter. What mattered was that she wasn't under his thumb for the time being. She was the freest she had been in three years and wanted to savor every minute of it as best she could. The air was saturated with the scent of stale sweat, pot, and booze, but it was possibly the sweetest air she had ever inhaled.

Everything about tonight was supposed to be about freedom, even her clothes. Her shirt was low cut and stopped above her navel, showing off her hourglass figure while still concealing the marks her husband had left on her. Her skirt was short, and her black heels added an extra three inches to her height. It was the type of clothing that Casimir would never let her wear outside the apartment anymore, even if she still kept some of it hidden in the back of her closet.

But he was nowhere near here tonight, and what he didn't know wouldn't hurt him. Or her.

She took a long swig of her drink as she took in her surroundings. It didn't feel like much had changed in three years, even if she herself had. The club, with its overly crowded dancefloor and patrons screaming over the music, felt like a time capsule, and it was easy to feel as though none of the past three years had happened, even if the fading bruises still twinged when she moved the wrong way.

She was about to go onto the dance floor when a muscular figure slipped into the seat next to hers. She glanced over, and he smiled.

The smile was ravishing, but that wasn't the only thing she noticed. He was tall—definitely over six feet. His broad shoulders and toned arms made him seem even bigger than he already was, and it was easy to see just by looking at him—even through his shirt—that his entire body was perfectly sculpted. His dark eyes crinkled at the edges as he grinned at her, accentuating high cheekbones and a strong jaw.

He was, in short, one of the most beautiful men she had ever seen.

"Hey," he said. The man had a deep voice that had a slight huskiness to it. It fit him perfectly.

She forced herself to stop ogling him. "Hi."

"Do you mind?" He pointed at the chair he was sitting on. Glancing down the metal counter, it was clear there were several free open seats at the moment. He could have picked any of them.

"No," she found herself saying before she could think better of it. The man nodded his appreciation before signaling the bartender.

"Are you here alone?" he asked when the bartender slid a beer in front of him. She looked up and down, taking in more of his appearance. The clothes were crisp and, despite being fairly simple, clearly expensive. The midnight-blue shirt that complemented his dark complexion had two buttons undone, enough to see chest hair and a simple gold chain. The Rolex on his wrist was new.

"Yeah," she said.

His eyebrows raised. "That's hard to believe." His eyes glanced down to her left hand, where the large, fake diamond rested. "Oh, sorry. Are you married?"

"Yes. I mean, well, it's complicated."

"That's always fun." The man took a swig of his beer. He glanced over at her again. "Shame, because I was gonna ask you to dance."

Heat flooded Carmella's face as she processed his words. It had been a long time since she had danced with anyone, even Casimir. And, after nearly three years of being called *ugly*, *worthless*, a *bitch*, and being told, "you're lucky someone even married you," it was hard for her to feel wanted. The way the man was looking at her right now made her feel attractive for the first time in years. Butterflies suddenly burst into her stomach and fluttered swiftly, their wings matching the rapid speed of her beating heart.

"You still can," she said, surprising even herself.

He glanced back down at the ring in question.

"He won't mind," she lied. "Like I said, it's complicated."

The man looked her up and down again, a faint smirk on his lips. His eyebrows were raised.

He knows, Carmella thought, and a thrill shot through her at the realization. *He knows I'm lying, and he doesn't care.*

The knowledge did nothing to steady her legs or stifle the burning desire smoldering below her stomach. It was his eyes and the way he kept looking at her, drinking her in as if she were the most beautiful thing he had ever seen.

Casimir.

The name was like a bucket of ice water dumped on her head. There was no telling what he would do to her if he found out. He would be livid. He would beat her worse than he ever had before. Hell, he might kill her.

But as the man stood from his chair and held out his hand to her, she took it instinctively. Her hand looked small in his, but his palm was warm and comforting. He pulled her onto the dance floor, his hands going to her hips and moving her back and forth gently as they got a feel for one another. At first, she stayed back from him a bit, worried that if their bodies touched too much it would send her over a precipice that she'd never be able to return from. But by the second song, she had taken half a step closer, and she could see every one of his eyelashes as he looked down at her. Her own hands ran up and down his arms, following the defined curves of his hard muscles. By the fourth song, their bodies were pressed against one another, and his hands had slid downward to her ass, cupping both cheeks as they moved together.

"You've got a great bod," the man said. She still didn't know his name, and something about that sent even more thrills through her body.

"I could say the same thing about you," she said, one nail running down his bicep.

"I'll bet you look even better without any clothes," he muttered into her ear.

She glanced up at him. This was it: her one chance to back out of the situation and leave. She could pretend this never happened. She hadn't done anything she might regret. She could walk away now, and Casimir would never be any the wiser.

But she didn't want to back out. Not anymore. She wanted her life back, some semblance of control. And she could get that here and now.

And by God, she was going to take it.

"Do you want to see?" she asked.

—

THE MAN'S APARTMENT WAS NICE and modern and in a far nicer area than her own. She stepped inside and had enough time to see the spacious kitchen and the living room with large windows that overlooked the Hudson before the man grabbed her by the waist with strong hands and pulled her toward him. Their lips met, and she all but melted in his arms. The embrace was pure lust and need, and all she wanted in that moment was for him to fuck her senseless.

He broke the kiss long enough to yank off his top and help remove hers. It fell to the ground as he drank her in.

For a moment, panic washed over her. There were still bruises, even if they were faded and healing well. But they were unmistakably present. Would he mention them? Ask about them? She wasn't sure how to explain them. Or maybe he would think she was too damaged, too weak.

But if he did notice them, he didn't say anything. Instead, he just stared in admiration, and she could see him beginning to stiffen beneath his pants.

"Fuck," he said. "You're even sexier than I thought."

Heat flooded through her body, from her head to her toes, all of it rushing to settle between her legs as her hands ran along his taut stomach, exploring his body as he bent forward to kiss her again.

Her fingers slid down toward his pants, and she grasped his cock over his jeans. He bucked slightly, and she could feel him grin against her lips.

"You like that?" she asked.

He nipped at her neck as he took hold of her breast. His fingers flicked tantalizingly across her already hard nipple, making the burning sensation growing inside her blaze even hotter. "You know I do."

She squirmed against him as he continued playing with her. It had been years since she had felt this way. She had forgotten what it was like. And now that she was remembering, she wasn't sure if she would ever be able to go back.

But then his fingers slipped below her skirt, and she found it hard to think of anything at all.

"No panties tonight?" the man asked, his voice close to her ear, his breath caressing her skin and sending shivers of longing shooting through her. "If I didn't know any better, I'd say you wanted to get fucked. Is that right?"

She couldn't say anything; all she could do was nod. Even if it had been on a subconscious level, she realized now that half the reason she had gone to the club was to feel something like this again.

He grinned. "I think I can help with that."

If she waited any longer, she might explode. She fumbled with the buttons of his jeans and pulled them down along with his underwear.

His cock was massive, and she wanted nothing more than for it to be inside her. She grasped it, stroking it experimentally, getting a feel for it. Despite the girth, it felt nearly perfect in her hand.

"Where do you want to get fucked?" he asked. "Bedroom? Living room? Kitchen?" He grinned mischievously. "All three?"

That nearly sent her over the edge right there.

"Table."

He grinned.

"I don't mind the idea of having you splayed out like a fine meal for me," he said. Then he hoisted her up by her hips, lying her down at the edge of the table before stripping off the skirt. He eyed her hungrily as he stroked himself before moving closer to her. His hand reached out, his fingers circling her pussy, seeing how wet she was. When he was satisfied, he ran his cock between her lips, sliding back and forth but not going in.

"You're a fucking tease," she said. "You know that?"

The man chuckled as his thumb fondled her clit. "I've gotten that once or twice," he said. "I like my women revved up and squirming."

She was certainly that. All she wanted was for him to thrust inside her and fuck her senseless. She didn't think she could wait much longer. At this point, she'd finish before he even slid inside her.

"You got that already," she said. "Now fuck me."

But she hadn't even gotten the last word out of her mouth when he thrust inside her, making her cry out in surprise and delight.

And that was how their night began, though it didn't end there. He must have made her orgasm three times—something she hadn't realized was possible for her. He alternated between fucking her hard and gently, pushing her against the wall and lying her on the bed, spreading her legs apart before moving forward to eat her pussy. And she returned the favor in stride, riding him in as many positions as they could manage in the hours they had.

By the time they finally flopped onto the bed among the tangled bed-sheets, the dark of the night had begun to shift to a slightly lighter shade, the dawn only just threatening to emerge in an hour or so.

Years later, Carmella would think back on that night. She never learned the man's name. Not when she woke up in bed beside him the next morning, not when she slid on her club clothes from the night before, not even when they sat and had coffee together before she left. There was an unspoken understanding about what they were and what they were doing. This was never going to be anything more than a one-night stand. Both knew it, and both were content with it.

But that night was the point of no return for her. In a strange, warped way, it gave her back some of the worth that Casimir had surgically and methodically stripped from her. And though she didn't know his name, she would always thank the man for approaching her at the bar that night. It set her on a path that would ultimately change the course of her life.

For better and worse.

CHAPTER 22

Alexa

A LEXA MUST HAVE REFRESHED her email a dozen times. But so far, all she had gotten was an email saying that she had won a million dollars, and all she had to do was send back her bank account details.

It was stupid for her to be this impatient anyway. It had only been two days since her meeting with the PI. Winston had told her it would probably be a few days before he got back to her. But she had never been good at waiting. And even then, the odds of him sending an email instead of calling seemed fairly slim. Still, refreshing her email felt slightly more productive than staring at her cell phone.

So she kept waiting. And waiting. And waiting.

It wasn't until a week had passed that she got a phone call.

"I haven't gotten it yet," Winston said when she asked about the progress. "But I'm close. Only problem is that I've hit the twenty-hour limit."

Alexa's eyes narrowed to slits. "How do I know you aren't hustling me?" she asked.

"I can send you what I've got so far if that'll make you feel better," he said. "But it's not much. At first glance, the guy seems clean. But there are a couple of red flags that tell me you might be right. Meeting with unsavory people and things like that." When Alexa didn't say anything, he continued. "How about this: I keep searching. If I don't find anything, you don't pay."

"And why would you do that?" she asked. "No offense, but I'm sensing some red flags of my own here."

Winston snorted over the phone, and Alexa could almost see him shaking his head in amusement. "It's an ADA. I think it's interesting. Of course I want to keep looking into it. Think of it as a professional curiosity."

Alexa considered, brow furrowed as she stared at the floor of her office. It looked dirtier than normal. She'd have to make sure the cleaning crew came in at some point to take care of that. Finally, she looked back up. "All right," she said.

The next week should have flown by. She had court three of those days, meetings with clients and other attorneys, date night with Joe, and wine night with Michelle and some of her other friends. But instead it dragged on sluggishly, hour by hour, day by day. And it drove her crazy. She checked her phone every ten minutes, hoping for a text or missed call, even though she knew there was no way he would be reaching out that soon. She just couldn't help it. Time was running out, and she needed to get O'Brien off this case before he did any real damage.

Then there was another call.

"I've got it," Winston said smugly as soon as she answered her cell. "I think you'll be happy with the results."

"Where do you want to meet?" She would have dashed off right then if he had suggested it. Hell, she was already reaching for her keys.

But just as she was about to leap from her chair and walk out her office, he said, "How about this evening, 6:30? There's a café not too far from you that should work for a meetup."

She scowled. It was only twelve. She was going to have to wait over six hours. "Sure it can't be sooner?" she asked.

"Sorry," he said. "I have business to take care of for some other clients. That's the earliest I'm free."

She grimaced. "If that's the best I can get, I'll take it." She tried and failed to hide the sigh of frustration. "I'll see you then."

She arrived at the café at six. She hadn't been able to wait any longer.

The knowledge that Winston had found something made it nearly impossible for her to sit still. Her leg jiggled impatiently as she clutched the cup of coffee in front of her.

"You should lay off the coffee if it's giving you the jitters like that," Winston said when he materialized next to her. He nodded down at her leg.

"It's decaf." She took another sip. "What'd you find?"

"Not one to dawdle, are you?" he asked, sitting down across from her.

"Never been my strong suit."

"Well, hopefully what I've got for you is worth the wait." He plopped his messenger bag on his lap and began rummaging through it. "I'll tell you, the man's careful. He knows how to hide his tracks and keep a low profile. He's good." Winston flashed a grin. "But I'm better."

And he slid a manila envelope across the table to her.

She tried not to seem too eager as she opened it, trying to keep her face as stoney as possible. But she was unable to hide the shock on her face when she pulled the contents out of the folder.

She splayed out dozens of photos across the table. Each of them had O'Brien somewhere in view. Some were innocuous: him walking down the street, talking on the phone, and eating dinner at an overpriced restaurant. But others . . . those were the interesting ones.

One of them showed O'Brien talking to a burly looking man outside of a sketchy-looking door in an alley, and another—presumably taken immediately after—showed him going inside. Winston tapped the photos.

"You know where this is?" he asked.

She squinted, then memories came flooding back to her, and she nodded. "Gryphon's Den," she said. "Gang hangout. Suspected drug den as well, but every time the cops try to bust it, they can't find anything. Probably because they have someone on the force. There's a lot of hiding spots for illegal stuff in there, too."

"That's right," Winston said. "I'm surprised you know that."

"I know a lot of things," she said, looking back down at the photos. "Part of being a prosecutor."

"Right."

For a moment she thought he might press her. But he didn't; instead, he pointed at another photo. "You know who that is?"

She leaned forward to see a large, white man with a bald head sitting at a restaurant across from O'Brien. There were several photos from that encounter, and in nearly all of them both men were smiling and laughing. Her eyes narrowed in recognition and distaste.

"Richard Davidson," she said. "Big-time drug lord. He's been arrested a couple of times, but it never stuck. I guess I can see why now."

"I got this last week," he said, tapping one of the photos of the two men. "That was when I realized there was something to what you were saying."

"Photos of the two of them don't prove he's doing anything illegal," she said. "It's just scummy."

"That's why I said I needed more time," he said, then pointed to the last set of photos. "I think you'll like these."

It was O'Brien and an unfamiliar man sitting in Washington Square Park at night. They were sitting next to one another near the fountain, the spout of water shooting over their heads. Winston was a good photographer, and even in the dim light of the streetlamps, you could see both figures clearly. In the series of photos, O'Brien handed the other man something that looked like money. The other man tucked the bills in his pocket before passing something over to O'Brien. Winston had zoomed in on the hands. Dangling between the fingers of the other man, about to drop into O'Brien's palm, was a baggie of white powder.

"Fuck," she said. "Fuck."

Winston nodded. "That's what you call *the money shot*."

She stared at the photo, still processing what she was looking at. She had always had her suspicions, but this was undeniable proof that O'Brien was crooked. And what was more, this was exactly what she needed in order to get him off the case.

She was so giddy she nearly laughed. It was too perfect.

Winston was still talking, and she forced herself to refocus.

"There are a few other goodies in that envelope," he said, reaching over and pulling the other items out. "Nothing quite as good as those photos there, but some of it is pretty interesting. I did a thorough background check and ran all the normal reports, which you can see in these. My time spent on the case, broken down so you can see exactly what I was doing, is in there, too." He pointed to the stack of papers he had just placed on the table. Then he dug inside the envelope and pulled out a small flash drive. "This guy's got all the photos here on them, so you have backups, and a few videos you might find interesting as well. It's also got PDFs of all the documents you've got here."

Alexa nodded, taking it all in as she looked at all the items.

"So, how about it?" Winston asked, sitting back in his chair with a shit-eating grin. He looked more like a college kid after finals than a hard-boiled private detective with that look. "Was it worth the extra hours?"

Alexa cut him an amused but slightly stern glance. "You know it was," she said. "Hell, I think you earned a bonus, too."

"If you want to give me one, I'm not going to argue." His smile faltered, and he leaned forward in his chair. "I haven't told the police," he said, "about the drugs. I don't know what you're planning on doing with this information, but I wanted you to at least know that."

Alexa's jaw twitched, and she nodded. "Appreciate it," she said.

"Any idea what you're going to do, if you don't mind my asking?"

The question gnawed at her. Should she report O'Brien? Turn him in instead of just blackmailing him? She chewed her lip as the arguments for both sides raced through her head. But ultimately, she knew what she had to do. There was really only one answer, and she should have known that the minute she hired the PI.

"He's getting reported," she said. "I don't want a guy like him prosecuting any more cases. Who knows how many he's thrown already?"

Winston nodded as if this was what he had expected her to say. "Well, I wish you luck."

She handed him a check. "You too. Thanks."

After Winston left, she stared back down at the papers and photos, all still splayed out in front of her. And as the realization of what would happen after she handed this information over to Barrow washed over her, a smug, triumphant smirk spread over her face. There was still a long way to go, but she had just cleared one of the major hurdles.

You're not going to get away with it this time, Casimir, she thought.

—

SHE WAITED A DAY BEFORE STROLLING into Barrow's office, trying to determine the best way to present the news. She wanted that scumbag out of the picture, and not just so she could take over the Johnson case. Anyone associating with people like Richard Davidson had no business being in the DA's office unless they were being brought up on charges. But she wanted to make sure she showed Barrow the information in a way that was irrefutable.

Finally, right after lunch, when she knew Barrow would be in his office and in a much better mood after eating, she grabbed the envelope and marched over. As she did, her eyes caught O'Brien's, and she smiled at him like a cat who had just caught its mouse. His eyes flickered in alarm when he saw the expression, as if he knew it spelled *trouble*. His own smug smile faltered, and his face filled with an uneasiness. That look alone was worth the thousands of dollars she had spent on Larry Winston. It was all she could do not to laugh.

"What can I do for you, Alexa?" Barrow asked as she stepped inside and closed the door behind her.

"I've got something you might find interesting," she said and handed over the folder with all the photos. She kept the personal documents and the flash drive in her desk drawer. There wasn't much incriminating in them, and she didn't think she would need them anyway.

Barrow frowned as he pulled out the photos. He flipped through them, his eyes narrowing as he saw what was in them. He glanced up.

"Why do you have these?" he asked.

"An interested party gave them to me," she said. It was half true, at least. Barrow didn't have to know she had hired the interested party. "But I think you should keep going through them."

Barrow returned his attention to the photos. He flipped through them idly but still paying attention to the contents. Then he froze, sitting up straighter as he looked at one of them. She didn't have to be a genius to know it was the one with the drug exchange. He glanced up at her.

"And you're sure these aren't doctored?" he asked. His voice had a plaintive, almost pleading tone, as if he were desperate not to believe what his eyes were showing him.

"I'm positive," she said. "But if you don't believe me, have him take a drug test. I doubt he's clean at the moment."

Barrow sighed and ran his fingers through thinning hair, gaze locked on the photo in front of him. He suddenly looked very tired and years older than he had moments ago.

"Fuck," he mumbled, barely audible.

Alexa waited, not saying anything as Barrow continued to process the information. She could see the gears in his head turning. It was the same thought process she had gone through two days before. Part of her felt bad for Barrow; this sort of thing was the stuff of nightmares for district attorneys. It was going to involve a lot of paperwork and a lot of headache. And the worst—or best, in Alexa's mind—part about it was that he had to act. Another of his attorneys had brought the information to him; he couldn't just sweep it under the rug like he might have if he was the only one who knew about it.

Finally, after a long moment, Barrow looked back at her.

"You realize you're ruining a man's career and life here," he said. "He probably has enough coke stashed away to slap him with a felony charge."

"I know," Alexa said. "But you can't just let him get away with this, Andrew. I wouldn't be bringing this to you if I didn't think it was serious."

Barrow frowned, narrowing his eyes suspiciously. "And you're sure this doesn't have anything to do with you wanting the Johnson case?"

Alexa opened her mouth, prepared to lie. But something told her that was the wrong idea. "It might have been part of it," she admitted, if a little reluctantly. "But that doesn't change the fact that he's on drugs and probably crooked. You can see who he's spending time with."

"And you know that if I take him off the case, that doesn't mean you're going to get to take his place, right?" he asked.

"Of course," Alexa said. "But I still think you should give me a chance when it comes time."

"*If*," Barrow emphasized.

"*When*," Alexa corrected. "You know that he can't stay on the case anymore, even if you want to pretend otherwise."

Barrow gritted his teeth but didn't respond. "Regardless," he said, "this doesn't mean you get the case."

"Sure," she said. "But that's a conversation for another day. And I still think we can get an exemption from the judge."

Barrow scowled. "Fine, fine," he said. "We're going to talk about this later. For now, leave me alone. I need to figure out what I'm going to do about this."

Alexa turned to leave. But just as her hand was on the handle, she paused, looking over her shoulder.

"Just so you know," she said, "I do have copies of those photos. And more."

Barrow's mouth parted slightly as the implication behind her words struck him. But then he clamped his jaw shut and nodded.

"Trust me," he said. "On something this important, I wouldn't fuck around like that."

"I know," Alexa said. "But I figured it was worth giving you extra incentive to be honest."

And with that, she walked out the door.

When she left, a nagging concern in the back of her head rose to the forefront: What if Barrow decided to do nothing? What would she do then? She could always report both of them to someone else, but she didn't like the idea. It didn't seem likely, but the thought plagued her all the way back to her office.

The fears turned out to be unwarranted, however. Less than an hour later, Sally poked her head into the office, her eyes alight with stunned excitement.

"You're going to want to see this," she said. Her glasses swished back and forth around her neck as if she had run there. "It's like Christmas came early."

Alexa stood and darted out the door. She didn't even pretend not to know what was about to happen. She pulled up short as she heard indignant cries coming from O'Brien's office.

"This is the stupidest fucking thing I've ever heard of," O'Brien shouted. Despite the closed door, his words were crystal clear, and a small group had formed nearby, all listening intently, barely uttering a sound so they could hear every word.

At a much lower, more reasonable volume, Barrow said, "We have evidence, Jacob. I wouldn't be here if we didn't. You know that."

"What the fuck kind of evidence are you talking about?"

There was a quiet rustling sound, and Alexa knew Barrow must be handing over the photos. She could just imagine the scene unfolding behind the closed door. Two uniformed police officers waited patiently by the door. One of them held handcuffs loosely in one hand as they regarded O'Brien, waiting to determine just how much of a threat he was. Meanwhile, Barrow was standing off to one side, having taken a step back as an angry O'Brien began rifling through the photos. And, as O'Brien flicked through them, his face was growing paler and more panicked by the minute.

When O'Brien finally spoke a few moments later, he said, "Where the hell did you get these?" His voice was far quieter and more subdued, tinted with an edge of dread. But it was still perfectly audible through the closed door.

"An anonymous source," Barrow said. "That's not important. Right now, until this is sorted out, you're suspended without pay. Now, I suggest you go with the officers before they have to drag you out."

"This is ludicrous," O'Brien said. "I can't believe you're doing this."

"I'm not going to say it again," Barrow said, and Alexa heard the steel in his voice, the tone and authority that had gotten him the role of DA in the first place. "Get whatever you need, then leave."

Loud rustling sounds emanated from the office, and a moment later, O'Brien flung the door open. He stared at the gathered crowd, all of whom were staring unabashedly at him, and his face reddened.

Then his eyes found Alexa in the throng, and his face turned the color of a tomato. "You," he snarled. "I know you did this, you bitch. You'll pay for this."

A chill shot down Alexa's spine at the words. They sounded far more ominous than she would have expected from the man. But before she could respond to the threat, one of the uniformed officers who had been in the room placed his hand on O'Brien's shoulder and steered him through the crowd and toward the exit and out of sight.

—

"HEY, ALEXA?"

Alexa glanced up from her paperwork to see Sally peeking into her office. Her hair looked slightly messy, and her cheeks were pinker than normal, as if she had just been running or doing some other form of exercise.

"What's up?"

"Mr. Barrow wants to see you when you're available," Sally said.

Alexa stood instantly, unwilling to wait as excitement pulsed through her. "Now's as good a time as any," she said. "Thanks, Sally."

She hurried past Sally and down the hall, trying not to seem too desperate or eager. She knew what this had to be about. There was really only one thing Barrow would want to talk to her about right now: Casimir's case. But that didn't mean he was giving her good news on the subject. For all she knew, he could be telling her he was giving it to Christine Clark, another ADA. She tried to ignore the fact that her palms were sweaty or that her heart had leaped into her throat. She needed this, needed it more than anything. She wanted to be the one who ran Casimir into the ground and threw him behind bars. There had been a time when she had wished he would drop dead. But death was too good for him. He deserved to live a long, boring life behind bars for what he had done.

She bit down on her tongue to try and get herself to calm down, to bring her back to reality. No use thinking about it until she knew what Barrow was going to say.

He was standing hunched over his desk, flipping through pages, when Alexa strolled in. He glanced up. He looked pale and haggard.

"Morning, Alexa," he said, picking up a cup of coffee and taking a sip. He grimaced. "Were you the one who made the coffee this morning?"

"Guilty."

"You always make it too strong; you know that, right?"

"I consider that a matter of opinion," she said. Barrow gave her an annoyed look before putting the drink back on the desk. "How are things with the O'Brien debacle?" she asked.

He sighed. "Annoying," he said. "I can't really get any of you to prosecute him. Conflict of interest and all that. So I'm trying to figure out how to handle that. He made bail almost instantly. I'm sure you can guess who he's using as his attorney?"

"Henry Thompson." She didn't even have to think about it.

Barrow nodded. "I really hope you're not going to ask to prosecute him as well."

"No," she said. "I'll let that one go."

"Which brings us to the reason I called you in," he said. He straightened, stretched, and walked around the desk. "I'm planning on giving the Johnson case to someone else. O'Brien had a lot of cases, and I'll let you take the pick of any of the othe—"

"Andrew," Alexa interrupted. "You can't do that to me. You know I'm the best person for this one."

"You are," he admitted, if a little grudgingly. "But the judge isn't going to—"

"Who's the judge?" she asked.

He gave her a look that told her she needed to stop interrupting, then said, "Dillon Putotelli."

She tried not to keep her eyes from lighting up. "If I can convince him to give me an exemption, would you let me take the case?"

Barrow let out a puff of air as he considered. "If you can get him to say yes," he said, "then I'll give you the case."

"Excellent." Alexa began to saunter out of his office. "I'll have that for you by the end of tomorrow at the latest."

As she wandered into the break room to grab another cup of coffee, she pulled out her phone and found the number she was looking for.

"Putotelli," a man's voice said when the line connected.

"Dillon!" she said. "It's Alexa. How are you doing?"

"Alexa, good to hear from you. I'm doing all right. And yourself?"

"Just great," she said. "Are you free for lunch? I was hoping we could meet up."

"I think I can schedule you in. How about one?"

"Great! I'll meet you at that sandwich café you like."

There was a chuckle on the other side of the line. "Trying to butter me up, are you?"

"I don't know what you're talking about," Alexa said. "But I'm buying."

—

A FEW HOURS LATER, Alexa was lounging in front of the café at one of their tables, basking in the sunlight streaming between the tall skyscrapers surrounding her. There was a scrape of a chair directly across from her, and she opened her eyes before giving a wide smile.

"Good to see you, Dillon," she said. "How's the courtroom been?"

"About the same as always." He yawned, then gave the young waitress a warm smile as she took their order. "Though I haven't presided over any of your court cases lately."

"I know," she said. "I've missed it. But that actually brings me to something I wanted to talk to you about."

Putotelli raised a gray eyebrow as he waited for her to continue. Putotelli was well into his sixties, probably closer to seventy, though Alexa wasn't positive. He was short and a little pudgy, though his face had thinned with age over the last couple of years, and the wrinkles on his face had carved themselves into deep chasms. His shoulders were hunched, making him look shorter than his five feet, ten inches. But his watery, blue eyes were kind and alert, and he still moved with the agility of a much younger man, and she knew his mind was as sharp as any.

"Don't hold me in suspense," he said.

Alexa took a sip of water and then leaned forward. "You're presiding over Casimir Johnson's case, aren't you?" she asked.

"Ah."

Their sandwiches came, and Putotelli fell silent. He picked up a fry, considered it, then plopped it into his mouth.

"How much do you know about last time?" she asked.

"Not much. But I know the important parts." He tapped a second fry against the side of his plate as he studied her. Then he swiped it in ketchup before biting it in half. "God, this place has the best fries."

Alexa nodded, fighting her impulse to steer the conversation back to where she wanted it to go. She knew the judge well enough to know that trying to get him to talk about something before he was entirely ready was a recipe for getting on his bad side.

And the one thing she couldn't afford right now was getting on Judge Dillon Putotelli's bad side.

He had been a judge since his midthirties, one of the youngest judges ever to be appointed to New York City's Criminal Court. And Alexa was fully aware of the fact that the only reason he hadn't risen higher in the court rankings was because he had no desire to do so. If he had wanted to, he no doubt would have been on the state Supreme Court by now or a federal judge. He was fair but ruthless and strict, and any lawyer knew that if they didn't conduct themselves appropriately in his court, he had no issue with throwing them out.

But Alexa had never had an issue with him. In fact, over the past few years, they had actually become friends. She found she enjoyed his company and his sense of humor. But just because they were friends didn't mean he had ever given her any favoritism in the court, and just because they were friends didn't mean she couldn't get on his bad side if she said the wrong thing.

"So, let me guess," Putotelli said, holding his Reuben in one hand and preparing to take a bite. "Now that O'Brien is currently under criminal investigation, you want to take over the case."

"You know me too well," she said.

"And you know that constitutes a rather blatant conflict of interest." It was a statement rather than a question.

"Naturally. Which is why I came to you. Barrow won't give me any sort of leeway unless you okay it first."

He waited until he had swallowed his rather substantial bite before saying, "Are you sure it's wise? What if you lose?"

"Then I lose, and a scumbag asshole goes free," she said, then gave him a pointed look. "But you know I won't let that happen."

Putotelli sighed and put down the sandwich. A few pieces of sauerkraut fell out and plopped onto the plate. "Alexa," he said, "I can understand why this is important to you. But that doesn't mean I can just give you permission to prosecute the case. And you know Thompson will use it against you."

"I know," she said. "But that doesn't mean it'll work. You know what the guy is like."

"I do," he admitted. "But that doesn't change the fact that you know I've got a point."

"Dillon," she said. "How often have I asked you for anything?"

"There was that one time you asked if I could get my hands on a bottle of Macallan Lalique for your husband when I went over to Scotland," he mused.

"That was a joke!" she said, unable to stop herself from laughing. "I didn't think you'd *actually* bring me one back. At least I didn't make you pay for it."

"Fair," he said, grinning as a sparkle of mischief glinted in his eyes. "And to be fair, you've never asked me for anything when it came to a case."

"I wouldn't ask if it wasn't important to me," she said gently.

He chewed on a fry, and Alexa waited with bated breath.

"All right," he finally said. "I'll do it. But that's the only favor you are ever allowed to ask me when it comes to a case. And you know that I'm going to be a hard-ass."

"I know," Alexa said, smiling as an overwhelming sense of relief washed over her. She could have kissed Putotelli for what he had just done. "It's one of the things I like so much about you."

CHAPTER 23

Carmella, 2009

CARMELLA WOKE UP IN A BED that was far too comfortable to be her own and rolled over onto her side. She took in the tidily cluttered room with unfamiliar pictures on the walls and hardwood floors as opposed to the dirty carpet in her own room.

Looking over her shoulder, she saw a lump beneath the sheets next to her: a white guy who had introduced himself as Peter the night before at the bar she and Georgia had been at. He'd been a little on the short side but good-looking and with a runner's physique. All she could see of him at the moment was red hair peeking out from beneath the covers.

She sighed and fumbled for her phone. It was just after eight. Casimir wasn't supposed to be back from his latest trip until after noon. She had time.

The man next to her in bed stirred and rolled over. His eyes blinked blearily before focusing on her.

"Hey there, sexy," he said, scooting over and putting his hand on her arm.

"Morning," she said, yawning.

Ever since that night of no return, she had gone out more and more frequently whenever Casimir got too drunk and passed out at six p.m. or went to some random place for the weekend to score blow and hookers with his friends. It was her small way of rebelling against him, of getting back at him for the last four years of emotional, psychological, and physical abuse.

At first, she had been terrified that he would find out what was happening. But he was so oblivious that, as long as she fucked him and still gave him head whenever he asked, he didn't notice anything had changed. She still cleaned, and he still beat her whenever he felt like it, so it wasn't as though much had changed. There was a savage pleasure in fucking complete strangers behind his back without him having a clue. There was no way he would ever let her leave. At least she could do this one small thing.

"You want some breakfast?" he asked, then raised his eyebrows. "Or maybe some other way of waking up?"

"Mmm," she moved closer to him, close enough to feel him hardening beneath his underwear. "What did you have in mind?"

Later, she would wonder what might have happened if she had just left when she woke up, if she hadn't taken the time for that last fuck. But ultimately, she supposed it didn't matter.

—

THE MOMENT SHE WALKED THROUGH her front door, a meaty fist slammed into the side of her jaw. She stumbled and probably would have fallen if that same meaty hand hadn't snatched the front of her skimpy halter top and shoved her into the wall with so much force that the drywall behind her head caved in with a spray of old plaster and dust. When she stopped seeing stars, her stomach clenched in terror as Casimir's livid face, his mouth curled in a sneer, shifted into focus.

The only thought that pierced through the cloud of terror fogging her mind was that *he had come home early.*

"Where the fuck you been, cunt?" he demanded, his breath smelling as putrid as it ever had. "I come home early and you ain't here, then you come in looking like a fucking whore?"

Her stomach clenched and her mind froze up and she said the first thing that came to her mind. "I was out with Georgia at the grocer—"

He punched her in the stomach, and she would have doubled over if he weren't still holding her shirt.

"Fucking liar," he snarled.

He threw her to the ground. The side of her head collided with the coffee table and more stars burst across her vision as her forehead screamed out in pain.

"Who you been fucking, huh?" he asked, stalking toward her.

"No one," she said, staggering to her feet as her hand went to her temple. It came back bloody. Everything was swimming, and she could barely think straight through the pain. She swayed unsteadily when she finally stood fully up. "I ain't—"

He hit her again before grabbing her by the neck and dragging her over to the kitchen counter. She was so dizzy she couldn't even fight him. He shoved her against the counter, slamming her stomach into the edge so hard that the breath rushed out of her. She gaped like a fish, trying to get air back into her lungs even as Casimir held her in place, pushing his body against hers. Her ass clenched in fear as her head throbbed painfully. She was more terrified than she had ever been in her life, and she wondered with horror just what Casimir was about to do.

It'll be fine, she thought as she struggled to regain her breath and Casimir continued pushing her into the counter. *He's done things like this plenty of times before. It'll be like all the other times.*

She had only just managed to breathe deeply again when she heard a clink of metal and the rustle of leather against denim from behind her. And before she even realized what was happening, Casimir's belt was around her throat. He yanked, and it cinched tight, giving him a makeshift leash and collar that she was helpless against. She could only take shallow, rasping gasps, and the edges of her vision turned black. Her fingers scrabbled uselessly against the leather, trying to pull it away from her neck at least enough so she could breathe. But it was useless.

"You like that, bitch?" he asked, pulling even tighter.

"Casi . . . stop . . ." she rasped. "Can't . . . breathe."

He slammed her head into the counter.

"Shut the fuck up," Casimir snarled in her ear as he jerked down her skirt. "You wanna be a whore, you're gonna be treated like a whore."

And he shoved himself into her.

She cried out in pain, her hands curling unconsciously into fists as she squeezed her eyes tight.

Just let him take it, she told herself through the pain as his thrusts rammed her into the kitchen counter again and again. His flabby stomach clapped against her ass as he pumped back and forth. *He's done it before. Just let him take what he wants and get it over with.*

But she didn't entirely believe herself. Something felt different about this one. He'd never choked her with a belt before, and even when he'd hit her, he'd never been this rough. Her head felt like someone had split it with a meat cleaver, her stomach ached, and her throat was going to have marks on it for a week. Tears filled her vision, and she could barely think through the storm of terror and pain. The blood from her temple trickled into her eye as she waited for him to finish. But part of her worried that it would go on forever. That he would never stop, and she would forever be stuck with this belt around her throat and Casimir's dick pumping in and out of her as she began to chafe.

But eventually he did, and her shoulders sagged with relief when she felt him finish inside her. Her entire body relaxed as she waited for him to let go of her and loosen the belt.

But instead of releasing her and ordering her to clean herself up like he always did, he yanked hard on the belt, jerking her away from the counter and dragging her to the couch. He was naked from the waist down, and his cock was fully erect. She choked as she stumbled behind, trying to keep up with him.

Panic set in as she realized he wasn't done with her. She had to act, to protect herself before things got too far. She needed to find a way out. Even though she was in pain, she lunged toward him, desperate to claw at him with her nails, kick him in the nuts, to do anything that might let her get away. But when she lunged forward to attack him, he just slammed his fist straight into her eye, and stars filled her vision again as new pain blossomed across her face.

He flung her face-first onto the sofa, and before she could scramble off, he was sitting on her, crushing her beneath his weight and sending dull pain along her lower back. He shoved himself into her again and began thrusting himself into her once more.

Finally, it was done. One last pump and squirt. She collapsed, closing her eyes, panting and trying to calm her pounding heart, reassuring herself that it was over with now.

And that was when the baseball bat came out.

CHAPTER 24

Maria and Tony

TONY AND MARIA DIDN'T HAVE to wait long. They had only just sat down in the chairs that the secretary had kindly pointed to when the door to the office opened, and a beautiful Black woman stepped out.

Tony blinked, brows furrowing. There was something familiar about the woman that he couldn't quite place.

"Hi," the woman said, sticking out her hand as Tony and his sister stood. "I'm Alexa."

"Tony," he said, shaking her hand.

The prosecutor's head tilted to the side, as if the name struck a chord. "Tony," she said, rolling the name around on her tongue. Then her eyes lit up. "You wouldn't happen to work at the Rooftop Plaza, would you?"

Tony paused, taken aback, when the final piece clicked into place. "You're the woman who gave me that huge tip a few weeks ago," he said.

Alexa laughed. "I'm surprised you remembered that."

"I don't forget 300 percent tips," he said. "Thank you for that."

"You looked like you were going through a rough time," she said. Her eyes flicked over to Maria, and the smile died. "I guess I can see why now."

Maria didn't flinch, but she did look at the ground and shift uncomfortably from foot to foot. Color rose to her cheeks as her hand unconsciously went to her cheek, where the bruise had finally faded, even if the interior scars were far from healing.

Alexa noticed the reaction, and her eyes narrowed. "You have nothing to be ashamed of," she said. "That asshole's done this before, and he'll do it again unless we can throw his ass in jail. But none of this is your fault."

"That other lawyer . . ." Maria muttered.

"Was a cokehead and as big an asshole as Casimir Johnson," Alexa said, and her tone brokered no argument. "And you don't have to worry about him anymore."

The honesty was such a shock and so refreshing that Tony barked out a laugh. Alexa glanced over, and she gave a small grin.

"Why don't we go in my office and go over things?" She gestured for the other two to go ahead of her.

"If you don't mind my saying," Maria said as she and Tony sat across the desk from Alexa, "it seems like you know Casimir pretty well."

Tony watched as Alexa's fingers twitched on the desk as if she were about to curl them into fists. But the fingers halted before the fist could fully form. Though she wasn't able to hide the anger in her eyes quite as easily.

"I've had dealings with him in the past," she said. "I know how brutal he can get and how much of a piece of shit he is. Like I said, he's done this before."

Tony frowned. He wasn't sure why, but his instincts were telling him that she was holding something back, but he had no idea what it was.

But that train of thought was broken when she pulled out a recorder and said, "All right, Maria, why don't you tell me everything that you remember from that night."

Maria squeezed her eyes shut, took a deep breath, and began.

—

"THANK YOU FOR YOUR HELP," Alexa said as she opened the door to her office. "I know how hard this is, and you're being incredibly brave. I'll be in contact with the next steps, okay?"

Tony nodded. "Thanks, Mrs. Montgomery."

She laughed and shook her head. "Alexa, please," she said. "Mrs. Montgomery feels so stuffy."

"Alexa, then."

As he and his sister walked down the hall, he mulled the meeting over. He couldn't help but like Alexa. There was something fierce about the woman, and the bluntness was so refreshing after dealing with that O'Brien lawyer, who had constantly sidestepped questions and worn a smug smirk whenever they talked. And he had only offered them the one meeting. Every time after that, whenever Tony had tried to reach out to him, all he had gotten was voicemail.

"I have to run to the bathroom," Maria said and hurried off into the ladies' room. His eyes followed her until she disappeared behind the door, and he wondered if she actually needed the restroom or if she was composing herself after having to relive everything again. He wouldn't question her about it, though. She needed her privacy.

His eyes swept around the hall as he leaned against the wall, watching the people walking past. None of them paid him any mind.

Well, that wasn't entirely true. One person paid him some mind.

A tall, absurdly attractive man glanced at him as he strolled past. He was pale, but it suited him. He had high cheekbones and an angular face. The dark hair fell around his eyes in an intentionally messy way. He looked wiry but fit, as if he ran a lot but didn't do much else—the type of frame that Tony liked best. The button-down shirt and nice pants suited him, but it was easier to imagine him in tight jeans and a T-shirt. His piercing, green eyes regarded Tony, and full lips quirked upward into a smile as he saw Tony looking back.

For a moment, Tony was captivated by the look, as if the man's gaze were pinning him in place. It was an intense, scrutinizing look. And though it lasted only a minute, some sort of spark seemed to shoot between them, the type of jolt that told you that the person you were looking at was going to be important in your life.

Then the man looked away, and the spell was broken.

Tony watched the man's back, the swelling balloon that had filled his chest rapidly deflating. It had been one-sided, then.

As he watched the man walk away, a pencil clattered to the floor behind him. But the man kept walking, oblivious to the fact that he'd dropped something.

"Hey," Tony called, trotting over to the pencil. The man turned around automatically, despite the fact that the hallway was crowded, and Tony could have been talking to anyone. "You dropped this." He bent down and picked up the pencil.

"Thanks." The man reached out and took it from Tony's hand. Their fingers brushed briefly. "I appreciate it."

"Not a problem." Tony paused awkwardly, trying to think of something that might keep the man there for a bit longer. "Uh, I'm guessing you work here?"

"Paralegal," the man said. "I'm guessing you don't?"

"Had a meeting with one of the attorneys," he said.

"Ah," the man looked him up and down, raising an eyebrow. "Bad boy from the wrong side of the tracks or upstanding citizen?"

"Waiter."

The man laughed. "Clearly an upstanding citizen, then." He stuck out his hand. "I'm David."

"Tony."

"Nice to meet you, Tony." He tilted his head. "So why are you here, Mr. Waiter?"

Tony's face fell, and he could see the almost guilty surprise on David's face as the other man realized it wasn't a joking matter. "I'm here for my sister," he said. "She, uh, got attacked, and the prosecutor wanted to talk to her."

"I'm sorry to hear that," David said. "That's awful. Is she okay?"

"As okay as she can be," he said, running his fingers through his hair as he glanced at the bathroom.

"Who's the prosecutor?"

"Alexa Montgomery."

David let out a low whistle. "That woman is ruthless," he said. "You're in good hands. Trust me. I've never met any lawyer that stubborn and tenacious, and that's saying something."

There was something about the words that put Tony at ease. His shoulders relaxed slightly, and he gave a soft smile, nodding his appreciation. "That's good to hear," he said.

"So does that mean I'll get to see you around again?" David asked, his eyes flicking up and down in a way that made Tony blush furiously. It had been a long time since he'd dated anyone, and he didn't think any of his exes could compare to the Adonis in front of him right now. His mouth was very dry, and for a moment he forgot the man's question.

"Possibly," Tony finally managed to say. And he realized that he desperately wanted that to be the case. The man standing in front of him intrigued him. He wanted to learn more, wanted to spend more time staring at his beautiful face. He wondered what the rest of his body looked like, if it matched the handsomeness of his face.

Tony had just opened his mouth, just barely mustering the courage to ask David for his number, when Maria appeared beside him. She glanced between the two of them politely.

"Are you ready to go?" she asked.

He tried to hide the creeping blush. He loved his sister, but he was too embarrassed to ask for a guy's number in front of her. She was very aware that he was gay, and she didn't mind. And that wasn't what made him self-conscious. It was just weird to him. That, and he wasn't sure how she would feel about him blatantly flirting in front of her after all she had been through.

"Yeah," he said, a bit reluctantly. He turned back to David. "I'm sure I'll be around at some point in the future," he said. "I hope I get to see you again."

"I do too." David turned and walked away, waving over his shoulder. "Nice to meet you, Tony."

Tony kept watching the other man's back, unable to stop until the man rounded the corner. Then he turned to his sister.

"Come on," he said. "Let's get going."

CHAPTER 25

Carmella, 2009

A FRANTIC POUNDING ON THE door roused Carmella from the void of unconsciousness. She let out a soft moan as all the aches and pains came rushing back to her. Her stomach was bruised, and her wrists and hands were still raw from where she had been tied up. Her neck and throat hurt, too. Her arm was on fire, and her head pounded painfully. Her eyes opened in narrow slits, and the light screamed at her. She was nauseous, too, and she vaguely realized she probably had a concussion before the thought slipped away. She couldn't even remember why she was on the floor or in so much pain at first. All she wanted to do right now was fall back asleep into oblivion.

"Carmella?"

The pounding on the door hurt almost as much as the rest of her body. She just wanted it to go away.

"Carmella! Get your ass to the door, or I swear I'll break it down."

Groaning, she got shakily to her feet. She took two steps and stumbled. She would have fallen if she hadn't grabbed onto the couch with her good arm.

She finally managed to stagger to the door, wincing as the pounding continued. She fumbled with the dead bolt before pulling the door open.

"Oh, thank go—" Georgia cut herself off as she saw Carmella, her eyes widening in horror. "Jesus fucking Christ."

Carmella opened her mouth to respond, then groaned and slumped against the door frame.

"Think I might lose a tooth," she muttered. It was all she could think to say.

"We're getting you to a hospital," Georgia said, taking Carmella gently by the arm.

Not half an hour later, they were clambering out of the taxi, Carmella far slower than Georgia, and stumbling into the ER, Georgia propping Carmella up. The receptionist paled when she saw Carmella and hurried the two women through check-in, bypassing the waiting room entirely. Georgia stayed by her side the entire time, unwilling to leave Carmella for a minute.

"How'd you know to find me, anyway?" Carmella asked when the latest nurse finally left them alone after asking the same twenty questions the other three doctors had. She was lying on a hospital bed, hooked up to all types of machines that read her blood pressure and heart rate. She'd already gone to get an X-ray of her arm and ribs and a CT scan for the concussion all the nurses were positive she'd gotten (they'd been right). Her arm and three of her ribs were broken, but her skull, mercifully, hadn't been fractured. It had been the one part of her body that had been spared the baseball bat. Her head was less fuzzy than it had been an hour earlier, at least. She snuggled down and closed her eyes, exhausted. It was going to be a long day.

"You didn't text me this morning that you got back safe from that guy's house like you were supposed to," Georgia said, gently brushing a strand of hair out of Carmella's face. "I waited just to make sure you hadn't forgotten, but when this morning came and I still hadn't heard from you, I got worried."

It was the next morning? It seemed hard to believe.

"Got a bit distracted," Carmella muttered, poking at the bruise on her face and wincing.

"I can see that." Georgia's face turned grim. "I'm guessing that wasn't the guy from the bar who did that to you?"

Carmella hesitated for a moment, her gut instinct to lie making her pause. But then she said, "Nah. It wasn't him."

"That fucking asshole . . ." Georgia took a step back and shook her head. "Why didn't you ever tell me?"

"You wouldn't've believed me," Carmella said.

"You're my best friend. Of course I'd've believed you." Georgia shook her head. "It don't matter. You're safe, and that's all I care about. Once we get you taken care of, we'll make sure that asshole gets what he deserves."

"I don't know if I want to press charges," Carmella said.

Georgia stared, shocked. "That asshole nearly beat you to death, and you're worried about reporting him?"

"He could come after me," Carmella whispered, her voice uncharacteristically timid. Her entire body ached. She wanted nothing more than to curl up and go to sleep, but the pain was too much to do even that, even with the medication.

Georgia shook her head. The beads at the end of her dark tightly braided hair clacked with the motion. "He ain't gonna touch you, girl," she said. "You're staying at my place from now on. I'll go back to your apartment when I know he ain't there and get your stuff. Just leave me a list."

Overwhelming warmth and gratitude washed over Carmella, and she smiled even as her face protested the movement. Georgia's hand reached out and entwined it with Carmella's, squeezing gently. "You're a good friend, Georgia," she said.

"And don't you forget it. You can repay me by never putting yourself in this type of danger ever again."

"Deal."

There was a gentle rustling of the privacy curtain, and a beautiful woman poked her head around it.

"Carmella?" the woman asked. She smiled warmly, revealing perfect, almost blindingly white teeth. "My name's Soleil. I'm going to be your attending physician. How are you feeling?"

"Like I've been hit by a truck going eighty." The words were out before she realized it.

Soleil gave a sympathetic smile. "I'm sorry about that. Hopefully the pain medications will kick in soon. Let me know if they don't, and I'll prescribe something a bit stronger."

"Thanks."

The smile vanished as the doctor glanced over at Georgia. "Do you mind if I have a word with Carmella alone?"

Georgia's eyes narrowed. "I ain't leaving her by herself." The grip on Carmella's hand tightened.

"It's fine," Carmella said.

Georgia glanced back and forth between Carmella and the doctor. "I'll be in the waiting room," she said grudgingly.

As soon as Georgia left, Soleil came and took her place by the bed.

"Your friend told the nurses what happened while you were getting your X-ray," she said. "I need to let you know that we're required to report any domestic abuse to a victim assistance organization."

"What about the police?"

"Right now? That's only minors and vulnerable adults. The elderly, mostly. But whoever is going to come talk to you will probably recommend you file a police report. I would too."

Carmella was about to shake her head in panic as nauseating fear overwhelmed her. "I don't—"

"He'll do it again," she said. "If he hasn't already. Both to you and to others. You got lucky this time. Next time, you might not be. And think of anyone else he might do this to."

Carmella went quiet as she thought back to how easily and ruthlessly Casimir had hurt and raped her to the degree that he had, as if he had done it a thousand times before, and to more than just her.

"He'll find me," she said. "And we're married. He's not going to let me divorce him."

"There are ways to get around that. Whoever comes to talk to you from that organization can tell you how to go about a unilateral divorce," Soleil said. "I'm betting he didn't let you get too close to anyone who might've told you that."

Carmella shook her head.

"Ultimately, it's up to you, dear," Soleil said. There was a pause. "Did he rape you?"

"He's my husband," Carmella said automatically. But Soleil shook her head.

"It can still be rape if it's without your consent. Did he rape you?"

Carmella hesitated, a wash of panic hitting her again. But then she nodded. Soleil took a long, deep breath.

"I'm going to get someone to do a rape kit as well," she said. "And I know it's hard and scary, but think about reporting it, okay? Either way, we'll get you in touch with someone who can help you through this."

Carmella nodded vaguely, her mind still foggy as she tried to process all the information she'd just received. There was a way out of this for her. Suddenly, a ray of hope blossomed inside her chest—something that she hadn't felt in nearly five years. There was a chance she could be free forever, and there was something she could do to make sure this never happened again. She just needed to get the courage to do it.

"I'll report it," she said, her voice barely audible.

Soleil gently squeezed her hand. "Good for you," she said. "I'm proud of you. I know it's not easy. Don't worry. I'll contact the police for you."

Carmella nodded gratefully. Even as she did, her eyes felt heavy, and all she wanted to do was sleep.

"I'm tired," she murmured.

"Get some rest," Soleil said, standing. "I'll have your friend come back in and stay with you. We'll move you to an actual room here in a bit, but we'll let you get some sleep for now, okay?"

Carmella barely heard the other woman as her eyes closed, and she finally drifted into blissful unconsciousness.

CHAPTER 26

Sally

"HEY THERE, SALLY."

Sally glanced up from her computer to see the young, attractive janitor at the corner of her desk, looking her up and down and smiling. "How are you doing this fine evening?"

"I'm doing well, Luca. How are you?"

"Much better now." He glanced down at his watch. "Are you free to help me with something?" he asked.

Sally tapped her lips in mock consideration as her eyes darted to the clock: 6:15. Glancing around, she saw that the entire office was deserted except for the two of them. An excited pressure began building between her legs, and she forced herself not to squirm.

"I think I can help," she said. "What is it you need?"

"Just getting something from the supply closet." His eyes raked up and down her body again as she stood, and she saw the glint of lust in his eyes. "I think you're dressed perfectly for it, as well."

She was in a skirt and button-down blouse, deliberately so. She hurriedly took her glasses off and walked toward the closet, Luca half a step behind her as if making sure she couldn't get away. Her heart pounded excitedly as she reached the storage closet and pulled open the door.

The storage closet was large and very familiar to Sally now. She stepped inside.

"Now then," she said, her voice innocent and curious. The door closed behind her as Luca stepped in. "What is it you needed help wi—"

Her words were cut off with a soft gasp as Luca grabbed her arms and pulled them behind her back. There was a rattle of metal before cold handcuffs encircled her wrists. Then Luca spun her around and kissed her passionately on the mouth.

"You wore something easy to take off," Luca said as he began to unbutton her blouse. "That's good. You listened to my orders." He pulled the shirt away from her breasts so that it fell down her arms to rest against the handcuffs. "And the bra, too. You're a good little slut, aren't you?"

"Yes, sir," Sally muttered breathlessly as he unfastened the front clasp of her bra.

"You been wanting my cock?" he whispered in her ear as he fondled her breast. He bit her earlobe and sent delightful shivers of longing through her.

"Yes," she said. And, God, it was true. She'd been fantasizing about it the last three days, ever since their last meeting. Just the thought was enough to get her wet. It had been so intense that she had barely been able to think or do work.

"Yes, what?" he asked.

Again, another jolt of excited longing pierced through her.

"Yes, sir," she said.

"Good girl." He kissed her deeply, making her feel his own longing all through her body. "You have been a good girl, right? You haven't been touching yourself, have you?"

"No, sir," she said.

"Damn," Luca said, kissing her neck. "I was really hoping to punish you."

Her toes curled as the pressure between her legs began to build. They had played this game before. Sally had never played with bondage or anything remotely like BDSM until Luca. Up until then, it had been vanilla missionary and the occasional doggy style. But the thought of being tied up and having to submit to the young, attractive man currently unfastening his belt was the most erotic thing she had ever imagined. She had never thought she would like this sort of thing, but the first time Luca handcuffed her and ordered her to obey him, she had come within seconds of him slipping inside her, and it was the wettest she had ever been.

Luca's cock sprung out fully erect, and he lowered her head to it, his fingers tangling in her hair and forcing her head to move back and forth. Her hands bound behind her back, all she had was the skill of her mouth and tongue, which flicked eagerly along the head. She closed her eyes, loving the taste of him and moaning around his massive cock.

"Good girl," he said. He pulled her back and spun her around, unlocking the handcuffs quickly and expertly. "We'll come back to those later," he said at Sally's disappointed expression. "I'm nowhere near done with you yet. But I want you comfortable while I fuck you."

He lowered her to the ground. Sally was vaguely aware of the fact that the smell of her arousal was mixing with the cleaning supplies all around her, but she didn't care. All she wanted, all she cared about, was Luca, and she needed him inside her.

His hand went to her clit, and his thumb flicked delicately across it while his other hand played with her tits. He gripped her nipple and twisted.

"I was thinking of bringing nipple clamps next time," he said as her back arched at the sensation. "Or maybe you should come over to my place, and I can show you the rest of my toys. I think there are a few you'd really like."

She groaned as her imagination ran wild at what he might do to her if she went to his place. He'd tie her to his bed and toy with her for hours, making her edge over and over again, never letting her climax.

"Please fuck me," she said.

Luca raised an eyebrow.

"Please fuck me, sir," she amended.

He obliged. He plunged inside her, filling her entirely. She gasped in delight as he pumped over and over. His hand stayed on her clit as the thrusts got faster and deeper, stimulating her in both places. Her heart raced, and all she could think about was the growing fire and need. Every thrust brought her closer and closer to the edge, and she knew she might break at any second.

"You feel so good," Luca whispered. "I love how wet you are."

"It's all for you," Sally said.

"I half want to stop fucking you and just taste your pussy."

"God, please, don't stop." She didn't think she could bear it. She needed his cock, needed it inside her. She was so close.

"I think I might," he mused, even as he continued thrusting.

"Please don't, sir."

"I'll tell you what." He leaned forward until his mouth was right next to her ear. "Come for me in the next thirty seconds, and I won't."

She groaned, relishing the command. The thought of having to come on demand, along with the constant thrusting and stimulation to her clit, kept that fire building and building until it reached a crescendo. She cried out, writhing delightedly beneath Luca as she rode the wave of her orgasm. Luca didn't last much longer, and a second later she felt his cock pulse, filling her with his cum.

He rolled off her, panting, his breath heaving and him slick with sweat. He turned toward her, his eyes sparkling.

"You okay?" he asked, his hand brushing a strand of hair from her face.

She smiled and nodded. She always loved that he asked this, that he made sure the games they played behind locked doors and the submissiveness didn't negatively affect her.

"You?" she asked.

His eyes glinted. "Oh, I'm more than okay," he said. His eyes raked up and down her body. "In fact, I think I've still got some more in me. Assuming you're up for it."

Glancing down, Sally could see him hardening again already. And just the thought of it was enough to rekindle her own fire.

"I think I can do that," she said, fluttering her eyelashes. "Sir."

Luca grinned and hauled her to her feet before pressing her up against the wall. His lips went to hers, and she began to melt again.

And they didn't hear the door open.

CHAPTER 27

Jacob

"SMILE," JACOB O'BRIEN said cheerily as he held up his phone and snapped the photos.

The old lady and the janitor spun toward the door. The man's dick was hanging out, still wet from being inside the woman, but slowly deflating. The woman—that bitch Alexa's secretary—looked mortified and squealed as she tried to cover herself. Not that he was interested in her wrinkled tits. What he was more interested in was what these photos would give him.

He had only come in to gather a few things from his office. He still had his keys and figured it would be easier for him not to have to deal with the crowd. So he decided to sneak in after work. He'd been going to his office when he heard the moans coming from the closet and decided to investigate. It was a complete coincidence, though a delightful one. And he could already see how it might be of use. His mouth curled into a smirk.

"Hmmm," he said, flipping through the photos. "Ooh, that's a nice one. Do you wanna see?" He turned it around and showed the photo. The secretary paled in horror.

Luca lunged toward Jacob, who stepped back, laughing. "That's not going to do anything," he said in a singsong voice. "These photos are already in the cloud. You can destroy the phone, but that's not going to do anything about the pictures. Here, look at this one. I think that's one of my favorites."

"Please don't," Sally said.

"That's right," Jacob said as if he'd only just remembered. "You've got a husband, don't you? And kids. Man, it would be a shame if they ever saw these, wouldn't it? Think her husband will divorce her when he sees these, Luca?"

"Come on, Mr. O'Brien," Sally said. "Please be reasonable."

"Reasonable?" He scowled and gripped the cell phone tighter. "Was it reasonable when your bitch of a boss ratted me out to Barrow and got me fired? Was it reasonable when she decided to throw me to the cops? I got arrested because of her."

"And you're taking it out on Sally?" Luca had put on his pants and wrapped his arm around the secretary, who had mercifully put her shirt back on. "You realize how much of an asshole that makes you?"

Jacob laughed maliciously. "The ends justify the means," he said. "It's nothing personal against your fuck toy. But I think she can be useful to me."

The secretary's eyes widened, and she wrapped her arms tighter against her stomach. "Please don't," she said.

Jacob made a gagging noise. "Not like that, idiot," he said. "I don't have any use for a shriveled pussy."

"Hey, don't talk to her like that," Luca said.

"I'll talk to her however I want," Jacob said. "I might not have as much leverage on you, considering everyone already knows you're a manwhore. But the prim, demure secretary of the bitch who ruined my life? Oh, I can think of several ways she can help me."

There were tears in the old lady's eyes. "What do you want?" she asked.

"I want you in my back pocket," he said cheerily. "From now on, you're my bitch. Based on what I overheard, you tend to like that." She winced, but he kept going. "Whenever I ask you to do something for me, I expect you to do it. Unless you want your husband to find out. And right now . . . I want you to give me your boss's address."

Sally's eyes widened. "Why?" she asked.

"Doesn't matter to you now, does it?" he asked, chuckling. "I've told you what I want. Now get it for me."

"I don't have it," she said. "That's confidential."

"Then find a way to get it, or I'll make sure your husband and your kids find out all about this. How long have you two been married? Forty-something years now?"

The secretary winced again, and Jacob couldn't help but get a savage pleasure from seeing the woman's misery. So maybe he was a bit of a sadist. It didn't matter. It definitely wasn't the worst of his habits. And right now, it was going to do him a shit ton of good.

"Please don't do this," Sally said.

"We could report you, you know," Luca said, eyes locked on Jacob as they narrowed. "I doubt you're allowed in here at all, considering you were fired and arrested."

"Suspended without pay," Jacob corrected. "I can still come here to grab things if I need them. It's still my office."

"And now you're a blackmailer on top of being a cokehead?" Luca shook his head. The anger was actually rather adorable. He thought he could do something about this.

"Why yes, I am," Jacob said cheerily. "And I would remind you that you will certainly lose your job if these photos get out. I forget the rules on interoffice relationships, but I don't think they're going to look particularly kindly on this one. Do you?"

Sally and Luca glanced away, and the entire thing might have been the most beautiful thing he had ever seen. He could have cackled.

"Well?" he asked. "Do we have a deal?"

CHAPTER 28

Carmella, 2009

THE PHONE RANG.

Carmella stared at it for a long time. She knew the number. But that didn't mean she wanted to answer, not after their last encounter. Still, it was probably important. Otherwise, she wouldn't be calling.

Taking a deep breath, she accepted the call and put the phone to her ear. "Hello?"

"Carmella, hi," the voice on the other line said. "It's Alexa. I wanted to check in and see how you were doing."

"Uh-huh." It was impossible to keep the skepticism out of her voice. "I'm doing fine. Better than last time I saw you, at least."

It has been nearly two weeks since Carmella had first met Alexa and their rather terrible meeting. Carmella had half-hoped she wouldn't hear from the lawyer again until after the trial. But she knew how stupid that hope was. No matter how much she wished it, it would never happen. There was too much to do.

"I was hoping that you and I could meet up today," Alexa said. "Or sometime this week. I wanted to schedule your video interview and go over a few things that are easier to talk about in person. Are you free for lunch? My treat."

Carmella glanced at the clock on Georgia's oven. She had been staying at her friend's apartment ever since the incident. Casimir didn't know where her friend lived, so it was safe. He couldn't find her.

"Sure," Carmella said. "Where?"

—

SHE ARRIVED AT A FANCY-LOOKING restaurant with white tablecloths and waiters in suits. She suddenly felt very, *very* underdressed in jeans and a T-shirt. She shifted back and forth on her feet.

She was about to step back outside and make sure she had gotten the right address when a figure already sitting at one of the tables waved at her.

"Carmella," Alexa called. "Over here."

"So glad you could make it," Alexa said when Carmella sat down opposite her. "Thanks for meeting for lunch. I've been absolutely swamped, so this is one of the few times I can squeeze in meetings. Plus, I'm starving. Have whatever you want. Like I said on the phone, it's on me."

"Thanks."

"You're looking a lot better," Alexa said as she poured Carmella a glass of wine and handed it over.

"That ain't saying much considering what I looked like."

"There hasn't been any trouble, has there?" Alexa asked, her face creased with concern.

"No. My friend is taking care of me," she said.

"That's good."

They talked about nothing like that for a long time, to the point where Carmella started loosening up. But she was still waiting for the hammer to fall. Because there was no way this was all it was.

It didn't happen, though, until after they had nearly finished their meal. Alexa put down her fork at the edge of her salad and wiped her mouth.

"So," she said, leaning over to pull a few pages out of her satchel. She held them in her hands, not handing them over. "I think the best time to schedule the interview would be sooner rather than later. Definitely before you get the cast off."

"Why?" Carmella answered her own question. "You want to play up the sympathy. You want them to feel sorry for me."

"That's a crude way of putting it," Alexa said but didn't disagree. "Are you free on Friday?"

"Why didn't you ask me when all the bruises were fresh?" she asked, gesturing at her face. Some of the cuts were still healing, and she was fairly certain she'd have a scar on her temple, but the bruises were almost entirely gone now. She looked a great deal better, and she knew that a steel in her eyes that hadn't been there previously had emerged. It felt like something had broken inside when Casimir had tied her up for hours on end, and more than just a few bones.

"You weren't in a great position when we last spoke," Alexa said. "I wanted to give you time to recover before I made you relive everything."

"Thanks," Carmella said. And she meant it. She reached out to take the papers, but Alexa held onto them.

"Have you reconsidered testifying in person?" she asked.

Carmella narrowed her eyes suspiciously. "Not particularly."

"It would help a lot," the lawyer said. "I know that it's hard, but—"

"I thought you just said the broken arm and bruises help," Carmella said, folding her arms. Her fingers tapped against the plaster of the cast.

"For a video, yes," Alexa said. "But that doesn't mean nearly as much as being in person. I'd take the latter any day of the week."

"If I say no, are you going to leave me with the bill?"

Alexa was genuinely shocked. "What? Of course not. I'd never do that to you, or anyone for that matter. I'm not that kind of person."

"Hmph."

"But," the lawyer continued, "you testifying could be the difference between Casimir Johnson going to jail and going back out on the streets. And if he's out there, that means he'll be able to find another victim. And that woman might not be as lucky as you."

Carmella winced, glancing away. That old guilt gnawed at her.

The truth was, she had thought about it. She'd thought about it quite a lot. Because a part of her knew that Alexa was right. But she didn't want to admit it. And the truth was, no matter what she tried to tell herself, she was still afraid of the man.

"We can't let that happen to someone else," Alexa said.

"I know that," Carmella snapped. "That's why I agreed to meet with you. But that don't mean I agreed to testify in court."

"I'm just asking you to reconsider," Alexa said. "He's going to do it again. He might even come after you."

Carmella remained silent. She stared at her fist, clenching and unclenching in frustration. She could still feel the ropes on her wrists, even if the marks had long since faded away. She could feel them cutting off her circulation, her fingers going numb as her nail beds turned blue.

She squeezed her eyes shut as a war began in her head, two sides trying to fight back the other. She knew the right thing to do was what the lawyer was urging her to do. Knew that it was the best chance of getting Casimir locked away for good. But the thought of seeing him again was too much.

But then she imagined him doing it to another woman. To Georgia, to her sister, hell, even some random girl on the street. She imagined him going further, imagined him grabbing a knife or bashing the poor woman's skull in with the bat and leaving her to die. She imagined what might have happened if Georgia hadn't come by when she did and gotten her to the hospital.

"I'm afraid," she whispered.

A hand reached out and went to her fist, covering it soothingly. "I know," Alexa said. "I would be too. But sometimes you have to move past that, or you'll let it consume you. I'll be in the room when you see him. So will a bailiff and a bunch of other people. It'll be okay. I promise. And no matter what you decide, I'm still going to do my best to put that asshole away for a long, long time."

Carmella stared at the tablecloth, at the remnants of her food, at the crumpled napkin still in her lap. Anywhere but at Alexa. Because even though she knew what she was about to do, she didn't want to see the woman's face in case it changed her mind.

Clamping her eyes shut, she nodded.

"Thank you," Alexa said, giving Carmella's hand a reassuring squeeze.

"You better put that asshole behind bars," Carmella said.

"I can't make any guarantees," Alexa said. "But I can promise that I'm going to do my damned best to make sure that happens."

CHAPTER 29

Jacob

JACOB WHISTLED AS HE sauntered down the darkening street, feeling the best he'd felt since that bitch got him fired and arrested. He had leverage on her secretary, and the bitch's address was burning a hole in his pocket. That, and he was about to get his first hit of coke in three days. Things were looking up. It was after ten p.m., and the crisp air was beautifully refreshing. He took in a deep lungful before continuing whistling.

But the tune died away—blown away by the wind—as he neared his destination, suddenly more anxious than he cared to admit. Despite all the good things that had happened, he had still pissed off the wrong people when he'd gotten caught. Even with his apology gift, things could get dicey for him. He rounded the corner and stepped into a clean but still somehow seedy alley. A man was leaning against the wall next to a metal door, looking bored but alert. His head turned when he heard Jacob's footsteps, and he straightened. One hand moved toward his hip, where Jacob knew he kept a gun he definitely hadn't gotten by any legal methods.

Jacob stepped into the flickering alley light, and the doorman relaxed, his hand moving away from the hidden pistol.

"O'Brien." The doorman nodded.

"Heya, Frank," Jacob said. "How're things."

"Fine for me. Probably not as fine for you." The bouncer regarded Jacob. "Heard you got arrested and got kicked off Cas's case. He isn't too happy with you. Reggie isn't either, for that matter."

Jacob tried to push down the lump growing in his throat and keep his cool. Casimir was one thing, but Reggie was different. While Casimir was dangerous only because of who he was close to, Reggie was dangerous because he had power. He could order him shot in an alley, and it'd be done by the end of the day. He was one of the worst guys you could cross, and Casimir clung to him like glue. Reggie being mad was ten times worse, and he'd have to tread carefully.

But Jacob didn't let on that he was nervous. He shrugged, hands in pockets to keep them from fidgeting nervously. "Shit happens," he said.

"I don't think they're gonna want to see you," Frank said.

"Trust me," Jacob said, grinning widely. "They will."

The bouncer looked him up and down, considering. Then he stepped away from the door.

"I don't have any orders keeping you out yet," he said, slipping a cigarette into his mouth and lighting it, "so you're good to go down. Just don't say I didn't warn you if you get the shit beaten out of you."

"That's not going to happen," Jacob said, a little more confidently than he felt. The other man regarded him impassively.

"If you say so," he said as he exhaled a puff of smoke. Frank opened the door, revealing a long set of cement steps, and Jacob walked down the stairs and into Gryphon's Den.

Gryphon's Den was a large underground space with wooden floors and cement block walls. A long bar that was always slightly sticky was in one corner, a bartender currently fixing some cocktail for someone standing behind it. Tables were spread out across the space, though room had been cleared for two pool tables, both of which were currently in use by large, burly men. Over in one corner, someone was clearly tweaking out on something. The air was filled with cigar smoke despite the fact that smoking indoors hadn't been allowed in NYC for something like twenty years.

Jacob scanned the room until his eyes landed on a group circling a table. Poker chips dotted the table. As he watched, one of the men flipped over two cards, and the other men at the table scowled. Taking a deep breath, Jacob steeled himself and walked over.

The men around the table glanced up as he approached. None of them said anything. Jacob tried not to let that bother him and put on his best smile.

"Boys," he said. "Good to see you. How are you doing?"

"You got some balls coming here, O'Brien," a muscular Black man with dreadlocks said around his cigar, his eyes narrowing.

"Come on, Reggie," Jacob said, spreading his hands out. "How many times have I helped your boys get out of a jam? Least you can do is let me stay for a few minutes."

Reggie grunted in reluctant acknowledgment. "The fuck you want?"

"Lots of things," Jacob said. "But a seat, first of all."

The men exchanged glances. At a slight nod from Reggie, they scooted over, and Jacob pulled up a chair.

"Deal him in, Cas," Reggie said. "We're playing Hold'em."

Jacob's eyes found Casimir's, who was currently glaring daggers at him. But the man still dealt him two cards face down before flipping over three in the center of the table for everyone to see.

"Heard that bitch got the better of you," Casimir said.

"Ten," Reggie said, tossing a chip into the small pile. "Also heard he was dumb enough to get arrested."

"Call," the man to Reggie's left said.

"Call," Jacob said. "She thinks she got the better of me. But I've got a leg up."

Casimir raised an eyebrow as he tossed his own chip in there. "That so?"

"Oh yeah." Jacob grinned as Casimir flipped over the next card. "I've got some information you especially might be interested in."

Casimir grunted but kept his eyes glued on Jacob. In fact, all the men at the table were looking at him. Even Reggie seemed mildly interested.

"You gonna tell me what it is?" Casimir asked.

Jacob shrugged. "For a price." He tossed a poker chip worth fifty in the pot.

Reggie's eyes narrowed, and he pulled the cigar from his mouth. "And what's that, exactly? Don't feel like I should owe you anything right now."

"Just some coke," Jacob said. One of the men raised, and he called, putting another few chips in the growing pile to match the bet. "Police took mine, and I burned through my hidden stash."

"Seems like a you problem," Reggie said. "And why the fuck should I give it to you for free?"

"It isn't free. I'm paying you in information."

"You're in deep shit, O'Brien," Reggie said, leaning forward and staring intently. His lips were a thin line of distaste, and his body was coiled. It reminded Jacob of a viper about to strike. "You got yourself kicked off the case, and now my boy's gotta deal with a bitch who's had it out for him for years. That information better be fucking gold if it's gonna be worth a damn. Let alone coke."

Jacob could feel his face pale, but he forced himself to keep a neutral face. Instead, he smiled.

"I've got the bitch's address."

A hush fell over the table. Even Reggie looked surprised. Casimir looked fucking delighted.

"You're shitting me," Casimir said.

"Nope," Jacob said. "Think I'd be shitting you right now? I happen to like my head without bullet holes in it."

Reggie had a much better poker face than Casimir. The boss flipped another two chips in the pile, and Casimir followed suit. They were the only two still in. "And what the fuck are we supposed to do with an address?"

"Anything you want. But you're not going to be able to get it anywhere else. She keeps that shit private. So I want two grams of coke for it."

Reggie's eyes narrowed. "One. It ain't worth that much."

"One and a half."

Reggie looked over at Casimir, and it was impossible to mistake the hunger in his eyes. He wanted that address. He wasn't even trying to hide it.

"Tell you what," Reggie said, turning back to Jacob. "I'll give you an eight ball if you sweeten the deal."

Jacob's mouth went dry at the thought, and a twinge of excitement and longing tugged at him. But he was smart. He hasn't been a prosecutor for nothing. And he knew Reggie well enough to know that whatever he was offering wasn't going to be simple. But he wanted that coke.

"And what do I have to do exactly?" he asked.

Reggie told him. Casimir's eyes lit up. Jacob considered for a long moment before nodding.

"Deal," he said. He flipped over his cards to show the ace of diamonds and a nine of clubs. "Full house, aces high."

"Good." Reggie turned over his own cards, revealing the eight and ten of spades. "Straight flush," he said. "I win."

CHAPTER 30

Sally

SALLY WAS CRYING AGAIN.

Her eyes were bright red, and she sniffled quietly, hovering over the sink. Her hands were shaking violently as they clutched the porcelain sides.

She needed to get a grip. She knew that. But the guilt was drilling a massive hole in her. It had been ever since she had dug into Alexa's personnel files—thanks to Luca's key to the HR department—and found her boss's address.

She had told herself that it was the only option. She couldn't let her husband find out. She didn't think she could bear the shame. She had grown up in a time when cheating and divorce were almost as scandalous as murder. She couldn't let anyone know what she had done. What would Vlad say? What about her children?

And yet, she couldn't help but feel as though she'd made a massive mistake by giving O'Brien the information he wanted. She wasn't sure what he was going to do with it, but there was no way it was good.

Fear clenched her stomach. Had she just subjected her boss—someone she had worked with for years and had an incredible amount of respect for—to something terrible? But what could O'Brien do with her address?

Plenty of things, a terrible voice in her head whispered. *There are lots of things you can do if you know someone's address. And you're the one who gave it to him.*

The tears burst through again, and it was a long moment before she managed to regain her composure. Finally, she took a deep breath and walked back outside and returned to her desk.

—

"SALLY?"

Sally jumped ten feet in the air at the sound of her name, then turned around in her seat to see Alexa poking her head out of her office door.

"Yes?" Sally squeaked. Alexa had found out. How had she found out so soon? She was about to get fired. She deserved it, but how was she going to explain it to her husband?

"Would you mind rescheduling my meeting with Henderson?" she asked. "Going through some paperwork, and it's taking a lot longer than I expected it to."

"Of course," Sally said, trying not to let the shock and relief show on her face. "Any date in mind?"

"Any time after tomorrow works fine," Alexa said. She frowned at Sally. "Is everything okay?"

"Yes, of course," Sally lied.

"You just look a bit upset. I know you had something going on at home. Did it get worse?"

"No, no," Sally said, trying to hope she at least sounded mildly convincing. "I've just got a headache."

"I'm so sorry. Do you need to take the rest of the day off?"

It took a lot of willpower for Sally not to burst into tears again or wince. Why did she have to be so kind? "No, no," she said. "I'll be fine. I'll get right on rescheduling that meeting for you."

"All right. Be sure to take some Advil if it keeps up. And don't feel bad if you need to leave early. Okay?"

"Of course. Thanks so much."

It was a relief when Alexa went back into her office, and Sally could breathe again. She tried to swallow the nauseating guilt bubbling through her, with minimal success. But she forced herself to focus on her work, if only because it gave her something to do.

It got worse when she ran into Luca.

It was after four p.m. Sally had readjusted her work schedule so they wouldn't overlap nearly as much, and it was the first time in a week that she had seen him. She froze, eyes wide and stomach churning as she saw him. He was as attractive as he'd ever been, but it was dimmed with the knowledge of what their infidelity had caused.

Luca's intense blue eyes met hers, and she turned to run the other way. But she had barely gone two steps when a hand grabbed her arm.

"Sally," he said. "Can we talk?"

"I don't think that's the best idea," Sally said, trying to extricate her arm, but Luca wouldn't let go.

"I don't want you to keep avoiding me," he said.

"What else did you expect?" she asked. "Do you realize what our fucking in secret ended up doing?"

"I'm fully aware," Luca said. "And I can see how much it's hurting you. I want to make sure you're okay."

"Of course I'm not okay," Sally said, and her eyes started to water again. "I've betrayed a friend. And I wouldn't have had to if I'd been able to keep it in my pants."

"It's not your fault, Sally," he said.

"Whose is it?"

He didn't answer. Instead, he asked, "Did you tell her?"

Sally's eyes darted to the ground, and that was enough of an answer. Luca swore softly.

"You have to tell her," he said. "She needs to know—"

"I can't," Sally said, and it was hard to keep her voice down when she could feel herself getting more and more hysterical. This was all her fault.

She knew that, and she hated it. She wrapped herself in a blanket of fear and self-loathing. Because even though she hated what she had decided to do, she also knew that there was no way she could have done anything else. "My husband would find out."

"Do you really want to be with your husband?" Luca asked. And it was a genuine question, which honestly made it worse. Because part of her wasn't sure. She was so used to being with him. It was comfortable staying in such familiar territory. But that didn't change the fact that she hadn't been happy with Vlad in a long time. If being with Luca had taught her anything, it was that. And that somehow made it worse.

"I don't know," she whispered. "But what will happen if I leave him?"

"You're a smart, capable woman, Sally," Luca said. "You'll figure it out. *We* can figure it out, if you want that."

The offer was so subtle and so surprising that it barely registered, and she had no idea how to react. So she just remained mute. Because up until now, Luca had been a casual fling. That had been the whole appeal. She wasn't sure if she wanted a relationship with him, and she wasn't entirely sure he wanted a relationship with her, either.

She didn't respond, and it seemed Luca didn't expect her to. He just released her and took a step back.

"Think about it," he said. "I'm not going to tell you what to do, and it's not my place to tell anyone and jeopardize your marriage. I respect you too much for that. But if you need to talk to someone, or if you need help in any way, you know where to find me."

He walked away, leaving Sally alone and feeling even worse than she had before.

CHAPTER 31

Alexa, 2019

"YOU LOOK SO BEAUTIFUL!" Michelle squealed. She clapped her hands together excitedly, bouncing up and down on the balls of her feet. Which was an accomplishment, considering she was in three-inch heels. Her baby-blue dress swished with the movement as she admired her friend.

Alexa smiled, looking down at her white dress. It clung to her frame, the creamy fabric spilling out behind her in a long train. The strapless top pushed up her breasts, making them look larger than normal. An ornate silver necklace wrapped around her neck, spilling down to just above her cleavage. A veil was nestled tightly into her hair, which had been pulled up into a tight, elegant bun.

"Seriously, Joe is gonna flip when he sees you. Or just faint in shock." Michelle reached down and rubbed the fabric between her fingers admiringly. "God, I just can't get over this."

"It's hard to believe," Alexa admitted, fidgeting as she tried to get used to her heels. "Honestly, I'm a little nervous."

Michelle gave a sympathetic grimace. "I know," she said. "It's a big step, especially for you. But I've thoroughly vetted the guy. And I threatened to cut off his balls if he even thinks of hurting you in any way."

"He believes you?"

"Of course he did." Michelle grinned wickedly. "I can be very persuasive."

"Would you actually?"

"If he does anything to my best friend? Hell yes."

Alexa laughed warmly, some of the tension vanishing from her shoulders. She never would have admitted it, but she was worried. She knew how marriages could go wrong, how bad men could seem decent at first until something shifted. She'd seen it before.

"Your friend wasn't able to make it?" Michelle asked, mercifully distracting her from that train of thought.

Alexa's features fell slightly. "She tried," she said. "But she's wrapped up in her job in LA. She wasn't able to get away."

"Price of attempting to become an actress, eh?" Michelle said. "Well, I'm sure she'll be here in spirit."

"Oh, I know she is."

A woman poked her head into the bridal suite. "Everything ready?" she asked. She was in a black uniform and had an earpiece in: their attendant. "We're about to get started."

Glancing in one of the many full-length mirrors, she saw a woman she barely recognized. Her makeup was immaculate, and the heels made her even taller than she normally was. Her hair pulled up made the angles of her face more prominent and elegant. Behind her in the mirror, she could see her sister and Michelle, both in baby-blue bridesmaid dresses. They both looked beautiful and were beaming up at Alexa.

"Let's get going, then," Alexa said, smiling as her heart began working double-time.

As they walked through the halls to where they would line up for the procession, she thought back to her relationship with Joe over the last year.

It had been what felt like a whirlwind. They had spent nearly every minute of the conference together, laughing and talking with one another over dinner and drinks. It had felt like reconnecting with an old friend rather than getting to know a stranger. On the way back, Joe gave up his business-class seat, taking Michelle's spot and giving her the more luxurious spot, purely so he could spend more time with Alexa. By the end of the flight, they were holding hands, and she had fallen asleep on his shoulder. When the flight landed, they exchanged numbers, and she called him the next day, asking if he wanted to grab dinner.

Since then, they'd been inseparable, effectively moving in with one another while still keeping their own places. They shared everything with one another, from their past to their fears and what they wanted out of the rest of their lives. She got to know his kids, who, though it took a while for them to warm up to her, eventually grew accustomed to her, even growing to like her.

It was a year before he got down on one knee. She remembered it perfectly. He had taken her to the rink at Rockefeller to ice-skate. They had been on the ice for maybe twenty minutes when he stopped in front of the grand Christmas tree overlooking the rink. At first she thought he'd fallen, until he pulled out a small, black box and held it out. There, in the twinkling lights of the Christmas tree, he told her how much he loved her and how he'd known since the moment he met her. By now people had stopped to watch, some pulling out phones to record, others whispering excitedly to one another as they pointed.

She was nodding yes before he had even finished asking the question. The cold froze the happy tears on her face, biting into her cheeks, but she didn't notice. She didn't even hear the crowd cheering and applauding as she took off her glove so he could slip the elegant diamond ring onto her finger. It wasn't massive or flashy, but she could see the love and care that he'd put into designing it.

"It's beautiful," she had said. It was all she could think to say. She couldn't find the words to express how much she loved him, how happy she was in that moment, or how excited she was that she got to spend the rest of her life with a man as incredible as he was. And then he pulled her into a kiss, and she didn't have to say anything at all. She was able to communicate it in other ways.

All this went flashing through her head as she waited to walk down the aisle and the music flowed to her.

Then it was her turn.

As she walked down the aisle alone, her eyes found Joe's. His green eyes were glittering with affection as he drank her in. And as she got closer, she could see there were tears in his eyes. And something about that vulnerability made her love him even more. He wasn't afraid to show his emotion. And she could see the love and affection there as he beamed at her.

They said their *I do*'s, and the kiss they shared after would forever be the best kiss of her life, one that would be burned into her memory for the rest of time. They embraced as people cheered and clapped. Then they turned to the crowd, Joe holding their entwined hands up in the air as they hurried down the aisle.

The reception was simple but perfect. Their first dance, in the middle of the grand room and watched by all their friends, was to "So Amazing" by Luther Vandross. And as Joe pulled her in close, swaying them back and forth to the music, he whispered the lyrics in her ear in a melodious voice she had never realized he'd possessed.

"'It's so amazing to be loved. I'd follow you to the moon and the sky above.'"

By the end of the song, she was crying too. And she knew then that she would know how it felt to be that loved for the rest of her life. To be followed to the moon and the sky above.

CHAPTER 32

Tony

"THANKS FOR MEETING with me, Alexa," Tony said, standing and shaking her hand. "I really appreciate it."

"It's my pleasure. Always happy to clear up confusing details. Things make sense now?"

Tony nodded, giving a slightly sheepish, embarrassed smile. "As much as they can," he said. "I'm new to all this law stuff, and the internet sometimes has too much information, so it's impossible to find the answer."

Over the last couple of weeks, Tony had been trying to look into the laws and court proceedings around Maria's case. But, despite all of the information he'd found, he still couldn't figure out all the proceedings and what would happen when. It seemed like everything was vague and had contradictory answers. Way too many of them seemed to boil down to *it depends*. Which was when he had called Alexa, who had been more than happy to meet with him.

Alexa chuckled. "I know that feeling," she said. "That said, you actually picked it up quite easily."

"Really?"

Alexa nodded. "It took me years to wrap my head around some of the specific minutiae. You just grasped them in a few seconds."

Tony felt his face go a bit red. "Well, it's easy when you only have to focus on certain things for a case," he said.

"True. But you still picked it up quick."

"Well, it's interesting," Tony said. "I appreciate you taking the time to explain it all."

"I was more than happy to. And feel free to set up an appointment with my secretary any time you want more information. And, either way, I'll be in touch about going over your witness statement and all that."

"Will do."

Tony strolled down the hall, and he couldn't ignore the fact that his heart was beating a bit faster, and that he'd had a second motive for wanting to come to the DA's building instead of continuing to surf the web for his answers.

But as he neared the exit, his stomach began to plummet as there was no sign of the absurdly attractive man from last time. It'd been stupid to think he might run into David again, of course. But ever since their first meeting, he hadn't been able to get the other man out of his mind.

Still, there was no sign of him today. He was probably busy. He might as well—

"You wouldn't happen to be looking for me, would you?" a vaguely familiar voice asked.

Tony turned, and his stomach lurched as he came face-to-face with a grinning David.

"I don't know what you're talking about," Tony said, but there was no real conviction in his voice.

"And here I thought my charisma and good looks brought you back to me," David said, sighing dramatically. "I really was hoping you'd swing by."

"It was purely for business purposes," Tony said, though the smile on his face made it clear he was lying through his teeth, and it made David grin even wider. "I definitely didn't have any ulterior motive in coming here instead of sending a few emails back and forth."

"Are you sure about that?" David teased.

"Well, it wasn't as though there was a large chance that we'd run into each other again," Tony said, still trying to play coy. "It's a pretty large building."

"In that case, I guess we'll have to thank fate."

"Never been sure if I believe in it. Maybe just thank coincidental timing."

"Well, whatever it is I'm supposed to thank, I'm still glad you came by again. How's your sister?"

He was surprised and appreciative that the other man had remembered. "She's doing okay," he said. "Or as okay as she can be, given the circumstances. She's strong, though. She's already getting back on her feet."

"That's good." David looked him up and down, head tilted. "What about you?"

"What about me?"

"How are you doing?"

"Oh." Tony considered. He honestly hadn't thought much about it; he'd been too worried about Maria and the trial to think about it. He sighed. "I'm doing okay. Tired, mostly. And I think I need something to distract myself from all this. It's all I think about, really."

"A distraction?" David smirked. "Would a date count?"

"Huh?"

David laughed, his arm going to Tony's shoulder. "I'm asking you out, Tony. Are you free Saturday night?"

He was so startled by the blunt offer that it took him a long moment to answer as everything clicked into place.

"Yeah. Yeah, I'm free."

"Excellent. Here, give me your number. I'll text you the details."

Tony rattled off the number, and he could feel his face growing hotter and hotter. A second later, his own phone buzzed, and he fumbled it out of his pocket.

Heya cutie ;)

He hadn't thought he could get any redder, but he did.

"You're cute when you blush," David said. "I've got to get back to work, though. I'll see you Saturday."

CHAPTER 33

Alexa

THERE WAS A KNOCK ON the office door, and Alexa said, "Come on in."

The door squeaked open. Alexa, who still hadn't looked up from her computer, where she was compiling notes about the discovery for the Johnson case, heard a soft, timid shuffling sound. Frowning, she glanced up.

Sally was standing on the other side of the desk, and she looked terrible. Her face was pale, and she wasn't wearing her normal makeup. Her normally tight bun was loose and limp, with stray hairs shooting out from all angles. She looked as though she'd lost weight, too. How had Alexa missed that? But more than anything, she saw that her secretary's eyes were red from crying, and the tears were still coming.

Alexa stood immediately and ran to the other side of the desk to embrace Sally. "What's wrong?" Alexa asked. "What happened?" She thought back to what Sally had said a few weeks ago about personal things. "Did something happen at home?"

"No," Sally hiccuped. "Well, yes. It's . . . I don't . . ." It was hard to hear the woman through the sobs, but Alexa waited patiently as Sally choked out the words, not wanting to startle her into clamming up. It was clear Sally needed to get whatever it was off her chest.

Finally, the secretary managed to say, "I left Vlad. We're working on the divorce papers now."

Alexa's mouth dropped open. "What?" Out of everything Sally might have said, this was about as far from what she had expected as possible. She'd always been under the impression that Sally and Vlad were happy together. She'd even met him a handful of times, and he'd seemed nice. What had happened to make Sally leave him?

Sally nodded. "I wasn't sure if I was going to," she said. "I was too ashamed to. You know how people my age look on divorce."

Alexa didn't say anything, but she was all too aware of how the older generation reacted to the concept, having seen it plenty of times before. "If you're unhappy, then you're unhappy," Alexa said. "You're doing what's right for you."

Sally shook her head. "You don't understand," she said. "I've put you in so much danger."

"What are you talking about?" A creeping sense of unease began crawling up Alexa's back. Whatever Sally was about to say was the real reason she had come in here today.

"I don't know if you know Luca," Sally said. "But we've been having an affair."

Alexa tried to keep her features composed, but she was unable to stop the soft "oh" of surprise from coming out of her mouth.

"Jacob O'Brien found out," Sally said, now staring at the floor. "He— he took pictures and threatened to send them to Vlad and everyone in the office if I didn't do what he asked. I didn't—"

"That fucker," Alexa was so startled and so angry that she inadvertently interrupted Sally. Her fists clenched, and her eyes narrowed. "That piece of shit. If I ever see him again, I'm gonna wring his neck."

Sally shook her head. "It's all my fault," she said. "If I hadn't had the affair—"

"You're not allowed to blame yourself for this," Alexa said. "This is on him."

"You don't understand." The tears intensified as Sally continued the story. "I listened to him. He told me he wanted your address, and I snuck into HR to get it."

That surprised Alexa. She took an unconscious step back as the implication hit her. He knew where she lived now. Who knew what he was going to do with that information? He could sell it to the highest bidder—she'd made plenty of enemies in her journey as a lawyer—or he could use it himself to get revenge. Spiders crawled up her spine.

And then the anger washed over her, as it always did. But she wasn't angry at Sally. It was impossible for her to be mad at the woman, even if she'd made a mistake. It was clear how guilty she felt, and getting mad at her wouldn't make the situation any better. No, she was angry at O'Brien. He was a petty man who was obsessed with the idea of revenge and only cared about money and power. He was making a kind woman miserable for his own gain.

But even through the anger, that kernel of fear remained. She had no idea what O'Brien had in store, but it couldn't be good.

"I know you can't forgive me," Sally said, "and that you could turn me over to the police for breaking into HR personnel files. But I was scared, and I didn't know what else to do. But I was wrong to do it. And because of that, I'm turning in my formal letter of resignation. If you want to turn me in, too, that's fine. I would understand."

"I'm not turning you in," Alexa said firmly. "And I'm not accepting your resignation. You're good at your job, and I happen to like you. We'll figure this out, okay?"

Sally's eyes widened with shock before she burst into fresh tears, the flood even stronger than before.

"Why are you being so nice to me?" she asked.

Alexa hugged the woman again. "Because you're my friend and I like you," Alexa said. "And I know plenty about making mistakes. It's obvious you feel bad about it. I'm not going to make you feel worse."

Sally shook her head violently, still sniffling. Alexa reached over to the edge of her desk and grabbed the box of tissues, handing it to Sally.

"I'm sorry," Sally blubbered. "I shouldn't be getting any sympathy right now."

"That's not how it works," Alexa said. "Do you have a place to stay?"

Sally nodded.

"Take the rest of the day off," Alexa said. "I'll handle the O'Brien issue, okay? And I better see you here first thing tomorrow like always. I'd be lost without my secretary."

Sally's head bobbed up and down, the lower half of her face concealed by a fresh tissue. "Thank you," she said.

Alexa wrapped her arms around the woman again. "Get home safe," she said. "I'll see you later."

As Alexa watched Sally walk down the hall, still dabbing her eyes, Alexa's warm smile faltered and turned into an uneasy frown. Now that she was alone and she could show her real emotions, fear and uncertainty crawled over her body like insects, and something gnawed unpleasantly at her stomach. She didn't know what O'Brien might plan to do with that information, but it wasn't anything good.

Her mind went back to the last time she saw the disgraced lawyer. The hatred and loathing that had twisted his features into a snarl had been unmistakable and undiluted.

She let out a deep exhale, fingers tapping against her leg. She couldn't tell Barrow. She would have to explain how Alexa found out O'Brien had her address and how he'd gotten it in the first place, and there was no way she was going to put Sally under fire. She could always move or stay somewhere else, but she wasn't going to let a coward and a drug addict run her out of her house. But there were other precautions she could take.

More than anything, she needed to be prepared for whatever was about to happen.

CHAPTER 34

Tony

"SO HOW DID I DO?"

Tony blinked, brow furrowing as he looked over at David, who was sitting across the table and had a Cheshire cat grin on his face.

"Huh?"

"The pencil. How convincing was it?"

There was another long pause as the pieces finally fell into place. His eyes widened, and his jaw dropped. "You did that on purpose?" he asked.

"Of course I did." David took a long sip of wine, looking incredibly smug. "I needed an excuse to talk to you. If you grabbed the pencil and came after me, it either meant you were interested or a good guy, or both. If you didn't, then, well, I hadn't embarrassed myself by coming up to you."

"I didn't realize it was possible for you to ever be embarrassed," Tony said. "You always seem so confident."

David snorted. "Do you know how embarrassing it is to accidentally hit on a straight guy? My gaydar has glitched on me in the past, and I wanted to hide in a hole for days after the last time."

Tony laughed, some of the tension in his shoulders from nerves easing. "Last time I did that, the guy nearly decked me," he said. "Not the most pleasant of experiences."

"Yeah, that's never fun."

"But to answer your question," Tony said. "Yes. It was very convincing. And obviously rather effective. You use that trick often?"

"Only when it comes to cute guys wandering around my work." David speared a piece of salad on his fork. "It isn't nearly as effective when you're walking through Times Square."

It was late in the evening, and the two of them were eating at a restaurant. Nothing super fancy, but there was a nice wooden bar and decently priced cocktails. The dim lights allowed for a modicum of privacy for those who wanted it. It wasn't particularly crowded for a Saturday night, but more people were trickling in regularly, and it was clear it was about to get a lot busier.

They were tucked in a corner at a high table. A plate of mostly eaten fries and a platter of nachos, along with two mostly empty glasses of some gin-based drink, sat on the table. Over the course of the dinner their chairs had moved closer together, and both of them now sat almost shoulder to shoulder, their knees touching gently whenever one of them shifted.

"Well, I guess I should be flattered that I merited the pencil test," Tony teased.

"Oh, you should be," David said it. "I only try that with the really handsome men."

Tony turned a brilliant red and took a long sip of his drink, draining the dregs. David laughed.

"I'm sorry," he said. "I'm not trying to make you uncomfortable."

"Yes, you are." Tony nudged David under the table with his foot. "So what do you do besides torment guys you're going on dates with?"

"I've got a black belt in martial arts," David said. "And I play guitar."

"Really?"

David nodded and held up his left hand; the tips of his fingers were all heavily calloused. "Since I was eight."

"I've always loved guitar," Tony said. "We couldn't afford it when I was growing up, but I would have loved to take lessons."

He remembered hearing his mother sing as they worked together in the kitchen, and he remembered an old man in Colombia who had played guitar on a street corner nearly every day. Tony would go out to sit and listen to him for hours whenever he got a chance, fascinated by how his fingers danced along the neck of the instrument and picked at the strings with ease and incredible dexterity. He'd always wanted to learn how to create magic like that.

"It's never too late," David pointed out. "I can lend you one of my guitars. I have a couple that I don't use. And I can always give you a few pointers. Assuming you want to see me again."

"I think I can make that happen," Tony said.

"What about you? I'm guessing that waiting tables isn't your entire life."

"No," Tony said. "I like going on runs and rock climbing, though gym memberships aren't cheap. I'm also a massive cinephile."

"Oldies or modern movies?"

"Both, but I've got a soft spot for black-and-whites. *The Maltese Falcon* and *Witness for the Prosecution* are two of my all-time favorite movies."

"I've never seen the second one," David mused. He polished off his drink, glanced at the bar as if considering getting a second one, then decided against it.

"We'll have to change that. It's a classic."

"What about now?" David asked, raising his eyebrows as a smirk played on his lips. "Unless you have another date after this."

"Well, I have about three," Tony joked. "But I can always cancel."

"Then why don't you come over to my place? We can watch the movie. And I could always teach you some basic . . . fingering."

Tony's stomach lurched as his heart began moving double-time. There was no way this was happening. There was no way this absurdly attractive man was offering to take him home. Tony wasn't bad looking necessarily. But he was a six compared to David's nine or ten. David could do far better than him.

"You're really cute when you get flustered, did you know that?" David asked, eyes sparkling.

"I do now."

"So I take it that's a yes?" David gestured at the drinks. "I'd say we should get another round, but I've got plenty of booze at my place. And I make a mean Manhattan."

"What about an old-fashioned?" Tony's eyes widened in horror as he realized the innuendo in what he'd just said. "I meant the drink," he stammered, suddenly hoping that the earth would open up and swallow him whole.

David's lips tucked in as he tried not to laugh. It didn't work. After a minute, Tony began laughing too.

"Yes," David finally said. His grin was gorgeous, reaching all the way to the eyes and crinkling the edges. "I made a good old-fashioned cocktail." He paused. "*And* I'm pretty good at the other type, too."

"Let's start with the first one," Tony said.

"Fair enough." David gestured toward their server. "In that case, I think we should probably get the check."

CHAPTER 35

Alexa

ALEXA STOOD UP, STRETCHING AS she glanced down at the papers scattered all around the table. She knew everything on those pages front and back. A few of them she could have recited by heart. But she still wanted to go over them again. Tomorrow was the beginning of Casimir's trial, and she wanted to be ready. She knew him, and she knew his lawyer. They'd pull every trick in the book, try and make Maria out as a liar and a whore, maybe even claim that he had paid Maria for sex. She needed to overprepare. She wasn't going to let that asshole get away.

But she still needed a break. Her eyes hurt from squinting at the legal jargon, and her brain had turned to mush. She wasn't retaining anything at the moment.

She glanced around the empty kitchen; the silence, save for the occasional car driving past outside, was a little unnerving and isolating. Joe was gone for a few days at a work conference, and so she was alone for the time being. She didn't mind being by herself. It wasn't the first time it had happened, and it certainly wouldn't be the last. But the timing was terrible. More than anything, she wanted to talk to Joe about how she was feeling, how truly nervous she was about the case, despite claiming otherwise. She was worried about what would happen if she failed, if she couldn't convince the jury that this monster deserved to be locked up for the rest of his life.

She sighed. There was no reason to worry about it now. She just had to be ready.

But right now, she needed a break.

She walked over to the small collection of red wine and picked out a bottle, pouring herself a very generous pour. She took a sip and closed her eyes, savoring the taste as her shoulders untensed.

There was a loud *thunk*, and her eyes flew open.

It sounded as though it was coming from the backyard. Frowning, she tentatively walked in that direction. Her heart was thudding in her throat as the hair on the back of her neck stood on end. Something wasn't right.

When she peered through the French doors, all she saw was the swimming pool, the water glistening in the moonlight as it rippled gently in the wind. She drummed her fingers against her leg. Even though there was nothing there, she couldn't help feeling that something was amiss.

She turned away, preparing to check the front, when the glass shattered behind her.

She stumbled forward. The glass of wine slipped through her fingers and fell to the floor, the thin shards joining those from the large French door windows on the ground. Wine pooled around her feet as she turned to see what had happened. The red liquid looked like blood.

A tall, lanky figure, clad in all black and wearing a mask, stepped through the makeshift opening. His shoes crunched the glass as he trod over it, heading directly toward the frozen Alexa. Her mouth was open in surprise, and she could barely think as she took in the man approaching her.

Then the figure raised his arm, and the glint of the pistol barrel spurred her into action. There was no time for her to be afraid, no time for her to think beyond basic instinct. She ran, getting out of the way just in time before the gun went off.

Without thinking too hard about it, she lunged for her cell phone, currently resting on the table among the scattered pages. But then the gun went off again, and her phone exploded as the bullet slammed into it.

They didn't have a landline. The only way she could call for help was if she managed to get out and to a neighbor's house. But something told her that wasn't going to be as easy as it sounded. The man was still blocking their back entrance, even as he slowly approached and raised his gun for a third shot. And the front entrance was locked and dead bolted. She'd lose precious time while trapped in a small hallway. There was one option, even if it was risky.

These thoughts rushed through her head in a split second, and before he could shoot again, she was running. The gunshot sounded, and there was a searing pain in her upper arm. She cried out in pain as the burning sensation spread to her shoulder and elbow. She didn't look, because if she looked, she was fairly certain she would lose her nerve, stumble, and die.

She had just managed to get to the bedroom and close the door when the fourth bullet shot from the pistol. There was a faint, muted cursing as she locked the door. The voice was vaguely familiar, but she couldn't place it, and she didn't have time to consider it. She needed to get to the nightstand.

After her own past and her mild paranoia, she had learned how to use a gun not long after she started law school. Until she got it, she would have nightmares of the same person breaking in one night and killing her while she slept. It had never happened, and she had grown to accept that it would never be needed, even if the gun made her feel safer. It turned out she had been right the first time.

She flung open the drawer on her nightstand and fumbled for the pistol. She managed to grab it as the locked door shattered, sending splinters of wood everywhere.

Without giving herself any time to panic, she spun and fired.

The bullet went wide, but the man ducked. She fired again.

The man doubled over, clutching his stomach. He gave an unintelligible grumble, and his hand rose shakily toward Alexa.

She fired again, striking the hand with the pistol. She had meant to shoot his shoulder, but she would take it.

The man screamed in agony this time. But it was nearly drowned out by the wailing sirens echoing in the distance. His head shot up, swiveling toward the growing cacophony, before turning back to Alexa. Her gun was steady and aimed directly at the man's head. She smirked.

"This is a nice neighborhood," she said. "People tend to call the cops fast when they hear gunshots."

The man fled.

Alexa didn't move her hand or leave her spot. She listened for the crunch of breaking glass that would tell her he had run through the backyard, the way he'd come in. When she did, and the sirens grew even louder, she lowered her hand and took a deep breath. She stared down at the blood on the hardwood floor, her stomach clenching as she realized that could have been her.

But it wasn't, she thought.

And as she processed it more and more, something nagged at her unpleasantly. Another thought pierced through the fog of disbelief.

This wasn't an accident, she thought. *This has something to do with Casimir.*

She supposed she knew what O'Brien had done with that information after all.

CHAPTER 36

Jacob

JACOB O'BRIEN STUMBLED through the streets, eyes squeezed shut in pain as he clutched his stomach. He could feel the blood coating his hand and soaking his shirt as it spread across the dark fabric. His other hand wasn't in much better shape.

What he needed was a hospital. But there was no way that was going to happen. The instant he walked into any ER in the city, the nurse or doctor or whoever would report the gunshot wounds to the police. And it wouldn't take much for them to connect the injuries to the break-in. There was only one place to go. The question was whether they would be remotely happy to see him. Who was he kidding? He already knew the answer.

That fucking bitch Montgomery had gotten the better of him. He had no idea how she'd gotten so lucky, but she had gotten out of the situation in far better shape than he had. It was supposed to have been a quick in and out: One shot and the bitch was dead. Make it look like a robbery gone wrong. But no. Instead, she had gotten away. He hadn't even realized she owned a gun, let alone knew how to use it.

Now he was in deep shit, and it wasn't just because of his mangled hand and the hole in his stomach. He was in deep shit because he had failed.

And the only person who might be able to patch him up was not going to be very happy with him.

But it would be fine. It had to be. Surely, he'd understand. At least, that was what he kept telling himself.

He staggered into the alley. If he'd had a free hand, he would have pressed it against the grimy walls for balance. He leaned his shoulder against it instead, forcing himself to keep moving forward.

He'd driven himself here but had parked some ways away. Reggie had a ten-block radius rule when it came to driving to Gryphon's Den. It was supposed to reduce suspicion and keep cops from having a better idea of who was visiting regularly. Normally, Jacob didn't mind it. Tonight, it was a massive pain in the ass.

Frank was at the door again. The burly man saw Jacob and his eyes widened. The lit cigarette fell from his hand and onto his shoe.

"Jesus fuck," Frank said.

"Shut the fuck up and let me in," Jacob snarled.

There was a long, agonizing pause as Frank considered. The bouncer's head was cocked, as if he was listening for sirens or some other sound that screamed danger. Finally, he opened the door, and Jacob stumbled down the steps.

Sound cut off as if someone had thrown a switch as Jacob stumbled down the steps. The silence was deafening, and he didn't have to look around to know that every single person was staring at him. It didn't matter. There was only one person he needed to see right now.

He found him at the same table as last time. He was staring daggers at Jacob. There was no shock on his face, only loathing and disbelief. And Jacob realized he'd made a very big mistake.

Reggie motioned to someone Jacob couldn't see. All of a sudden, a meaty hand grasped the back of his shirt and began dragging him to a door in one corner. He followed, knowing that trying to fight wouldn't work in his favor in the slightest. The man attached to the hand threw him into the room and slammed the door shut.

It was a bare room, one that might normally have been used for storage but clearly hadn't been in some time. The fact that there were dark stains and an unpleasant stench about the place did nothing to soothe the growing anxiety as he surveyed his surroundings. He licked his suddenly very dry lips, and for the first time since he'd been shot, the burning bullet holes weren't the focus of his attention.

It seemed like an agonizingly long time before the door opened again. Reggie, Casimir, and two other men stepped in. One of them stood in front of the door, blocking the only exit as it swung shut.

"You got some nerve coming here all shot up," Reggie said, and there was no mistaking the distaste and anger in his voice. "The fuck you thinking?"

"I—"

"You weren't thinking," Reggie said. "You were being a dumbass."

"You at least kill the bitch?" Casimir asked. He folded his arms, and the hunger in his eyes told him that was all the other man cared about.

For a moment he thought about lying. Because telling the truth was going to do shit for him. But one look at Reggie told him that lying was going to be even worse. And it wouldn't take long for them to find out he was lying through his ass.

"No," he spat. The pain was intensifying again, and it was getting hard to think. He pushed harder against his stomach.

"Looks like she got you good," Reggie said, arms folded as he looked on in amusement. His lips were curled into a smug smirk that could have been a sneer.

"No shit," Jacob spat. The pain ended up being too much, and he collapsed on the floor. He looked down at the blood spreading along the floor, joining the other stains all across the concrete floor, and it took him a minute to realize it was his. He began to panic. "Look, are you going to help me or not?"

"Why the fuck should I help you?" Reggie asked, his eyes narrowing. "My boy's still going to trial tomorrow. And the prosecutor is still the same woman who's got a bone to pick with him. You said you could take care of

it. Hell, I even gave you an eight ball in advance cause you were so sure."
He raised an eyebrow. "You still got my eight ball?"

"No." He had used nearly all of it by now. The panic intensified as
Reggie's eyes narrowed to slits. He was in deep shit. "I can pay you back."

His legs were trembling, and it wasn't because of the blood loss. He had
to tread very carefully.

"You got the money on you right now?"

"No. But I can get it to you first thing tomorrow when the bank opens."
He was stammering now. "Look, Reggie, I'm sorry. I need a doctor. If you
help me out, I swear I'll—"

He trailed off as he looked at all the men. Behind Reggie, Casimir was
snickering. The other two were looking at Jacob with cool indifference,
which was even worse.

"That gonna get Cas outta the trial?" Reggie asked.

"No."

"See, I could forgive all that," he said, his eyes chips of dark ice. "I
wouldn't be happy, but I'd let it slide. Except you did one really stupid thing."

A pit opened up in his stomach as he sat there, looking up at Reggie.
He was getting weaker and weaker from blood loss, and the pain was growing even as the terror mounted. The edges of his vision were going blurry.

"What was that?" His voice was hoarse.

"You got shot and had the balls to come here and ask for help. You
know, the one place that I've managed to keep the cops away from for the
last ten years? Anyone saw you, any cop that don't come here regularly or
any good citizen—if any of them saw you, I'd have people beating down
my door in seconds. You're a liability, asshole."

Before Jacob could react or say anything in his defense, Reggie pulled
a gun out and aimed it at Jacob's head. "And I don't fuck with liabilities."

The gun fired, and everything went black.

CHAPTER 37

Alexa

A LEXA WALKED UP THE STONE steps to the grand courthouse like she had dozens of times over the last ten years. She glanced up at the courthouse and took a long deep breath.

Her shoulder stung beneath the tightly wrapped bandage, and she was exhausted. The police and paramedics had kept her up for several hours: the paramedics insisting she go to the hospital, finally wearing Alexa down enough that she complied, and the police peppering her with questions, both at her home and the hospital. She'd barely had enough time to call Joe and tell him what had happened. He'd left the conference immediately and gotten the first plane home, but he wouldn't be here for another few hours.

When she'd told the officers she needed to get some rest and that she had court in the morning, the two men questioning her had exchanged exasperated looks.

"Ma'am," one officer said, and she hated the almost patronizing tone in his voice. "With all due respect, that's a terrible idea. I'm sure the judge will grant a postponement."

Her eyes narrowed to slits. Neither of the officers in front of her had been in court with her, neither had ever seen her in action. So neither of them were prepared for the death stare she unleashed on them, the stare that made witnesses and defendants crumble. Even while she was sitting in a hospital bed in the comfortable clothes she wore at home, that glare was intimidating.

"You must be out of your damn mind," she said.

They coughed and looked away. The second one shuffled uncomfortably.

"We'll, uh, let you know when we need to speak with you again," he said. "But I'd suggest a police presence for the rest of the night, if you're okay with that."

Alexa nodded stiffly, standing up from the hospital bed. She discharged herself, a police officer brought her home, and she went inside.

She had fallen asleep within minutes but woke up to a burning pain in her shoulder. She'd been hurt badly before, but she'd had no idea just how much a bullet wound hurt, even if it was just a graze.

She got up slowly and took the pain medication she'd been prescribed. Eventually the pain ebbed to a dull throb. And, gritting her teeth, she made herself coffee, gathered up all her documents, looked for her phone before remembering it had been destroyed, and walked out the door, preparing to go to court.

She was stopped halfway up the steps by a winded, red-faced Barrow. He'd clearly been running. He panted heavily, his chest moving in and out as he heaved.

"Thank god," he said between breaths. "I got a call this morning from a friend of mine in the force telling me you'd been shot." His eyes looked her up and down, as if searching for a giant bullet cavity. "It wasn't true?"

"Oh, it was." Alexa tapped her shoulder just below the graze, then instantly regretted it. She winced. "But I'm all right."

"The case . . ." He trailed off. "Are you sure?"

"Now more than ever." And it was true. She'd probably never be able to prove it, but she was certain Casimir was somehow tied to what had happened last night. He might not have ordered it directly—that wasn't his style—but he might have convinced one of his friends to order it for him. Regardless, he and this case had nearly gotten her killed last night. And she was not about to back down.

There was so much conviction in her voice that Barrow couldn't argue. He just nodded.

"If you're sure," he said. "In that case, good luck. I hope you put the bastard behind bars."

It was such a frank statement from the normally reserved man that it actually made Alexa laugh, deep from her belly and entirely genuine.

"I'm gonna try my best."

"I know you are."

She nodded and kept moving, continuing her path up the steps.

She sauntered into the courtroom, head held high. Henry Thompson was already there. He gave a curt nod to Alexa, one that was accompanied by pursed lips and obvious dislike, before glancing back down at his papers.

Soon after, Dillon Putotelli emerged from his chambers and moved to his seat.

"Your Honor," Thompson said, almost as soon as Putotelli had sat down. Alexa had been waiting for it. "Given Mrs. Montgomery's history with the defendant, I'm going to have to request that she recuse herself from the case and that Mr. Barrow have someone else take her place. We can postpone the trial until they are caught up on all the necessary information, but—"

The judge held up his hand. "I'm well aware of their past history, Mr. Thompson," Putotelli said. "However, after speaking with both Mrs. Montgomery and Mr. Barrow personally, I have been assured that Mrs. Montgomery will behave professionally and not let the past affect her duty as a prosecutor. I've determined that, as long as Mrs. Montgomery does not question Mr. Johnson, there will be no conflict of interest. And considering your client had pleaded the fifth, that isn't an issue, as you are well aware, considering that you and I had this discussion several months ago. Mrs. Montgomery has been given an exemption and shall be allowed to continue with the trial."

"In that case, I request a mistrial." Thompson's words were clipped and efficient. She knew how fast he could spin stories and unbalance witnesses. He was a good lawyer, even if he was a terrible person.

"Denied," Putotelli said, almost bored. "Now that we're finished with that, we can proceed with jury selection."

Alexa had to bite back a smile as Thompson's jaw clenched. He gave a jerky nod to the judge before sitting back down.

And now, it begins, Alexa thought, as several men and women filed into the courtroom, ready to be culled into twelve jurors who would decide Casimir's fate.

CHAPTER 38

Carmella, 2010

ARMELLA WAS BITING HER NAILS, her leg jiggling nervously. The courtroom was half full. Some of her friends had come, including Georgia, as had her siblings. But she still felt alone in the massive room, as if her brother, who was sitting next to her, was a mile away, and the bench had stretched to eternity. The wood-paneled and elegant room with its stone ceiling felt too large and too small at the same time.

It felt like agony, the waiting. She had no idea how long she'd been there. It had probably only been ten minutes, but it could have been a century. She hated it.

She was in the front row, which Alexa had told her to do. But it still felt like a horrible idea.

Eventually, Alexa walked down the aisle. She was stunning, her outfit crisp and professional. It was a black pantsuit with a red blouse. Her hair was pulled back, and her chin was up high. She looked so in her element that it was shocking, and somehow inspiring.

Alexa looked around, and her eyes met Carmella's. She smiled.

"Doing all right?" she asked.

Carmella snorted.

Alexa chuckled. "Thought you'd say that." Reaching out, she gave her hand a soft squeeze. Her dark, brown eyes looked into Carmella's. "It's going to be okay," she said. "You're doing the right thing. And you won't be on the stand for a few days. You don't have to be here if you don't want—"

But Carmella was shaking her head. Because she knew that if she said yes, if she left right then, she wouldn't come back. And deep down, Carmella was pretty sure Alexa knew it too. But she was still giving her the out if she wanted it. Even now, Alexa was giving that option, despite the obvious ruthlessness and how hard she had worked to get Carmella here in the first place. It made Carmella respect her even more.

"Nah," Carmella said, though her voice was a bit hoarse. "Nah, I'm staying."

Alexa smirked. "I hoped you'd say that."

Carmella smiled, but it was wiped away when side doors opened, and a large but short man strutted into the room. He was wearing a suit that didn't fit him quite right, but he was clean-shaven and had clearly showered. He looked almost presentable.

It had been months since she'd last seen Casimir—not since the day he had put her in the hospital. He looked almost the same. He had his normal self-assured, cocky smirk, despite the fact that two officers were flanking him as he walked to the defense table. As he sauntered, his eyes landed on Carmella, and he winked at her.

Maggots writhed in her stomach as she looked at him, her arm suddenly screaming in pain as if in memory. Her mouth was dry, and she grew tunnel vision, her entire being focused solely on Casimir as her pulse drummed in her brain, blotting out all thoughts.

A hand reached out and grabbed her left one, then another hand grabbed her right.

"We got you," her brother whispered. "You all right."

"He ain't getting anywhere near you," Georgia added. "Not without getting through us first. And I'm gonna put up a hell of a fight."

The reassurances warmed her, giving her more confidence than she'd ever be able to articulate in the future. She took a deep breath and watched as the trial unfolded before her.

The first few days went by in a blur. Carmella stayed for all of them. Every time Alexa spoke, Carmella expected the lawyer to summon Carmella to the stand, even though the lawyer had assured her that wouldn't be until the end of the prosecution's case. So Carmella watched, and the more she watched, the more enraptured she became. It was incredible, seeing Alexa move and talk so effortlessly. Every word she picked was perfect, everything she did—from the pauses to taking two steps closer to the jury—was calculated and planned out, even if they looked natural. Every so often, Carmella would glance at the jury. She wasn't good at reading faces, but it seemed to her like they were listening with rapt attention, hanging on to every word Alexa said. It was incredible, and a sudden tugging sensation began in Carmella's stomach, some inexplicable pull that she couldn't fully describe.

And then it came.

"Your Honor, I call Carmella Johnson to the stand."

Carmella stood, willing her knees not to shake. They didn't listen. She swore on the Bible and took her seat in the witness stand, trying not to look too nervous.

Alexa's portion went well. The lawyer had coached Carmella for days, and they went over the questions and answers for hours before the trial. Alexa had told her what the defense might say and how to handle it. She'd even gone so far as to tell Carmella what to wear and how to act in certain situations. So the first part went off without a hitch. She felt comfortable and relaxed as she began to tell her story, even the painful parts.

And then came Thompson's questions.

"Mrs. Johnson," Thompson began.

"Ms.," Carmella interrupted. She had divorced the bastard, and the paperwork had gone through two months ago. She hadn't gotten around to changing her damned name yet, though.

"My apologies. *Ms.* Johnson. You admitted in prior testimony to having an affair. Multiple, actually."

Alexa had warned her this was the defense's strategy. They were going to paint Carmella as a slut, an adulteress. They'd claim that one of her lovers beat her when they found out she had a husband and that she lied, saying it was Casimir to preserve some of her reputation.

"Yes, sir."

"How many times did you cheat on him?"

There was a silence as she hesitated, taken aback by the bluntness of the statement. "I don't—"

"You don't know. Okay, let me rephrase it: How many lovers did you have while married to my client?"

Carmella blanched, her cheeks turning red. She glanced over to Alexa, who was frowning at the prosecutor as she waited for him to continue.

"I don't know," she finally said.

Thompson feigned surprise. "You don't know?" he asked. "You had a lot of them, then. You expect the jury to believe you didn't keep track of them?"

"Objection," Alexa said, shooting to her feet. "Argumentative."

"Sustained," the judge, a man by the name of Peter Williams, said.

"When did the affairs begin?"

"A couple of years into our marriage," Carmella said. The smug smirk on his face made her want to crawl out of her skin. She didn't know what the man was playing at, but she knew it wasn't anything good. He had a plan, and though Alexa had warned her this would happen, nothing could have prepared her for the way Thompson was looking at her.

"Why'd you start?" he asked.

"I found out he was cheating on me," she said.

"Did you see him cheating on you?"

"No. A friend told me."

"Ah." He nodded sagely before turning to the jury. "You took this friend's word at face value, and so you decided the best way to deal with it wasn't couple's therapy or divorce. You'd just cheat on him instead. Even though you never saw it firsthand."

"He beat me, too," she muttered.

"So now you're saying you cheated because he beat you, even though you just said a moment ago that it was because he allegedly cheated."

"It was both." What was it about this man? He was absolutely ruthless, pulling no punches as he continued his deluge of questions.

"Let's go back to the beatings," he said. "How long was he beating you for?"

"He started a year into our marriage," she said.

"So you're saying that, for four years, he was hitting you, and you did nothing? Didn't tell anyone?"

"I was afraid," she said. Her voice was hoarse.

"You didn't even go to the hospital or tell your best friend," he said. "There's no record of you ever going to the hospital or any report of domestic abuse until that day."

"He did," she said, but her voice was cracking and sounded weak.

"Tell me," he said. "Were any of your lovers violent?"

"No, of course not."

"Tell me about the evening leading up to the beating and the day it happened." It was a sharp change in topic, one that caught Carmella off guard. She began stammering.

And so it continued.

CHAPTER 39

Alexa

"**Y**OUR HONOR, I'D LIKE TO CALL Tammy Washington to the stand," Alexa called.

A rustle of movement from the gallery and a young woman, who probably turned eighteen three months ago, if that, flounced over to the witness stand. She was all curves, with huge breasts and a round ass. Her pigtails flopped as she walked, bouncing in time with her steps. She might have been pretty if she wasn't wearing more makeup than anyone could ever need to apply at one time. And her attire, comprised of a skimpy, black dress that barely covered her cheeks, and five-inch heels, was more suited to a nightclub than a courtroom.

Alexa forced herself not to purse her lips.

"Miss Washington," Alexa said. "Could you explain to me the nature of your relationship with the defendant?"

"Who? Casimir?"

This time, Alexa had to force herself not to sigh. "Yes, that's the defendant."

"Oh we're real close." She was smacking her mouth, chomping up and down rhythmically, a soft squelch periodically accompanying it. Alexa frowned.

"Miss Washington, are you . . . chewing gum?"

"Oh, yeah." Tammy popped a large bubble and grinned. "Better than dip, ain't it?"

"Bailiff?" Judge Putotelli called, glancing over at him. "Get a trash can. Miss Washington, please spit that out."

"Okay, jeez." Tammy deposited the gum in the trash the bailiff held out for her. She pouted, slumping back in her seat and folding her arms like a petulant child.

"Miss Washington, could you clarify what you mean by 'real close.'"

"Means we're fucking," she said smugly.

"So not dating?"

"Objection," Thompson said. "Assumption."

"Sustained."

"Are you and Casimir dating?" Alexa amended.

"Course we are."

Alexa glanced over at Casimir, who rolled his eyes. "It doesn't seem like Mr. Johnson sees it that way."

"Objection—"

"Withdrawn," Alexa said, interrupting Thompson before he could finish. "How long have you been dating?"

"About six months," she said.

Alexa raised her eyebrow and exchanged a look with Thompson in a rare moment of comradery as they both shared the same thought: How likely was it that Tammy was legal when they started dating? Even Thompson had a slightly queasy look of distaste on his face.

"And do you know the name Maria Gonzalez?" Alexa asked.

"Only once all this bullshit started," Tammy said, bored.

"Miss Washington, please refrain from swearing while on the stand," Judge Putotelli said, as if explaining to a kid why he shouldn't kick the back of an airplane seat.

"Tell me, did you and Mr. Johnson have an open relationship?"

There was a pause. "I guess so," she said. "We're kind of on-again, off-again."

"And the night of April 13, when Ms. Gonzalez was attacked?"

"We was off," she huffed.

"You said he loved you," Alexa said. "If he loved you, why was he out with someone else? Namely, Ms. Gonzalez?"

"Objection, speculation," Thompson said behind her.

"Sustained."

Alexa nodded. It was fair. But she wasn't getting anywhere at the moment. She needed to change her strategy. "Tell me, did Casimir ever hit you? Or become violent in any way?"

An even longer pause, and Alexa watched something uneasy flicker behind her eyes.

"No," Tammy said.

"Ms. Washington, may I remind you you're under oath?" Alexa said.

"He didn't!" Tammy said. The outburst might have been convincing to some, but to Alexa it just looked like a desperate attempt to cover shame over something Tammy shouldn't have any shame about. Alexa knew how that felt. "He loves me. He would never do something like that."

"And what about those two times you ended up in the hospital?"

"Objection, irrelevant." Thompson wasn't going to let anything slide by if he could help it.

"Overruled," Putotelli said, glancing over at Tammy. "Miss Washington, please answer the question."

Tammy hesitated, her eyes glancing over to the left as she licked her lips. "Fell," she said. "That's all."

Looking over at Casimir, she saw him grinning maliciously as he stared at Alexa. He showed his teeth, and the grin turned wolfish.

Alexa knew Tammy had been abused; it was plain as day. But she also knew that Tammy wasn't going to give up Casimir. It was a dead end. He had won this round, and Casimir knew it, too. He winked at her, and it was all Alexa could do not to storm over there and punch him right in the face.

"No further questions, Your Honor," Alexa said, doing her best not to clench her teeth. She turned and sat back down at the prosecution table, doing her best to keep her expression neutral.

Thompson stood, stretching his back slightly as he slid his chair out from underneath him. He glanced over at Alexa and flashed a smug grin. They were back on opposite sides.

"Miss Washington," he said. "Thank you so much for joining us today. I have to admit, I don't see what your testimony has to do with this case—"

"Objection."

"Sustained."

"Regardless, I appreciate you taking the time to be here. I'll make this quick. You say Casimir is a good guy. Do you think he would ever stoop to something so low and horrible as beating a poor woman and leaving her in an alley?"

"Course not," Tammy said. Her shoulders had relaxed and the smug, self-satisfied tone and expression had returned. She reclined back in her seat. "He's a good guy. Besides, why would he need to fuck—uh, screw—some random slut when he's got me a phone call away? Don't make sense."

"So if he'd called you that night, you'd have agreed to have sex?"

"Of course." Tammy snorted.

"Why's that?"

"Because he's good in bed."

Thompson nodded as if Tammy had said something incredibly profound. "So do you think if, as the defense claims, Miss Gonzalez had intercourse with the defendant on the night in question, she would have enjoyed it?"

"Oh yeah," Tammy said.

Alexa stood. "Objection, Your Honor," she said. "Speculation."

"Sustained."

But Alexa knew it wasn't any good. Even if the jury was supposed to disregard the question and pretend it didn't exist, it was still going to be in their minds. No matter what, those words were going to affect the jury. It was human nature. Hell, studies had been done on it. And that was the danger Thompson had always posed. He understood the human psyche, and he knew how to manipulate the jury without them realizing it. She'd seen it before. And it was dangerous.

And the longer Thompson spoke, the more she realized what a battle she had ahead of her.

—

IT WAS A LONG, LONG DAY in court, and by the time Alexa finally got home, she was exhausted. Her body ached, and her thoughts were racing so quickly there was no way she would be able to ignore them. It seemed impossible that she'd ever be able to get to sleep, despite the fact that she'd gotten little sleep the night before and had been shot in the last twenty-four hours.

As soon as the door opened, Joe came rushing through from the living room. He enveloped her in a bear hug, only loosening his grip when she gave a quick grunt of pain as his arm pressed into the wound on her arm.

"Hey, babe," he murmured into her hair, seemingly unwilling to let her go. "I'm so sorry. How are you feeling?"

She leaned into him, wrapping her own arms around his waist. She took a deep breath, inhaling his cologne. Just being near him made the last twenty-four hours feel more like a fading nightmare she'd had a week ago.

She had told Joe not to come to the courthouse, knowing it would distract her. But he'd clearly been waiting anxiously for her to return home. She nuzzled into him briefly, closing her eyes and letting herself find comfort in his warmth.

"I'm better now that I'm with you," she said.

"Come on," he said, guiding her into the living room. "I've got a bottle of wine and some chocolate ready for you."

Thick foam insulation had been put up where the French door had been until they could get a replacement. In the kitchen was a full bottle of Chablis, a box of the most decadent-looking truffles (Ferrero Rocher), and a box of mixed chocolates from her favorite chocolatier.

"That's not *some* chocolate," she said, even as her mouth watered at the sight. "I should get shot more often."

He gave a hollow chuckle and kissed her on the head. "Please don't," he said. "I had a heart attack the entire plane ride home. I don't want to have to worry about that happening again."

"Sorry, bad joke." She leaned up and kissed him on the lips. It was a long moment before they parted. "But thank you. It means a lot."

He brushed a strand of hair from her face. "Anything for you," he said. He gave her one last lingering kiss before stepping back and pouring the Chablis into two waiting glasses. "How was the trial?"

She appreciated that he knew she wouldn't want to talk about the shooting, that he knew her well enough to understand that she'd bring it up herself when she was ready. How he knew her so well it sometimes astounded her even as it soothed her.

"Not as well as I'd hoped," she said. "But not terrible. Thompson is on his A game."

He handed her a glass of wine. "I know you'll take care of it," he said.

She hesitated before finally voicing a thought that had been plaguing her all day. "What if I don't?" she asked. "What if I fail and he goes free again?"

"It won't happen," he said.

"But what if it does?"

He took a sip from his own glass as he considered. "Then hopefully he's learned his lesson and will stop while he's still ahead. Or, knowing him, he could get shot and die in a gutter before he has the chance. And if it's neither of those and he tries this shit again, then he'll get caught, and you'll get him next time."

She didn't say anything, and instead took a long swig of the wine, relishing the taste as it ran down her throat.

"It took ten years this time," she said, looking down at the glass and running her finger around the rim. "I want that fucker behind bars."

"I know you do," he said, his fingers running along the length of her good arm. "If I know anything about you, it's how stubborn and tenacious you are. You'll get him behind bars, or you'll die trying." He glanced at her shoulder and made a face. "Uh, poor choice of words."

She laughed, doubling over and nearly sloshing her wine. It wasn't even that funny of a joke, but everything about the situation, coupled with those words, was so absurdly hilarious to her that she couldn't help it.

He's going to think I've gone crazy, she thought, and started laughing even more.

Eventually the laughter died. She glanced up at her husband. He was smiling at her affectionately.

"It's so good to hear you laugh," he said. And she knew the multiple layers behind the statement. It had been a while since she'd laughed, certainly. But if the killer had succeeded last night, she never would have laughed again, and that's what Joe had meant.

She kissed him, the taste of cool wine on both their lips.

"I'm still here," she said.

"I know."

He placed his glass on the table and began kissing her neck, his mouth moving down to her collarbone. She moaned at the delicious tingling sensation moving down her back. She put her own glass down.

Joe's hand moved to the hem of her shirt. He looked up at her with raised eyebrows.

"Is this okay?" he asked. "I don't want to reopen the wound or—"

"Shut the fuck up and take my shirt off."

Joe grinned and did as he was told. His fingers caressed the bandage on her shoulder gently, a slight frown on his face. He bent forward, his lips brushing gently against it. He straightened a bit, enough to whisper in her ear, "I'm so glad you're okay."

Warm, strong hands went to her waist as he took in her body, looking intently at her as if trying to reassure himself that she was real.

Words couldn't express how much she loved him and how glad she was that she was okay, too, if only so that she could see the man she loved again.

She brought him down to her, kissed him, and dragged him into the bedroom.

CHAPTER 40

Tony

"THE DEFENSE CALLS Tony Gonzalez to the stand."

Tony stood, swallowing slightly as he adjusted his slightly shabby suit. It pinched in places, but it was the best he could afford on a waiter's salary.

He got to the witness stand, and once he swore to tell the truth, the whole truth, and nothing but the truth, he sat, and Alexa approached. She smiled reassuringly, silently communicating that it would be all right.

"Mr. Gonzalez," Alexa said. "You are the brother of Maria Gonzalez, correct?"

"Yes ma'am." Tony wished he'd combed his hair again. It had gotten messy since his shower this morning. And he wished he hadn't cut himself shaving three times, giving himself unappealing red marks on his neck and chin. His razor was too dull, and he hadn't gotten the chance to get a new one. He felt entirely out of his depth. How would anyone believe him as a witness?

"What were you doing the night in question?" she asked.

"I was at home, waiting for my sister."

"Why?"

"She was supposed to come home at midnight."

"And she didn't?"

"No, ma'am."

"Why didn't you call the police?"

"I was about to when she came through the door."

"Could you describe what she looked like?"

Tony hesitated, his stomach clenching as he thought back to that night. He didn't want to think about it. He shoved it from his memory whenever he could. But he had to relive it.

His eyes darted around as he tried to get some courage. His eyes went from Casimir to Alexa to Maria. Then they swept across the gallery and froze as he saw a familiar Adonis-like man lounging in the back row: David. Tony had mentioned in passing that he was busy because of the trial, and the other man somehow had not only managed to find out what day Tony was testifying but also bothered to take the day off to come see him. David flashed Tony a grin and nodded. It was the type of nod that clearly meant *you got this*.

Something about seeing David, seeing the nod, allowed him to unfreeze. He took a deep breath and began to talk.

It hurt to go through again, but he pushed through, remembering Alexa's suggestions on what to say and how to explain it to convey the right message. Glancing over at the jury box, he saw it was working. The more he talked, the more he described how Maria had looked and how he'd brought her to the hospital, the more he saw the jurors' faces twist in sympathy and revulsion. Several shot pitying looks over at Maria, and others shot death glares at Casimir. It was incredible, seeing the way his words and Alexa's carefully phrased questions painted a clear picture for the jury, one that helped convince them Casimir was a monster.

The man was currently glowering at Tony, but he didn't care. He needed to do this for his sister. He spoke, and his eyes went to David whenever he needed some sort of comfort or reassurance. And he was always there, giving that encouraging smile.

Eventually Alexa finished with him, and it was Thompson's turn. But he threw softball questions, something that made Tony uneasy. Alexa had warned him that the defense was ruthless, but he only asked a handful of questions before saying he had no further questions. Something about it was wrong. Glancing at the prosecution's table, Alexa knew it too. Her eyes were narrowed, following Thompson like a hawk. Something was wrong and based on Alexa's expression when he got off the stand, he knew that she knew exactly what was coming next. He wanted to ask her, but he also knew she wouldn't tell him.

—

IT WAS MARIA'S TURN on the stand. She was sweet but clearly nervous. But she answered all of Alexa's questions easily enough, and Tony could tell the nervousness endeared her to several members of the jury. They were looking at her with sympathy, and when Alexa began showing photos of the battered and bruised Maria, they all looked horrified. *Good*, Tony thought. It was agonizing to hear his sister relive the details of her rape, but at least he wasn't the only one who couldn't stand hearing the words.

When Alexa, after several hours of questions, said she was finished, she walked back to the bench. Her eyes found Tony's and before she sat, she leaned over the railing into the gallery and whispered, "Whatever Thompson says, don't go punching the guy. And just remember he's spinning a flimsy story."

She sat back down. He had no idea what she was talking about or even how to react to the whispered words. He knew they were important, but he couldn't figure out what exactly she was trying to tell him.

And then Thompson began, and he understood completely.

"Miss Gonzalez," Thompson said, his voice as oily as a car salesman's. "When you went to the club, who came up to whom?"

"I was sitting at a table, and he came and sat next to me," she said.

"And did you know who he was?"

"Not at the time, no."

Thompson feigned surprise, taking a step back and making an exaggerated face of befuddlement. "But when you came home later that night, you told your brother that your assailant was Casimir Johnson."

"I found out later," Maria said. "At the club, he told me his name was Casimir, and when he . . ." She made an inarticulate gesture. "When he did . . . *that* . . . I figured out who it was."

"So, to confirm, Mr. Johnson never gave you his full name."

"No," Maria said. "But I'd heard it plenty of times before."

"Miss Gonzalez, how much did you have to drink that night?"

Her face turned a brilliant red. "I don't remember," she said timidly. "He kept feeding them to me."

"A ballpark."

"Several," Maria said.

"A bit more specific than that, please," Thompson said. His triumphant smile was almost wolfish, and Tony hated it.

"Um, maybe around six. Maybe eight."

"Is it possible that you mistook my client for someone else named Casimir?"

"It's not a very common name," Maria muttered. But her eyes had gotten that panicked, doe-eyed look.

"Answer the question, please."

"No," she said. "I picked him out in a lineup."

"Miss Gonzalez, you were incredibly drunk. Any positive identification would—"

"Objection, Your Honor. Opinion."

"Sustained."

"In my mind," Thompson continued, strolling away from Maria and toward the jury, "there are two options here. One is that you got drunk and went home with someone else named Casimir. Later, when things became clearer, you *thought* it was my client. You'd heard his name before, after all. No, don't shake your head. The second option is that this was a plot constructed by you, and who knows how many other people, to slander my client's good name. His name's been drug through the mud before, after all."

For some reason, his eyes flashed toward Alexa. He saw the woman tense for the briefest of moments.

"That's not true," Maria said.

"Objection. Badgering," Alexa said, half a second too late. Her voice was strained.

"Sustained."

"You said this person didn't give you his full name," Thompson said. "So either you knew it was Casimir Johnson before, meaning that you targeted him directly and are lying to us now. Or you're telling what you think is the truth, but you're misinformed."

"I didn't—"

"Did you get a rape kit done when you went to the hospital?" he interrupted.

Maria, who was clearly close to tears, shook her head, her gaze turned downward.

"Why not?"

"I was ashamed," she said.

"Now why would you be ashamed of being raped?" Thompson asked. The words should have been comforting, something to soothe a traumatized person. But from Thompson, it sounded scornful and accusatory. The implication being that if she had been raped, she wouldn't be ashamed. But that wasn't how it worked.

"Objection." Alexa's voice was a whip crack, and she was barely containing her rage. Her back was to Tony, so he couldn't see her facial expression. But he could see the way her nails dragged against the table as they curled into fists and the way her entire body was quivering. Clearly Tony wasn't the only one who needed reminding not to punch Thompson. "Badgering the witness. Again."

"Sustained." Even Putotelli looked disgusted. "Mr. Thompson, if you can't ask anything without antagonizing the witness, I suggest you sit down."

"Apologies, Your Honor," Thompson said, but he was smiling so wide it looked as though he'd already won the case. "No further questions."

But Tony knew the damage had already been done.

CHAPTER 41

Carmella, 2010

B Y THE TIME THOMPSON WAS DONE questioning her, Carmella was in shambles. The man had managed to systematically tear her down, gaslight her, and make her question everything that had happened over the last several years. He'd somehow managed to make it seem like Casimir was the victim, and that she was a sorry sack of shit and a compulsive liar. Her hands were shaking, and the lump in her throat was so large that she couldn't speak. She at least managed not to cry until after she had gotten off the stand. She hadn't even been able to look at the jury.

She stayed in the bathroom a long time, hunched over in a stall. Other women's heels moved in the gap between the stall door and floor, but none of the women to whom they belonged reacted to her crying.

After some time—though Carmella wasn't sure how long—the door opened. She expected the exact same thing to happen with the newcomer as had happened with all the other women. But instead, a voice said, "Carmella? Is that you?"

It was Alexa. Carmella gave a loud sniffle. "Yeah," she said. "It's me."

"Do you want to go on a walk?" she asked.

A long pause, then Carmella stood and unlocked the door.

"We've got a fifteen-minute recess," she said. "And it's a nice day out. Come on."

They walked for a bit in silence. It was indeed a nice day out. The sun streamed down between the giant skyscrapers, and there were shockingly few pedestrians. The air smelled clean for New York, and there was something about the entire thing that was strangely comforting.

"What'd I miss?" she finally asked Alexa when they had walked the entire block twice.

"The prosecution just rested," she said. "It'll be the defense's turn next."

"Is he going to call me again?" Carmella asked.

"It's possible. But I don't think so." Alexa gave a long sigh and looked up at the blue sky surrounded by tall buildings. "I don't know if I've done enough this time," she said. "I've been doing this for a while now, and this isn't going well. It isn't because of anything we've done. Just sometimes it happens. You can see it in the jurors' faces."

"So everything I just went through was for nothing?" Carmella bristled. "Me being called a *whore* and *slut* twenty different ways, and he's gonna get off?"

"We don't know yet," Alexa said. "And I hope not. I've won a lot of these types of cases. But he might. I just don't know."

Carmella didn't respond as she tried to quash the anger. But then Alexa said, "I'm sorry," and all the anger washed out of her.

"It's not your fault," Carmella said. "You did your best."

"Tried to, at least."

"How much longer, do you think?"

"A couple of days? Depends on how much evidence they give and how long they draw it out for. And then there's the jury's deliberation, and that can take anywhere from five minutes to five days."

Carmella nodded, chewing the inside of her cheek.

"He's gonna come after me if he gets out?" she asked. It was a fear she hadn't voiced yet, but it kept her up at night: imagining what would happen if she heard her apartment door open late one night, heard his voice and his footsteps from the other room.

It's payback time, whore.

"I don't know," Alexa admitted. Her eyes were hard and determined. "But I'll help make sure he doesn't."

—

THE DEFENSE RESTED TWO DAYS later. The day after, Alexa gave Carmella the call she'd been waiting for.

"The jury's reached a verdict," Alexa said by way of introduction. Even over the phone, it was impossible not to notice she was trying to keep the tension out of her voice.

Carmella felt her stomach twist with nervousness. "Is that fast?" she asked.

"About standard," admitted Alexa. "You ready to find out your ex-husband's fate?"

But it was a rhetorical question; Alexa already knew the answer.

A few hours later, Carmella was waiting in the courtroom with bated breath. Her chest hurt as her stomach did somersault after somersault. She had no idea what was about to happen, but all she could do was wait and keep her fingers crossed. She hated it. She hated feeling helpless, hated not knowing what these people were about to say. They held Casimir's life in their hands, and Carmella's in a way. If Casimir wasn't convicted, she would have to find ways to make sure he didn't come after her.

The judge sidled in as the jury took their seats. Time seemed to stand still.

"Has the jury reached a verdict?" the judge asked.

The foreman, a round, balding man with glasses, stood. "We have, Your Honor."

"For the charge of first-degree assault, we find the defendant not guilty on both counts."

Carmella's heart sank. She glanced over at Alexa, whose face was stone.

It's not over yet, Carmella told herself. *There are other charges.*

But already her stomach was tightening in dread. She could feel herself beginning to sweat as she held her breath, unwilling to breathe.

"For the charge of sexual battery, we find the defendant not guilty."

Carmella's entire body froze as she processed the words. There was still one more chance, one more opportunity for Casimir to be locked away.

"For the charge of rape in the first degree, we find the defendant . . ."

Carmella waited, her eyes locked on the foreman.

"Not guilty."

CHAPTER 42

Alexa

"THE DEFENSE RESTS."

"The prosecution may now make its closing argument," Putotelli said. His eyes locked on Alexa.

Alexa stood, steeling herself as she walked around the table to stand in front of the juror's box.

"Ladies and gentlemen of the jury," she said. "You've heard both sides of the story. The defense has created a ludicrous story about how Miss Maria Gonzalez is a liar and temptress, and that she coerced the defendant into sex and then later blamed him for an unrelated assault. The truth is, Miss Gonzalez, like so many other women over the years, is a victim. The person who did these heinous acts, who savagely beat and raped a young woman who was simply having fun with her friends, is in the courtroom right now, sitting at the defense table. You've seen the evidence. You've seen how savagely she was beaten. You've heard testimony both from the victim and her brother, showing the damage the defendant, Mr. Johnson, caused . . ."

Alexa continued, warming to her topic as she did. She watched each juror's face as she continued going, trying to determine how many of them were swayed by her words. Some of them were easier to read than others. It was enough to give her hope, but she knew from experience that compelling arguments didn't always work.

She finished her argument. There was nothing more she could do. She could only hope that she had done enough, that Casimir would finally get the justice he deserved.

As she sat down, her mind went back to the first trial, which felt like a century ago. She remembered hearing the verdicts, one after the other, her anger and frustration growing along with her fear. She remembered gripping the gallery railing, her knuckles growing whiter and whiter. She remembered the jury, all of them pointedly not looking at her, as if they felt some layer of guilt for their decision. And, worst of all, she remembered Casimir, staring smugly at her as he winked. It had felt almost like a threat.

She was so lost in memories that she didn't hear a word of what Thompson was saying as he made his own closing remarks. She tried to bring herself back into the present, forcing herself to listen.

"You have to keep in mind that my client is a good man," Thompson was saying.

Right, she thought. *And water is dry*. Casimir was more like Rumpelstiltskin, manipulating and deceiving everyone for his own gain. He was even short like the man from the fairy tale. She only wished that he would stamp his foot and explode into a million pieces like Rumpelstiltskin had.

"The last time my client was brought up on spurious charges, he was rightly acquitted. I hope that you will make the same choice. You have to understand that, when you are passing judgment on this man, you are impacting the rest of his life. You as the jury must look at the facts, and only the facts. Something like this can elicit very strong emotions, but you can't let the tragedy of the situation dictate your decision. What happened to Miss Gonzalez was terrible. But there isn't enough evidence proving that my client did it. The burden of proof is on the state. Your job is to determine whether the state has effectively proven that my client, beyond reasonable doubt, committed this terrible crime."

Alexa had heard this strand of argument before. She kept her eyes on the jury. Two or three looked uncertain, as if the defense attorney's argument was a compelling one. Which, in a way, it was. Others glanced into the gallery, at Maria, who Alexa knew was leaning against Tony, his arm wrapped around her in both comfort and protection.

And then the trial was over. The jury stood and walked out the side door, where they would be sequestered and go over the evidence. It could take two hours, it could take two days, before they came back with a decision. There was no way to be sure. And it was officially out of Alexa's hands, no matter what she wanted to do.

This was the worst part, waiting for the jury to return. She'd never been a patient woman, and it was these types of situations that pushed her to her limit.

"How long?" Tony asked as soon as they had both stepped outside of the courtroom. He didn't need to elaborate.

"There's no way of telling," Alexa said.

"Is shorter better?" Maria asked.

"Depends," a paralegal Alexa knew peripherally—David, she thought his name was—said. He was standing next to Tony. And as Alexa's eyes moved downward, she saw that the two men's hands were clasped together. Tony was leaning against the other man slightly, seemingly unwilling to let him go. "Mostly it means that the jury is convinced one way or the other and they don't need to go over all the evidence a hundred times. But that can mean they're convinced of his guilt, or convinced of his innocence."

Alexa nodded her agreement. "Well put," she said. "In short, we'll just have to see."

Her phone rang. "I have to take this," she said when she saw the number. She stepped to the side. "What's up, Sally?"

"Have you heard?" The secretary sounded breathless.

"I'm guessing not," Alexa said, her curiosity immediately piqued. "What happened?"

"I heard it through the grapevine, so admittedly, I don't know how accurate it is," Sally said. "But Jacob O'Brien was found in an alley last night. He was shot in the head. They think he'd been there a while."

It took a moment for the words to fully sink in. "He was . . . shot?"

"Several times, apparently." There was a significant pause. "People are saying he was shot in the hand and gut as well."

Alexa's ears began ringing as the pieces fell into place. She remembered her fight with the gunman, how there had been something familiar about him that she just couldn't place. It had been O'Brien.

So that was what he used my address for, she thought, strangely detached from the reality of the situation. She wondered if it had been on someone else's orders or his own initiative. She'd probably never know. She wondered whether that meant the danger was over or someone else would try. Strangely, she thought it was the former. They would know by now that she would have an inkling of what had happened. They wouldn't want to try again in case it failed, and she could point the police in their direction.

"Thanks," Alexa said. "That's good to know. How are you holding up?"

"Better," Sally admitted. "It was awkward explaining things to the kids, about what happened between me and Vlad and trying to get them to understand why I'd done what I did. I don't know if they've forgiven me yet, but at least they know now. How's the trial?"

"We just finished," Alexa said. "We're waiting on the jury."

"Good luck."

They didn't have to wait long. About five hours later, Alexa got the call: The jury had reached a verdict. She hurried back to the courthouse, every inch of her body tense with apprehension and fear. Though she had tried to remain composed for the sake of Tony and Maria, she was terrified that history would repeat itself. That the system would fail yet again.

The jury filed in, and she got that absurd sense of déjà vu. It felt so similar to what had happened fourteen years ago that goosebumps crawled over her flesh. But at the same time, it felt different. Things had changed. She was no longer the same woman she had been all those years ago. Casimir knew it too. She could see it in his eyes every time he glared at her.

"Has the jury reached a verdict?" Putotelli asked.

"We have, Your Honor," the foreman, a curvy woman with long, blond hair, said.

Alexa tried not to grip the table too hard as she waited.

"On the charge of first-degree assault, we find the defendant guilty."

Alexa breathed out a long sigh of relief.

"On the charge of sexual battery, we find the defendant guilty."

She nearly sat back and melted into her seat.

"And on the charge of rape, we find the defendant guilty."

Alexa collapsed back into her chair, all her muscles sagging in relief at once.

Guilty of all charges.

She had done it.

CHAPTER 43

Carmella, 2010

THE BRIGHT SUNLIGHT SHINING down on Carmella and Alexa as they stepped out of the courthouse seemed too cheery, incongruous with the disappointing verdict. They had failed.

"I'm sorry," Alexa said as they reached the bottom of the stone steps. The large throng of people moving on the sidewalk as they returned home from work was thick, and people shot the two stationary women dirty looks as they brushed by, clearly wondering why the two women were just standing there impeding traffic.

Carmella glanced back up at the courthouse doors towering some way above them, waiting to see Casimir strut through the doors, gloating over his victory. But, for the first time since she could remember, she didn't feel fear at seeing him. Something, some spell he had over her, had broken. She felt freer than she had been in years.

"Don't be," Carmella said, tearing her gaze away from the stone building behind her. "He can't hurt me no more."

"He doesn't know where you're living, does he?" Alexa asked.

Carmella shook her head. "I moved out of my friend Georgia's place a few days ago, actually. She's moving to LA anyway, so it wasn't like I was gonna be able to stay there much longer," she said. "I made sure that he knew I was gone so he wouldn't come after her, but that's all."

"How is the new place?" Alexa asked.

Carmella snorted. "It's a shithole the size of a shoebox," she said. "Bout all I can afford at the moment, given my new job don't pay shit. But it's mine, so I can't complain."

Alexa's mouth quirked upward.

"What's next for you?" she asked. "I'm guessing you aren't going to stay at a shit-paying job forever."

Carmella hesitated, feeling heat rise up her face. "There is one thing I was thinking about," she admitted. "But it's probably stupid, and I don't know if it'd work anyway. It ain't cheap."

Alexa tilted her head inquisitively. "What?" she asked. Something in the lawyer's expression told her that the other woman already had an idea what it might be. Carmella coughed uncomfortably.

"I was thinking about trying to get into law school," she said. "Seeing you do your thing was incredible. The whole thing was inspiring. We may not have won, but you've helped me a lot. And I wanna do the same for other people."

A wide smile spread across Alexa's face and her eyes glittered. "I think that's a great idea," she said. "You've got that stubbornness about you. And you're smart, even if that asshole made you feel otherwise for the past five or six years. I bet you'd be a great attorney."

Carmella flushed at the praise, momentarily feeling as though she were floating on air. But then she came crashing back down to reality.

"That's assuming I can get a loan or something," she said. "That shit ain't cheap."

Alexa tapped her chin as she considered Carmella. "You really wanna do this?" she asked.

"I think so."

"You got a bachelor's?"

Carmella nodded. Over the last several years, in an attempt to give herself a bit more freedom, she had been taking online college courses part-time. She had gotten her degree just before Casimir landed her in the hospital.

There was an even longer pause as the lawyer continued to study the other woman. "Tell you what," she said. "Pass the LSAT, and I'll help pay for law school. I'll write a letter of recommendation. Any school you want in New York, no matter the cost. Assuming you get in. Which I think you will."

Carmella gaped. It was all she could do.

"You fucking serious?" she asked.

Alexa chuckled, her brown eyes twinkling. The amusement and pride on the older woman's face, and the sun shining down on her, made the attorney more beautiful and radiant than Carmella had ever seen her before, and the first thought her mind went to was that the lawyer had to be an angel.

"You might want to curb the level of swearing if you want to go down this route," she said. "Well, at least in the courtroom. But I'll work with you on that."

Tears welled in Carmella's eyes, and she had to blink them away. No one in her entire life had done something like this for her. And a woman who was arguably a virtual stranger was offering her the chance of a lifetime.

"Why?" she managed to choke out.

"Because I see a lot of myself in you," Alexa said. "And I think that you'll be able to make a difference and make the world a better place. You just got that look about you."

Carmella's head was spinning. Even though she had thought about being a lawyer ever since seeing Alexa in court, it had felt like an idle fantasy, something that she wouldn't be able to ever actually do. It seemed too far-fetched, regardless of the dream. And here was this woman, effectively offering her the world, a change in her life that she had never thought could actually happen.

"I can't pay you back," Carmella said. "Not any time soon."

Alexa was shaking her head. "I have plenty of money," she said. "My family was pretty wealthy. Owned a lot of real estate. Truth be told, I have more money than I can spend in a lifetime."

"Then what do you get out of it?" Carmella asked.

"Knowledge that there's a new lawyer out there who's as stubborn as I am. And I get to be a bit of a mentor." Her eyes sparkled. "If I'm paying for your law school, I'm gonna get to bother you about it and give you suggestions." When Carmella still stared disbelievingly at her, Alexa added, "If you really want to pay me back, when you have the means, do it for someone else. Someday you're going to come across someone who wants to go down this path and who you think has potential. Help them achieve that dream. Even if you can't pay for their law school, at the very least mentor them and help them get through it. That's all I ask."

At first Carmella only stood there, still dumbfounded. Then she flung her arms around the other woman, holding her tight. This time, she couldn't hold back the tears. This woman had given her a once-in-a-lifetime opportunity. In later years, she would think about that day regularly, and even then, she would never be able to fully articulate how much that offer meant to her. It wasn't one many people got, and she promised to utilize it to the fullest.

"Thank you," Carmella whispered.

"I take it that's a yes?" Alexa asked, and Carmella could hear the smile in her voice.

Not saying a word, and not relinquishing the embrace, Carmella nodded.

"I'm glad." Alexa broke the embrace, taking a step back and holding out her hand. "In that case, it's a deal. And you better get studying for the LSAT."

They shook on it.

CHAPTER 44

Alexa

JOE WAS WAITING FOR HER when she stepped through the door of their house. He swept her into his arms, holding her tight.

"I just heard," he said. "I'm so proud of you, baby."

She leaned into him, taking a deep shaking breath. Her legs were shakier than she cared to admit, still overcome by the adrenaline. They felt like jelly, and she was surprised she had managed to get home at all. She inhaled his cologne, letting herself drown in the delectable scent of coffee and leather.

They stayed like that for a long time. Then he kissed her forehead. He stepped away enough to pull her into a real kiss. His lips were warm, the kiss one of the most passionate he had ever given her. She didn't want it to end.

But eventually, he broke it off. "How are you feeling?" he asked.

"Better."

Her mind went back to how the trial had concluded, the triumph she had felt as she watched the men haul Casimir out the side door of the courthouse, back to prison where he would rot for a long, long time. The sentencing would take place most likely in about three months, so she wouldn't know for exactly how long until then. But even if it wasn't for life, Casimir would be an old, old man by the time they released him. And that would do just as well.

"It's a breath of fresh air," she admitted. "It's loomed over me for a long time, even if I was able to push it away for long periods of time. But the fact that he was still out there always weighed on me. But now he's done."

"You did good work, honey," he said. He tenderly brushed a strand of hair from her face. His green eyes looked longingly at her with a familiar spark Alexa knew well. His hand slid to her waist, and he pulled her into him. A bulge in the front of his pants began to harden. Just the feel of it was enough to spark a flame between her legs and she moved against it, helping him stiffen even further. He smirked as she pressed against him, his fingers gently lifting her shirt.

His lips found her neck, and he trailed gentle kisses down to her collarbone, his magic fingers caressing her even as he lifted her blouse.

"God, you're so sexy," he said, standing back to drink her in. "How the fuck did I get so lucky?"

"You went to the right conference at the right time," she said. "And you were persistent."

He grinned lazily. "Oh, right."

Then he scooped her into his arms. She wrapped her own arms around his neck and began kissing every inch of him that she could get to, an overwhelming hunger and need for him building at an alarming rate. His right hand found her breast and squeezed, even as he continued carrying her to the bedroom. Even through the bra it was enough to make her jerk and twitch. She moaned softly against his neck.

He lay her down on the bed, and she flung off her bra as he began slowly to pull off her pants, revealing her toned, chocolate-colored legs. But he was going too slow.

"Hurry up," she said. "I need you now."

"I'm gonna take my time," Joe said wickedly. "I want to savor it. Besides, it's fun making you squirm."

She let out a string of halfhearted swears, though their effect was significantly lessened by the fact that she was moaning the entire time. He kissed the inside of her thighs, slowly moving upward to her sex. His mouth ran up her slit, already moist with desire, finding her clit and flicking, delicately at first, then more fervently. One hand reached up and grabbed her breast, while the other slipped inside her. Her eyes shot open, and she gasped and moaned in pleasure as his fingers began pumping, alternating between fast and slow. She groaned as he continued playing with her, building the tension, but it was never quite enough to send her over the edge like she needed. Her fingers gripped the bedsheet as she writhed beneath his touch, relishing every moment of it.

When he finally lifted his head and moved to crawl over her, she pounced, grabbing his shirt and pulling it off with so much speed it nearly ripped. She pushed him onto the bed and moved on top of him, unbuckling his pants.

His cock sprang forth as soon as she pulled off his underwear. She took it in her mouth, needing to taste it, to taste him. He groaned as her tongue flicked up and down his shaft, teasing him the same way he had her. Her hand pumped rhythmically as her mouth bobbed in time. His soft groans and obvious pleasure were just more fuel for the ever-growing fire between her legs. That pleasurable sensation kept building, and she knew it probably wouldn't be long.

His fingers grasped her hair tightly, pulling her up toward him. He kissed her, pressing her breasts against his body. Her hips instinctively began grinding against him.

Finally, she couldn't take it anymore. She sat up and impaled herself on his cock. She groaned as he filled her, and she began to thrust rhythmically. Joe's hands gripped her waist, helping guide her. She kept going, the pace growing faster and faster. Her own pleasure was intensifying with every pump as his cock glided in and out of her. She arched her back, throwing her head back and closing her eyes in pleasure as she continued to ride him like a stallion.

They moved together as one, each responding to one another instinctively, the way only two people who knew each other intimately on every level—physical, emotional, spiritual—could. It was, without a doubt, the best sex Alexa had ever had in her entire life.

One final thrust and she shattered. She cried out in ecstasy as the sensation shot through her entire body, sending her to oblivion and back. Joe kept pumping, thrusting in and out of her as she rode the wave of her climax. She could see in his eyes how close he was, and with a final moan, he finished inside her.

They stayed like that for a long time, looking deeply into one another's eyes as they panted, Alexa's hair cascading over her face as she stared down at him.

"I love you," she said.

He pulled her toward him and gave her a long, tender kiss that spoke more than words ever could.

Later, after they had showered and gotten into bed, ready to fall asleep, Alexa checked her phone. There were a handful of messages. But one drew her attention.

> *Girl, I just heard. Fuck yeah! It's bout damn time.*
> *Proud of you—G*

Alexa smiled at the message and sent back a reply. As she snuggled down into bed and closed her eyes, she felt more at peace than she had in years. A weight she hadn't realized she'd been carrying, one that she'd thought was shed years ago, was lifted. A chapter had closed.

And with that thought, she fell asleep, the smile still on her face.

CHAPTER 45

Alexa, Two Months Later

S ALLY WAS THERE EARLY when Alexa came in.

"How are you holding up?" Alexa asked.

"Better than I was," Sally admitted. "We're still working through the divorce proceedings, but I had a talk with Vlad a few days ago. He wanted to apologize, which felt absurd. He said he should have prioritized me more and that he understands how this happened. He's not happy about it, obviously, but he still gets it. I told him he was stupid for apologizing and that I was the one cheating on him, but . . ." Sally trailed off, struggling to find the words.

"It'll take some time," Alexa reassured her. "Divorce is rough. Trust me, I know."

Sally snorted. "Yeah, I guess you do."

"How is Luca?"

Sally let out a puff of air and began fidgeting with the glasses dangling around her neck. "No idea," she admitted. "After I got divorced, we tried to keep it going. But it just sort of fizzled out."

"I'm sorry," Alexa said.

"Oh, it happens," Sally said. "I still don't regret the divorce, even if it didn't work out with Luca. I don't think it ever would have been anything more than sex anyway, to be honest. And, truth be told, I think the deception and fact that I was married is half of what made it so tantalizing."

Alexa nodded, smiling. "I've definitely been there," she said. "But let me know if there's anything I can do, all right?"

Sally's smile reached her eyes, and it made her beautiful. "Of course. As long as you do the same."

Alexa gave Sally a brief hug that was slightly awkward, as the secretary was still sitting, but it was warm and genuine and said more than words ever could. Then Alexa straightened and strolled into her office. There was plenty of work to be done.

Later, as she was working on some of the minutiae of an upcoming trial, there was a knock on Alexa's office door.

"Come on in," Alexa said, expecting it to be Sally. But when she glanced up, she was pleasantly surprised to see it was Tony. He looked more relaxed than she had ever seen him, and there was something in his eyes. Something very familiar that tugged at an ancient memory.

"Hi, Alexa," Tony said.

"Tony!" Alexa put down her pen and stood, walking over to shake the man's hand. "How are you doing? How's your sister?"

It had been nearly two months since the trial, and she hadn't heard much from either of them in the previous weeks. She'd been worried about them, and had actually planned on reaching out soon, so she was glad to see him here.

"Maria's good," Tony said. "She's feeling a lot better and a lot more comfortable. She went out with her friends last week for the first time since the incident, and she's dancing again." He brightened. "She's actually considering applying to teach at a studio near our apartment."

"That's great! And how about you?"

"I'm good. I'm actually here to meet David."

"So that's still going strong, then?" Alexa asked. The blush Tony gave told her it was going more than just strong. She remembered how that felt.

It was how she had felt when she and Joe had first begun to date: that pull where you could tell deep down that this one was more meaningful somehow, on a subconscious level that ran more than just the surface flame that told you every relationship was different. On a deeper level, this one meant more.

"Yeah," Tony said, a fond, wistful expression spreading across his face. He was totally lovesick. It made Alexa smile. "He's a great guy. Anyway, I wanted to thank you again. I . . . what you did . . . it means a lot. Both to me and Maria. If that other attorney had stayed on the case, I know Casimir would still be walking free. And I think you putting him away did more for Maria's healing than anything else possibly could have."

"I was happy to help," Alexa said. "And I'm glad to hear that it meant that much."

"It's not just that," Tony said. A vivid blush crept up his face, one that was far more prominent than the one David's name had elicited. "I wanted to say . . . well . . . you've inspired me."

And there it was. She finally recognized that look in his eyes. That shining, excited determination mixed with anxiety.

"I'm, uh, I'm going to take the LSATs," he said. "I'm already looking into law schools."

"Are there any you like?"

"Well, I can't afford much," Tony admitted. "So I'm looking at ones that are more reasonably priced. Some of them are really promising."

"What if money wasn't an issue?"

Tony snorted. "I don't like thinking about that," he said. "It's wishful think—"

Alexa held out her hand and Tony instantly fell silent. "Humor me," she said, smirking. "Ignoring the money, which schools do you like?"

Tony coughed as he considered. "NYU, obviously," he said. "Columbia and Cornell also have good programs that I'm interested in. Fordham's supposed to be good, too."

"The top four law schools in the city, then," Alexa teased. "All of them are great. Mine was NYU. A letter of rec from me wouldn't be too shabby."

Tony shrugged. "A letter of recommendation from you would be amazing," he said. "But, like I said, NYU is out of the question. I'm thinking CUNY if I can get a loan."

"CUNY isn't a bad option," Alexa said. "And there's a good emphasis there on social justice for minorities and underrepresented people. I could see it being a good fit for you. And, to be fair, the most expensive law school isn't always going to be the best fit for someone, depending on their interests. More expensive doesn't always mean better. But I don't want you to be limited by funds. If there's a better option out there, you should apply."

"I don't—"

"Tell you what," Alexa said. "You apply to all the law schools you want. Any of them that seem like they would be a good fit, everything from CUNY to NYU. Then, when you get back your acceptance letters—cause I have a feeling you're going to get accepted in a few places—pick whichever one is your top choice. I'll pay your tuition."

Tony looked as though he'd been hit by a semitruck. He collapsed in the chair as her words washed over him.

"You can't," he said. "That's too expensive."

Alexa arched an eyebrow imperiously and crossed her arms. It was the type of pose she used in the courtroom. "I think I'm entitled to do whatever I want to do with my money," she said. "My husband and I have more than enough. Trust me. And before you say it, he'll have no issue with me doing this."

"This can't be happening," he said hoarsely. "There's no way this is happening."

Alexa laughed. "It is," she said. "Do you want me to write up a document? I know a pretty good lawyer."

"No, no," Tony said. "I believe you. I just can't believe it."

"Well, you better," Alexa said. "Think of it as an incentive to do really well on that LSAT."

Tony studied her, his brow furrowed. She stayed perfectly still under his scrutiny, waiting for him to ask the question that she knew he was about to ask.

"Why me?" he asked.

"Because you've got a spark in you that I think will get you far in law," Alexa said. "And because of the way you helped your sister. But mostly because I like you."

Tony shook his head. "That's not the question I meant," he said. "More just . . . why do something like this at all?"

Alexa's smile grew wistful, and she gazed out the window as clear sunlight streamed in. Her mind went far away, to years ago, to another life. She thought of a handshake in front of a courthouse. Of a promise she had yet to keep.

"Someone helped me once and didn't ask for anything in return," Alexa said. "Just told me to pay it forward. So that's what I'm doing."

CHAPTER 46

Carmella, 2010

CARMELLA PASSED THE LSAT with flying colors.

She remembered getting the letter in the mail and opening it with trembling fingers. It had been a 171. She couldn't believe it. She had studied for three months, but, given everything, she had expected it to be a 150, 155 at best. She never would have dreamed that she would get that high a score. She supposed she had Alexa to thank for that. Her mentor had made sure she was more than prepared for the test, giving her practice exam after practice exam and all the books she could possibly need.

With that score, as Alexa had pointed out, she could go almost anywhere in the country. But she was staying in New York, like they'd agreed. But now her options had expanded beyond belief.

It was a good thing it had come when it had, too. The final date for applications was coming up. She was later than she'd like, but she'd been limited by when she could take the LSAT.

Still, things were looking up more than they had in months. She hadn't heard from Casimir, though she still knew he was hanging out with seedy criminals and thugs. She'd heard from old acquaintances that he spent a lot of time at the Gryphon's Den, which wasn't anything new. It seemed as though he'd gone back to his old life, though, thankfully, she was no longer a part of it.

The apartment she was in was small but tidy and with better appliances and a shower than what she'd had with Casimir. It was cheap, and she could afford it thanks to the money she'd stashed away while she'd been married. It was in a relatively safe part of New York, and she'd found neighbors she really liked and even got along with. There was a nice man named Levi two doors down who lived with his partner, whom she wouldn't mind getting to know better. And it was easier now that she didn't have an abusive husband breathing down her neck.

For the first time in a long time, she was truly free. It wasn't just a facade of freedom, like it had been whenever she'd cheated on Casimir. It was true freedom. And it was like breathing fresh air.

And then the LSATs results came, and everything had seemed even better.

But that letter, that life-changing letter, was nothing compared to what she was holding in her hands right now.

It looked so official. Her fingers ran across the address for the Civil Court of the City of New York as her heart pounded. She stood there in the middle of the hall next to the mail slots, staring as her heart pounded excitedly.

Then she remembered she was standing in the middle of a walkway and blocking most of the mailboxes. So she closed her box and ran down the hall toward the dingy staircase to her apartment on the second floor.

She slammed the door shut as soon as she got in and stared excitedly at the letter, tossing the random magazine and junk mail on the counter. The magazine slid off and flopped on the ground. She tore the letter open, and the envelope fell unceremoniously to the floor. She unfolded it and read:

ORDER GRANTING LEAVE
TO CHANGE NAME

The print was small, but the words were clear. She skimmed it quickly several times, just to make sure that she was reading it correctly. Because it felt too good to be true. But there it was in black and white. She wasn't

Carmella Johnson anymore. She would be able to shed that name and the life that had gone with it. In a way, it felt like a new start, a blank slate, even though she knew that the memories would last forever, continuing to shape her for the rest of her life. But that didn't matter. The last link connecting her to Casimir—her name—was gone.

He would find out what her new name was eventually. But that didn't change the fact that it would be infinitely harder for him to find her. And by the time he did, he probably wouldn't care enough to come after her.

She stared at her new name, a wild giddiness spreading through her whole body.

She had thought about her name for a long time. She had wanted it to mean something to her. She didn't want to just pick a random name. She didn't even want to just pick a name she really liked or thought sounded pretty. She wanted it to be more than that.

It had taken her a long time. Eventually, her mind went to two different women, two people who had molded and inspired her in two very different ways. One of them was her mother, who had worked hard every day of her life to give Carmella and her siblings a chance at a good life. The other was the lawyer who gave her a chance at a new life, who was trying to help make her dream a reality.

She had asked her, of course, if she was okay with it, and she said yes. She even helped her through the steps of bureaucracy to get what she needed. And now it was here.

She had crafted the name carefully, using her mother's maiden name for her last. And now she stared down at her new name for the first time.

Alexa Montgomery.

She said the name over and over, rolling it around on her tongue to get used to it. It felt perfect, like a well-worn glove.

Alexa Montgomery looked out the window of the cramped apartment. It was a beautiful day. She had no idea what the future would hold, how she would do in law school, or how her life would change. She didn't know, but it didn't seem to matter.

Whatever happened, she would face it head-on.

Smiling wider than she had in years, she placed the documents on the small table. Then she walked over to the laptop she had splurged on to do more research on potential law schools.

She had a lot of work to do.

Her new life had officially begun.

A Word from the Author

Look at you now! Beautifully and wonderfully made! A mustard seed, once upon a time. A seed that he tells us is all we need, and anything will be possible.

We all fall short in life. The fear, the anxiety, the feeling that we can no longer go on . . . but one thing is for sure and will always remain the same—our FAITH!

Don't EVER let anyone take away your dignity. The mind can function in multiple dimensions. As a child, we are all born with our own individual mind, not knowing where it will take us. As we get older, it continues to develop so immensely until one day we realize the power that each and every one of us has, with such a dynamic capacity that can take us anywhere in life. With all that said, do not EVER compromise your self-esteem for anyone. "Feel your fear" and keep going. The sun will certainly shine again one day!

PLAN . . . ACT . . . BELIEVE . . .

About the Author

Marie Theodore is a mother of three who has lived in Long Island, New York, for the past twenty-four years. She is an entrepreneur and business owner who has worked with children for the past nineteen years. She holds a bachelor's degree in business management and a master's degree in early children education.

GOODNESS OF GOD

Trust in you, I will always
Here and now
Even when I fall
Greater is your name
Oh Lord, my savior
Overjoyed you've made me
Destined to protect
Never had you failed me
Even in my darkest moments
Surely you know
Singing your praise, I will never stop

Oh my Lord, how I love you
Faithful as you are

Grateful and kind
Omnipotent, without a doubt
Devoted to you, I will always be!